THE BLOOD COAST

JASON M. KENNEDY

FORESHORE PUBLISHING
London

Published by RiverRun, an imprint of
Foreshore Publishing 2023.
The Forge 397-411 Westferry Road,
Isle of Dogs, London, E14 3AE
Foreshore Publishing Limited Reg. No. 13358650

The home of quality fiction.

ISBN 978-1-7393949-1-2

Jason M. Kennedy worked in intelligence and paramilitary operations in the private sector, before becoming a private detective. He now lives in Kent, England. The Blood Coast is his debut novel.

1

ON THE FAR SIDE of England. Deep in the West Country. Things where winding down. Drawing to a close in a simple quiet Cornish way. The same as it always had. It was the end of yet another warm sunny day. And the night was slowly drawing-in. The sky was blood-red and seemed almost angry. But in the small harbour community nobody noticed. Things seemed the same and nothing out of the ordinary.

The last of the small fishing boats had already come in and landed their catch. And the seagulls had long since flown away to their roosts. And the last of the dockside trades had closed up. But further out, just past the point, another wasn't ready to come in yet. The calm gentle sea gently lapped against the side of the old fishing boat. Wave after wave rolled over, danced and fizzed as it chugged along. Silhouetted against the horizon and the pitch of the bruised red sky, it didn't look out of place.

It was probably one of many, that had past that day. And no-one ashore would think any different, even perhaps if it was seen. But it sailed on. It had a purpose. An intent. And the two men aboard were bringing to a close the final stages of a dark one. Banking around the boat sat broadside. The engine was cut and the small vessel was allowed to drift on the gentle current. The two occupants in the wheelhouse gazed out at the vast sea surrounding them. And surveyed the shore-line through an old pair of battered German Naval binoculars. They were alone. Totally alone. No activity in the harbour. No other vessels coming their way. Not even a seagull flying above. The sun continued to sink slowly and majestically into the sea. And now only the harbour lights and bluff-point were faintly visible in the hazy shadow of the fading light. The darkness was now starting to take hold. Becoming *'Witching-Hour'*.

The door to the wheelhouse creaked open and together the two occupants slowly strolled out onto the old, weathered deck of the little trawler. They stared hard in unison at the large grey parcel that lay there. They seemed to be gauging it. It was really no bigger than a small under-croft fridge. So at least perhaps manageable. They circled it. Several times. Then their hesitation vanished and they both stooped and grabbed the ends as best they could. It was heavy. Slippery and cumbersome. The contents were uneven and even appeared to move and fight back at being man-handled. They struggled on. Then heaving it up, landed it with a thud onto the stern-cover. Just above the now silent engine. They paused studying it. Then with a shove, rolled it over and it splashed-down into the sea like a depth-charge.

They both reeled, avoiding the spray, then finally leaned forward. Scanning the surf to make sure it had sunk. There was no mistake. It was gone. No sign of it. Only the tell-tale fizz and foam of where the sea had been broken in its wake. The older of the two turned and gave a slight nod. And the other sauntered back to the wheel house and started the engine and with a burble the little boat gathered pace and slowly moved away. The man on deck flexed his chest, taking in the salty breeze. Then reached in through his over-coat and pulled out a slim pencil-like cigar. He twirled it in his fingers then tore-off the wrapping and cast it out into the sea. With a flick of his silver Dunhill lighter, he breathed a spit of flame into it. And finally with a strong powerful exhale, kept a watchful eye on the last of the bubbles, just to make sure.

***

The turbulence was heavy. And seemed relentless. The 747 had a smooth flight. But as it neared the UK the bad weather kicked in and the sheer hulk of the plane rocked countlessly from side to side. Coupled with dropping attitude several times like a kite dancing in a gale. Those who weren't awake, were now. Nervously shook from their slumber by the cabin floor coming up and almost hitting them square in the face. But finally, the wheels of the 747 screamed as they touched-down at Heathrow. And seat belt clicks reverberated through the cabin like metal castanets. As everyone made a sudden and eager scramble for their bags and the exit.

But one person remained still. He wasn't in any hurry. And leaning forward from his seat, he glanced down the aisle. He could see the plane was almost empty. So realising this he finally made his move. He liked to hang at the back. As no one ever paid any attention to who was last. Everybody on board just wanted off. After almost 30 years of tirelessly serving the government. Peter Crane was ready for some leave. Indefinite! And long-overdue. Grabbing his bags at arrivals he sauntered through customs via a secret route. Being an operative for MI6 had its perks. Crane breezed on unseen down through a side corridor. And to his left through mirrored glass, he could see the holiday makers queuing-up. There were only two guys checking passports, so they would have a long wait. He'd seen this so many times. It was almost second nature. Tired mums and dads. Screaming kids. And grandparents who looked like death-warmed-up and ready to give-in and collapse were they stood.

Luckily, there was no sound. Crane was thankful for some small mercies and the genius of sound-proof glass was one of them. As he hated screaming kids almost as much as queuing. Finally stopping at the last door, he ran a card through a small metallic reader attached to the wall and the mag-lock cycled and clicked back. He pushed the doors hard and walked briskly through. Glancing at his watch it was a little after 2am. Heathrow was busy. As always. A collection of life from every corner on the planet. Either arriving or leaving. But no one paid him any notice. And dragging his small suit case behind him, that was the way he liked it. He didn't stand-out. To everyone around him, he was nothing more than another weary tourist. But in truth he was a spook hiding in plain sight. But that was just SOP for every agent. As one of their greatest strengths was to look ordinary. To blend in. Disappear. Just be just another person or weary traveller going about their business.

With a rumble of his case on the walkway mat. Coupled with some inaudible squawking through a tannoy, the large glass doors shooshed open. And then the cold night air hit him like a lightning bolt. Crane shuddered and mumbled under his breath. And hailing a cab, he haphazardly clambered in muttering his address. And he slumped down and peered out of the windows. There was no mistake he was back in England. It was dreary and the wind and rain seemed relentless. Shutting his eyes he pondered warmly on his recent assignment. For the last few years the weather had been good. As where the surroundings of palm trees and warm beaches. But after a lifetime of living out of a suit case, he'd had enough. Many operatives burn out after countless years in the field and some have even defected for the right price. So having done more than his quota. More than his fair-share. He knew, in some way, he was owed this. And it was time to collect his pension and stay-put for once. Angola. The Philippines. Sierra Leone. And then finally his favourite – 'Latin-America and Cuba'. He loved it there. Plus Crane loved Cuban cigars and he smoked as many as he could. His final bus-stop assignment was to meet up with a former Cuban secret agent and buy the plans to a new type of armour-piercing round. Crane knew full-well this wasn't new tech. Just a re-hash of what was already available. But this was apparently of Russian design. So his MI6 controller wanted to know what was going on. Wanted to know more. Even obtain one if he could. So he was assigned at the last minute.

This agent had supposedly been fired over embezzling. And had contacted a British sleeper-cell in Havana touting secrets for sale. Or so that was how the story went. And that was all he'd been told in his rushed briefing. Cuba was still basically a poor Communist country. But British Intelligence knew for certain that Castro had his sticky fingers in the till. And had been stashing money away in numbered accounts in Switzerland for decades. But no money ever filtered down through the ranks of his government. Or to the people at the sharp-end. As Castro had always traded on his country's patriotism to the Socialist cause. But cash was king and always gave an advantage in this type of negotiation. So this agent was definitely up for making some money and selling what he knew. Cuba may have been a poor country but their army is one of the best equipped in the world. And most of it Russian in manufacture and design. That was apart from some odds and sods that the CIA had left behind when they supported Castro's coup back in 59.

Cuba's army had Kalashnikov's. RPG's. Air support and full military infrastructure. The list just went on. And the Russian Cuban connection went further and deeper than the rest of the world really knew. The agreement was a simple meet and greet. Get the intel. Pay him and make a fast exfil. But Crane knew that meeting him in public was no safe cover option. The Cuban secret police wouldn't care if they started a fire-fight in down-town Havana. They were notorious for it. And any civilians caught in the crossfire were nothing more than collateral damage. And to some - target practice. Cranes plan was easy. He kept it simple. To him, involving too many operatives for an op like this only muddied the waters. And the Brit sleeper cell in Havana only collated intel and weren't really geared-up for any armed support if the shit-hit-the-fan.

Coming through customs at Jose' Marti airport he made his way to left luggage and paid for a locker-rental. Placing his small suit case in, he slammed the door and jammed a match-stick into the hinge. If anyone tried to open it, at least he'd know and he'd abandon it. It wouldn't be the first-time his luggage had been *'Jarked'* and a transponder had been hidden inside it. The last thing he wanted was anyone following him back to the UK. And back home. Crane jumped into a cab. If you could call it that. An old American Oldsmobile. More rust and gaffer-tape than anything else. And coughing and spluttering they made their way towards Havana. And glancing out of the window he took out his mobile and clicked the position-finder. This would ping at the sleeper-cell and they would know he was in Cuba and they would triangulate him. Stopping at St Martin Square, Crane got out and slowly made his way to the Bolivar Café. He'd used this place before and had come to know the owner well. Crane had found his teenage son in South America involved with the communist group 'Shining-Light Liberation Army' operating out of Peru. He and his brother had run away to join them. And he revealed to Crane an assassination attempt on a French diplomat had gone wrong and they had tortured and killed his younger sibling for supposedly being a traitor and the reason for its complete failure.

He was made to sit and watch. As they took great joy in setting about him with a chainsaw. Cutting his off his hands and feet and finally his head and then cooking the lot on an open fire. And finally making him eat the charred flesh from one of his dead brothers hands.

Unbeknown to him, Crane was on a joint intelligence mission and was there to take steps to prevent the hit taking place. And he now felt responsible in some way for his younger brother. So Crane got him out of there and back home to Havana. Moments before a squad of CIA *'Wet-Boys'* partnered with an SAS unit, went in there and took them all out. And secretly disposed of all the bodies in a mass unmarked grave. His father swore he was indebted to him forever and when he wandered in, his bear-hug and kiss on Cranes cheek still showed this and confirmed his gratitude.

'Good to see you my dear good friend.. Holiday..?' – he growled in a deep gravelly voice.

Crane smiled – 'No.. job .. one last job before home.. !

He grabbed up Cranes hand and warmly shook it in his bear-like paws - 'Anything you need.. anything my friend.. my home is yours.. !'

Crane straightened his eyes – 'I need a piece.. nothing too fancy.. but full.. yeah.. !'

He slowly nodded. And understood exactly what Crane meant – 'Coffee.. ?' – and he waved to a far table near a window. Crane sat down and placed his satchel on the seat next to him and again pulled out his mobile. No sooner had he done so than a text pinged onto the screen.

'POSITION NOTED – MEET & GREET IN 30' and then it vanished from the screen. Just as the burly café owner came back towards him. He neatly placed a cup of thick black steaming coffee down in front of him and gently passed Crane a heavily folded magazine. Crane took it and uncurled the edge slightly. Inside the folded pages was a shiny nickel-plated Smith & Wesson snub-nosed .38 special.

He looked up at the café owner and winked. He returned the same and slowly walked away and re-took his place back behind the counter. Crane glanced around. The café was almost empty. As most were sitting outside basking in the glorious mid-day sun. He slowly slid the magazine down into his lap and gently took out the revolver. He thumbed the side catch and popped out the chamber. It was full. A full six rounds. He clicked it back into place, leant forward and slid the .38 special into the small of his back. And reaffirmed his shirt. Picking up his coffee, he raised it in a cheers-like motion to the café owner. He glanced over and shot Crane a side-smile and nodded.

Just as he was browsing through the magazine a young man of around 20 came bustling into the café. Crane paid no attention and continued to gaze back to what he was reading. When suddenly the chair the other side of his table slid back with a metallic screech on the tiled floor.

'Why don't you make it more fucking obvious.. !' – Crane whispered in a hushed angry tone without looking up. The young lad sat down and tried to mouth something. But nothing came out. And Crane noticed out of the corner of his eye that the café owner had moved to the end of the bar. And was fixed on the new visitor. A small burner mobile was slid across the table towards him. And seeing this Crane laid his magazine over it and placed a hand under it to retrieve it. 'So fucking obvious.. where the fuck did they get you from.. Oxford ?' – mumbled Crane as he slowly looked up at him. His face blank and dead-pan. Again the young guy tried to mouth something when suddenly the café owner came briskly walking to the table – '*Yes.. ?.. Coffee..?.. Beer..?*' – he bellowed.

He looked up at him and again tried to mumble something. Then suddenly realising that was his que to leave. He hurriedly got up from his seat and stumbled away towards the door. Crane gently shook his head and glanced up at the café owner again. He returned the same with a surprised look and slowly wandered back to the bar keeping an eye on the door. Crane drained the last of his coffee and put the burner phone into his pocket and shouldering his satchel he strolled up to the bar. He out-stretched his hand again and smiled. The café owner grabbed it again with both of his paws and shook it warmly. 'Good luck my friend.. whatever you need.. I'm here.. !' – he said nodding. Crane gave a gentle smile. And finished with a thumbs-up.

Walking back up the Street Crane fished the phone from his pocket and thumbed the power-button and

11

the little phone bleeped into life. Jogging the menu, he found the pre-entered number for the ex-Cuban intelligence agent and pressed send. It only rang once and the agent came onto the line. And from the tone of his voice, he was obviously eager for his pay-day. Crane gave his simple pretext instructions and clicked off. And sliding the battery from the phone, pulled out the sim-card and snapped it in two. Then threw it all into a curb-side drain.

Crane put his plan into action and hired a small speed-boat. His pretext was going fishing. Plan B was If it all went boss-eyed he would pitch the Cuban agent over the side and then high-tail it to Miami. It was the only option as there were no black-ops for back-up. Once out at a safe distance the agent gave Crane an old mobile phone. His Government issue mobile. And Crane watched the footage and looked at the photos. Then transferred the intel to his own. Along with its address book as an added bonus. Happy. Crane shoved his mobile back into his trouser pocket and thrust a fat envelope towards the agent. He grabbed it greedily and tore it open and his face lit up like a pin-ball machine.

Five grand in English Stirling. All brand new fifty pound notes. Crane smiled inwardly and sniggered lightly. As he knew this was enough money for him to live well on for the next couple of years at least. The deal was done and Crane launched the agents mobile into the sea. There was no-way he could have kept it.

Even if he wanted too. The agent. The contact. Could have been a *'double'* working both sides for a bigger payday and his mobile could have been a transponder.

And the last thing he wanted was some Cuban sleeper-cell paying him a visit in the dead of night. So time was of the essence. And now the deal was done, Crane sped back ashore and slammed the speed-boat onto the rickety old jetty. He didn't look back. No pleasantries. No goodbyes. He just jumped onto it and walked briskly to the roadside. This was the most dangerous part of any op. The Exfil. As he could have easily been in the cross-hairs of a snipers rifle. An easy open target. Or a snatch and grab right on there on the road side. And heart pounding, hand on the .38 special, he stood momentarily. And no sooner had he appeared then an old rusty orange Chevy screeched to a halt beside him on the road.

Crane jogged around and grabbed the door and leap in and sat down on the thread-bare front bench seat. And the Chevy sped away as fast as it could. Coughing and farting black fumes as it went. 'Got it ?' – blurted the driver. Crane glanced around. He was an old friend. A retired CIA operative who had relocated to Cuba and was now growing coffee. Supposedly. Crane smiled broadly at him and gave a happy nod. He returned the same and handed Crane a nice fat cigar and he sparked-up.

'Mission accomplished' – barked Crane as he hungrily puffed away on his stogie.

It wasn't operational-prudence to use your own contacts. For the sake of own security. But Crane preferred using this tact to move around when he had no official back-up. He felt safer using people he knew and trusted. And retired agents are always willing to help each other. It was a private unwritten rule in the intelligence community for old spooks.

His friend drove him straight to the airport just outside Havana. And just as he pulled up, Crane leant forward and pulled the nickel-plated .38 special from the small of his back and slid it across the bench-seat towards him. His old CIA friend didn't even look down. He just snatched it up and slid it under his seat.

'Another one for the collection.. Eh Crane..!' – Crane turned briefly and smiled and winked. There was no need for any other words. The mutual respect was always there. And grabbing his satchel from the floor of the old Chevy. And retrieving his unmolested case from the locker. He got on the next plane home. But that; Crane decided, was his last for queen and country. And MI6, British Intelligence, would have to do without him. They would have to train someone else to steal or trade technical secrets and secret weaponry.

His late Grandmother had left him her little cottage in Cornwall. And this only heightened his want to now quit. And he'd decided that once he'd been de-briefed, he'd pack up his London flat and disappear to the West Country. He hadn't been back there since he was a kid. The last time he was about fifteen or sixteen. But he wanted to be there now. He'd missed her funeral. But he knew in his heart, that she would understand. And at least; forgive him hopefully. Arriving back at home seemed a blur at best. But no-sooner had he arrived than an alarm clock was screaming and he sat bolt-up in bed.

In the field you can please yourself as long as the jobs done. But now the unfamiliar routine of office hours kicked-in and leaping from the bed he headed for the shower. Throwing on a baggy crumpled suit from his un-packed case, Crane pocketed his mobile and retrieved his code-keys from his safe. And stomping on age-old mail that adorned the mat, he slammed the front door and made for the lift. Gliding effortlessly through the large glass doors to his apartment block, he stood and once again and shivered in the early morning breeze. It again gave rise to him being home. Home in London Docklands. He raised a hand and a black London cab screeched to a halt and he got in. But this was no ordinary cab. It was company transport.

'Morning Tibbett.. nice to see you' – blurted Crane.

'You-too Lieutenant.. good to have you back'.

Being called Lieutenant was a hang-over from Crane's days in army intelligence and it was a title he hardly relished anymore. But it was another sure sign he was back in England and decorum was perhaps in order. 'I haven't missed this place.. and I won't miss it when I go down to Cornwall'

Sitting at some lights Tibbett snatched a glance in the rear view mirror - 'Oh yeah.. you're up for early retirement!'

'Early !' - snapped Crane as he angrily looked round.

'I've done my share Tibbett.. I'm cashing in my pension and I'm off to spend the next couple of years fishing or gardening.. till I get bored.. then I'll think of something else.. Cornwall's peaceful.. and quiet.. and a world away from this damn place.. ! ' Tibbett snatched a backwards glance in the rear-view mirror and peaked his eyebrows at Cranes statement. Pulling away, they followed the rush hour and meandered down the South embankment. It was bumper-to-bumper. And Crane sighed to himself that soon he'd finally be able to leave all this hustle and bustle behind. Hanging a left over Chelsea bridge Tibbett swung the cab down onto a side road and drove through some barriers that gave way to what seemed to be a building site. Then at the end of the muddy roadway, pulled into an old disused railway arch near Vauxhall.

Flashing the lights twice a plain clothed security guard magically appeared from a small dark recess near the entrance. He stepped forward and peered into the cab. He smiled approvingly. Turned and waved his arm. Then with a shudder the cab seemed to lurch forward. Then with a loud metallic clank it started to sink almost submarine-like into the ground. Looking up Crane watched as the guard slowly disappeared. The last thing he saw was a glint of sunlight on the barrel of the MP5 that was slung over his shoulder.

'The Office still likes the theatrics'.. eh Tibbett'

Tibbett glanced around and smiled at Crane. Raising his eyebrows.

Coming to a sudden stop Tibbett let go of the hand-brake and pulling away he drove forward and parked in a space near a large ancient wooden door. And a blinking of sub-lighting flickered-on and Crane got out. Then he watched in silence as the cab spun around on a hidden turn-table. And once facing back the way it came in, a dull metallic rattle sounded and clanged, as it ascended and returned once more to the road above. Sliding the code-key from his pocket Crane sauntered forward and ran it through the reader. A piercing blue light shone into his right eye and then with a buzz, the large wooden door sprang open. Pulling it, he stepped in. And automatically, it clanked-shut behind him. There was a faint hum and another sinking feeling gripped Cranes as the lift started to descend.

Musing to himself, Crane turned just as the feeling abruptly stopped and the silver double doors in front of him slid open with a shoosh. 'Morning Lieutenant Crane.. Commander Matherson's expecting you' Crane didn't utter a word. No pleasantries. Nor acknowledgement. He just wanted to get his debriefing over with and go home and pack. A long glass corridor loomed before him and striding down he passed row after row of dark shadowy rooms.

Some were full of computers with people clad in white overalls, fussing over them. To Crane they seemed like mad professors on the cusp of some great discovery. Others were full of men in combats assembling and disassembling fearsome looking weapons. The types of which that have never been seen before. This was the Governments secret storage area for prototype weapon technology. Plundered from around the world.

What couldn't be snatched. Stolen and smuggled was bought from corrupt officials and most of it acquired by Crane himself. Such was his role within British Intelligence. Stopping at the last door. He didn't bother to knock. He just grabbed the handle and shoved it open. Matherson. Round and portly and some sixty years. Coupled with some 40-odd in British intelligence, sat almost throne-like behind a vast oak antique desk and was busily shuffling papers as Crane strode in.

He was a '*Walrus*' of a man with a temperament to match. Resplendent in an old moth-eaten Oxford tie that he always wore. Along with his three-piece tweed suit and brogues. To Matherson the tie was a medal. And he wore it like a medal. In an effort to note his hierarchy and position. And as he thought, his superiority. He looked up - 'Don't you ever blasted-well knock Crane ?'

'What's wrong Miles.. you think after all these years I can't keep the governments secrets !'

Matherson grinned sarcastically and sprawled back into his chair - 'No.. I just find you bloody rude.. always have.. but nonetheless !'

Dumping himself in an ox-blood leather Chesterfield. Crane crossed his legs and pulled a large Cuban Cigar from his inside pocket. He sniffed it warmly. Then clipping the end, he placed it into his mouth. And fisting some matches, he sparked up and breathed in hard. Then swirled it round and blew it out. The thick smoke bloomed into the air like a personal fog-bank. As he whirled the fat cigar back and forth in his fingers.

'I rest my case.. ' - said Matherson grimacing and waving his hand as the smoke meandered towards him. Retrieving the mobile from his inside pocket. Crane palmed it for a moment, then leant forward and threw it onto the desk.

'The Cuban job worked-out well ! Surprisingly !.. Everything's in there.. photo's.. video.. even got the agents address book as a bonus.. plenty of numbers that we can strip and evaluate.. the lot.. so if there's nothing else.. I'm going home.. you'll have to get someone else to acquire the tech for you.. or steal it as I've got no intentions on going back to Cuba.. or on any other blasted assignment for that matter.. !'

Matherson snatched it up and toyed with it. Ignoring Cranes statement and eagerness to leave.

And noticing his superiors lack of interest, Crane got up from his seat and made for the door. "Hang-on Crane.. I've not de-briefed you yet.. so sit down.. !"

Crane angrily re-took his seat - "Well get on with it will you Miles !.. I filed my C27 two months ago.. it's been agreed and authorized.. the Cuban assignments done so the moment I leave here I'm officially retired from active service.. I haven't got any firearms.. it was checked back-in.. just before I left Cuba.. all I've got is my ID's and key-card".

'Yeah well.. you can check those when you leave as well.. but until I say you can go.. you're not going any-bloody-where OK.. and I would have preferred you to have used our contacts for this Cuba job.. not the bloody CIA ! .. retired or not !' - barked Matherson as he finally looked up.

Crane shot him a stern glance – 'Firstly Miles.. Carson's an old friend and I trust him.. and I trust him to have my back in a tight-squeeze.. ! I'm certainly not gonna put my life in the hands of some fucking wet-nosed Oxford grad.. who's new to the game and I wouldn't trust with a fucking-potato-gun..! Matherson recoiled slightly. He knew in a way Crane was right.

Too many Ops had been blown by young inept field-agents who lose it when under pressure. Still after several cups of black coffee. Crane had said all he wanted to. But what he really wanted to do was drag him across the desk by his precious tie and give him a right-hander. And sitting there he recalled that in the past he'd come very close to doing it. But during his some-what enforced interrogation, Crane pondered on Matherson's tirade of questions. They felt odd. And cold.

He gently nodded, sipping his coffee and allowed his eyes to wander down. The face that lapped and shifted in the dark liquid almost seemed an omen of things to come. Things loosing shape. Things looking distorted. Taking him with them. For some reason Crane now felt very uneasy. Gulping the last, he slammed the cup down. 'Can I go now.. ?' - said Crane in a somewhat school-boy tone.

Matherson leaned back and sank into his leather chair. He folded his arms with almost military precision. Being mindful not to crease his precious tie. 'How you getting to darkest Cornwall.. flying down in your little Spitfire..?'

'Hadn't really thought about it.. but probably.. but then again that's none of your damn business.. is it Miles.. your authority over me ends now.. here and now.. !' Getting up Craned turned to leave. He'd had enough of Matherson. Over twenty years too-much.

'Don't forget.. ! code-keys' - bellowed Matherson. Crane didn't answer. He just slammed the door and sauntered back up the corridor. Breathing in the fumes as he emerged into the daylight Crane took the subway this time, back to his apartment. He hated it. Hated public transport. But it was just a precaution in case he was being tailed. Following anyone on trains, let alone the subway, was a nightmare for any surveillance operative and any surveillance operation. Too-close and your burned. Too-far away and you miss the next move. Miss the target. Just too-many people. Too-busy. It was a delicate juggling-act. That was hard to get right.

Spending a lifetime of looking over your shoulder would be a hard habit to break. He hadn't told the office or Matherson anything of his real plans. But he had a gut-feeling that they knew exactly what he was doing. British Intelligence sometimes has a habit of *'watching the watchers'* and retiring from active service was one thing. But he wanted out. Out of circulation. Out of contact. Out of reach! And after being away from London for so long. it didn't feel like home anymore. So leaving for the West Country was hardly a wrench.

Crane hadn't driven his car for some time and far as he could recall, it was still in storage below his apartment. But to him it could stay there. The caretaker had driven it more than he had. And he was welcome too. But he thought he'd better check. Crane got into the lift and pressed for the basement. Then rattling on the glass door, Charles the old carpark attendant made an appearance and he handed Crane the keys. And he sauntered off in search of his car. The underground carpark was massive and dimly lit. But Crane soon found his way to bay 35 and as he rounded a corner there she was. He gently pulled off the light grey cover and allowed it to parachute slowly to the ground in the light breeze.

The old black Porsche 911 SC Targa sat squat. Proud and almost sentry-like. And looked as good as the day his Grandmother had given it to him on his 21st birthday. Crane smiled. It was a hell of a present at that tender age and he couldn't believe his luck. And it still lightened his heart every time he saw it. And on her insistence, he promised her that he would never sell it.

He hadn't driven it for quite some time. The last was a good few years ago. During a summer sabbatical in France. And fishing the key into the lock, he opened the door and got in. The truly wonderous smell of old leather. Burnt oil. Coupled with a hint of pure German engineering, eclipsed his nose and he beamed.

He fired the engine and the flat-six engine roared into life like a clap of thunder. And he revved it several times and the widest smile again shot across his face. Then tapping his hand on the steering-wheel, he flicked the key and the engine spluttered and ground to a halt. Crane paused for a moment then clambered out and shut the door. He stood for a moment. Admiring it warmly. Then ran his hand up the windscreen and over the Targa roof top. His smile now broke into a contented laugh. Then re-affirming the lock, he pulled the cover back over it and made his way back to Charles and his little office. He stopped for a moment and looked back at the Porsche. Thinking; maybe I'll come back and get it sometime. 'Yeah' – he said quietly to himself with a smile. But with a rattle of the keys, pushed the door open and gently threw them onto Charles's desk. Matherson was right about one thing at least. He didn't plan on driving all that way and not long after he'd booked it, the intercom announced that his cab had arrived to take him to Victoria.

Apart from a few very personal items, his suit case had stayed pretty-much the same. Just some family photos and the odd sentimental piece were added and heaving it towards the ticket booth he was soon aboard the 12 o'clock train to Kent. The fog that was London seemed to stay with him. As Crane peered haplessly out of the windows at his surroundings. A never-ending Metropolis of tall buildings, buses and black cabs and a feeling of grey damp smog. He stared at the throng and hustle and bustle of people on a mission to get where they are going. But slowly the grey metal landscape gave way to green fields and tree's and he felt his mood lighten and his eyes became heavy. Thankfully the train jolted him awake and rubbing his eyes, he saw that they were just coming out of the last tunnel from Gravesend. And he knew he'd almost arrived at Chatham. Shouldering his small leather satchel, he bent to grip his case. Crossing the track he gave in his one-way ticket and was soon sitting in yet another cab, heading towards Rochester's little private airport. After many 'Hello's and 'It's been a long-time' Crane was finally standing beside his beloved plane. And placing his bags into the storage panniers he stood back admiring it. Checking the service roster. It was fully fuelled and had been serviced. But like any good pilot. He checked again. And double checked.

The silver and blue twin-engine Cessna Skymaster was an 'operational' souvenir. And one he truly relished. He'd stolen it at De Gaulle airport, brining over a weapon that Mattherson deemed vital and 'It must be in British hands at all costs..!'. Driving over from France was out of the question as French customs would have found it at Calais not to mention Spanish intelligence was hot on his heels and they wanted it back. And he didn't relish the idea of getting into another gun-fight halfway across the English Channel. The Spanish agents also wanted his head.

Crane had shot and killed at least one of their squad and wounded two others in a frantic car chase across the Swiss Alps. And they probably wanted revenge just as much as their weapon back. If they'd have caught him. He knew they would torture him first. Then used it on him. Just for the hell of it. Counter-Intelligence teams don't carry 'Sammies' surface-to-air missiles. So once he was airborne he knew he was relatively safe. You can't road-block an airplane in flight. But after almost running-out of fuel across the channel, Rochester Airport was the only place he could land and he'd stationed it there ever since. Manston was too near the docks. Matherson knew he had it but turned a blind-eye. Because in the end he knew Crane was a man who always got the job done. So it was deemed *'spoils of war'*.

Strapping himself into the cockpit he put the head-set on and with a flick of the key, the engines roared into life and settled on a steady beat and rhythm. All gauges ready 5 by 5 and he requested clearance to runway 4. A muffled OK buzzed in his ears and Crane taxied over and placed himself ready. Then heaving on the throttle, the little plane lurched forward and leaving it to the last minute he pulled-back and the Cessna climbed steadily into the air. The sat nav gave simple directions. The sky was clear. Crane steered Westward. And he settled-in for the flight.

It was noon and a bright warm day. And just off Bluff Point near Looe harbour, a father and son team were fishing. The same as they always had. Man and boy. They came from a long line of fishermen. Who once made a good living catching fish in these waters. But in these modern days, times had changed and what was once enjoyable, was now arduous. For some reason in this part of the Cornish Coast. In this stretch of water. Things had changed and the fish rarely took the bait. In Looe - the locals say it all changed just after the end of the war. Sam leant against the sorting-table and shrugged his shoulders and stared at the catch. It was nothing. Hardly worth the effort. Just a few crabs that had been caught in the wrong pots. 'Dad let's call it quits.. I'm cold !!.. and… bloody-hungry'

Sam's Dad peered out the wheel house and shot him a stern glance - 'I know this isn't a normal fishing route.. no-one ever fishes this stretch now son.. but you never know.. and then we'll go in.. OK!'

'After all.. with our damn-luck lately.. it's worth a try.. it's been a shit week !'

Knowing he wouldn't change his mind, Sam sauntered over to the launcher and flicked the main-switch. With a loud slop the net dropped off the stern and he lashed the line to the main cleat. Sam gazed at the shore-line and the harbour in the distance. His mind wandered. Pub tonight he thought. *Darts and fish and chips and I may get lucky again...specially if my Juicy-Josey from the café is going to be there !*

Suddenly the little boat was yanked to one side knocking Sam off his feet and sent crabs flying. And scrambling to pick himself up, he glanced around wildly. 'DAD.. DAD.. what's going on ?'

Sam's Dad ran to the stern - 'Get to the wheel and put her in reverse.. slowly'

Leaping to his feet Sam followed his orders. And he slowly reversed the engine and the little boat chugged backwards. 'Stop the engine..!' said Sam's Dad, waving his arm.

Cutting the motor Sam ran to the stern and stood next to him, gazing into the surf - 'What we hit.. ?'

Sam's Dad shook his head - 'Nothing.. we're too-far out to have hit a hard sand-bank.. but there are drifts around here.. and they can build-up over time'

'Reel it in !' - and he pointed at the winch

Sam made a grab for it and it whirred into life, slowly retracting the line. Staring over the side they both scanned the water to see if anything was there.

Suddenly the winch gave a high-pitched whine and started to back-up. Looking up at it Sam glanced worryingly at his Dad.

'Crikey.. what the hell have we caught ?'

Sam's Dad didn't answer. He was leaning right over the side, almost touching the sea. 'Get a bill-hook.. QUICK' – he shouted. Again doing as he was told. Sam grabbed a long hook-ended pole from the top of the wheel-house and passed it to him. 'Steady the line.' Placing his hands on the cleat. Sam took a loose end of the line and threw it over another. shifting the weight across the stern. 'Here.. grab-hold' - And passing him the bill-hook his Dad leant again right over the stern. His face was almost touching the water.

'What the hell's that.. ?' – said Sam, still struggling with the pole. And craning his neck to see. 'What ?.. what is it?' – he continued.

'Let go of that now.. it's secure'- said his Dad.

Placing the bill-hook down Sam stood beside him and peered over - "Crikey.. what is it ?"

'Dunno.. let's get it onto the deck' And reaching over they both grabbed the large grey shape by it's sides and heaved. Finally landing it onto the deck with a loud wet thud.

'What the hell is it ?' - asked Sam. Rubbing his numb hands up and down on his waders.

Sam's Dad was already making his way back towards the wheel-house and making a grab for the radio, he keyed the mic. 'Dunno.. but I'd better call this in !.' – he said staring at him. 'Maybe a merchant's been through here and lost part of a load! But whatever it is I don't like this at all.. that package or whatever the fuck it is.. smells really bad.. and what's that green shit leaking out of it too.. ?'

The radio squawked in the background as his Dad spoke to the harbour master.

'Lash it down Sam.. the winds getting-up and the tides starting to break..'.

Sam made a final knot in the rope and stared again at the parcel. The engine gurgled into life and they started to make for the coast.

He stood back and placed his hands on his hips. Then looked at his Dad. 'Well it's not crab.. and certainly not lobster.. or Mackerel for that damn sure..!'.

'Yeah.. and it's not the first time strange things have been found in this stretch of water, his father replied.

Sam glanced back in surprise – 'What do you mean..?'

Sam's dad snatched a look – 'Oh its nothing.. just years ago some of the other fishermen have found strange fish in this area..!'

Sam looked confused - 'Strange fish..?' - he called back.

'Yeah.. remember old Bubbsey-Low..?'

'Yeah.. he died years ago.. 20-odd years ago!' - nodded Sam in reply.

'The word was and they recon he ate some fish or crabs caught in this area.. two weeks later he died coughing-up some weird green-goo.. and that damn package is leaking something green..!'

Sam sauntered over to his dad in the wheel-house. He looked concerned.

'Don't worry son.. we'll get in and ole Nory can deal with it.. OK - and he gunned the throttle and the little crab-boat sped-forward churning the surf and trailing a line of blue smoke.

Far up on Bluff-point a small hidden camera was watching their every move. It tailed them perfectly and silently. Locked-on like a heat-seeking missile. And the person watching the screen didn't avert his gaze.

Merely picked up a small walky-talky and keyed the mic - *'44-Bravo.. this is control.. possible compromise.. !'*

'One of our packages has been found by some fishermen.. trawler logged and ID'd.. request tactical response.. !'.

Back in the harbour the alone occupant of a dark BMW picked up a small walky-talky – *'Received.. under-stood..'*

2

THE CLOUDS BROKE AND gave-way to a brilliant blue sky and peering down Crane could just make out the coast in the hazy distance. Glancing at his watch it had only taken him a few hours. Helped along by a strong tail wind. And hearing the approaching bouncer signal he knew he wasn't far from the little airstrip.

Banking around he radioed for a clearance vector. And feathering the engines he dropped gently out of the sky like a glider.

With a bump he touched down on a newly manicured runway and buzzed along to a clear birth. He meandered his way in and with a final flutter, the engines cut out and the propellers ground to a stuttering halt.

He flicked off the inertial dash-control, released his harness and fumbled for the door. And un-coiling himself from the cockpit, Crane wearily stood up and stretched himself.

He was glad to be back on 'TERRA FIRMA'. And glancing down, he stamped his feet several times in the thick plush grass and stretched hard to relive the cramp in his back and legs. Crane breathed in and flexed his chest. Then just as he lowered his arms, it hit him. He was in Cornwall. He recognised it. The smell of the sea and the dusty air and its surroundings. He smiled. A relaxed warm smile. Something he hadn't really done for a while.

Crane was somewhat lost in the moment. When to his complete surprise he was greeted by an old man shod in a tatty hi-vis, flat-cap and odd welly's - 'How do,' he beamed with a smile. 'That's a nice plane!'

And motioning with his head, the old chap pointed towards a battered old rusty tractor chugging away quietly. Happily belching plumes of black-smoke in the process.

'Oh.. Thanks..!' – said Crane returning the smile and warmly shaking the old-guy's hand. And after placing his case into the trailer and shouldering his satchel, he clambered into the back and sat on a make-shift seat.

Clumsily fashioned from an orange R-Whites lemonade crate.

Checking-in at an old shed that doubled for a control tower Crane wandered-off in the direction of a pub. He knew there used to be one near here. And he was sure he saw it when he flew over. He was parched

33

and his guts were rumbling. So a bite to eat would be a good move before he ventured any further.

He knew he was on the outskirts of Looe and just on the crest of a hill that lead through a small valley. In the distance he could see that it was still littered with the odd thatched cottage and bungalow just before reaching the harbour. And Crane again smiled to himself. He'd been away from here far too long he thought. And as he could recall, he was only a short bus ride away to where his Grandmothers cottage was. And strolling on, the 'The Seagull' came into view.

He remembered this pub clearly from his younger years. But they only ever rode past. Never in. As his Grandmother was not a fan of public-houses. And on those many times, Crane could see other children playing in the beer-garden. But he was never one of them.

He only ever went by it on the bus, sitting next to his Grandmother. On their way home after a long day-trip to Penzance. Or St Ives.

Standing for a moment outside. It didn't look the same as he remembered from his childhood. It had been painted and looked a lot smarter and cleaner than he could recall. A new pub with a theme. Like so many were in England now. But bowling through the front door, Crane was greeted with a smell that made him feel even more melancholy. Again it was Cornwall. His Cornwall. And it to him, it had a unique smell and aroma that reminded him of summer holidays and an almost forgotten contentment. The houses, the shops, the pubs. To him, they all had it.

The pub may have seemed new from the outside, but inside was like an old story book. The blackened oak beams. The horse brasses that hung from the walls. Old, faded pictures of fishermen in long-barges, standing proud by their days catch. Adorned every tar-stained wall.

Now this is a pub, Crane mused to himself.

And dumping his case and satchel down in a little alcove near a smouldering log fire, he strode up to the bar. And glancing back and forth he couldn't remember the last time he'd been in an old English pub.

Suddenly the landlord appeared from a side passage – 'Oh hello.. a new face ?'

Crane smiled – 'Yeah.. just moved back.. finally retired and going to live in my dear Gran's cottage.. just outside Looe.. not been back here for almost thirty years..' – he continued again, glancing around.

The Landlord wiped the bar top and frowned a little – 'Oh nice.. it is a lovely part of Cornwall that's for sure'. Then he pulled his head to one side – 'Not thinking of taking up fishing are you..?'

Crane gently shook his head – 'No.. not really.. hadn't thought about it.. just to relax.. that's all'

'Good' – blurted the landlord – 'Coz you won't catch much.. not around these waters.. the sea around

Looe ain't no good anymore.. and what was caught.. was funny looking..!'

Crane frowned at this statement - 'Funny.. how do you mean ?' - he said inquiringly.

The landlord leant forward and his expression seemed to turn a little serious – ' Yeah.. I've heard stories of strange looking fish with three eyes.. and odd coloured crabs.. people getting ill.. they say it ain't been right since the War.. !'

Crane grimaced – 'Oh OK.. so I'll steer clear of the fish and chips then..!'

The landlord offered a small smile and relaxed his posture – 'There's still fishing.. just the locals all steam-out further past the point and use the far North estuary..!

'What'll it be..?' - he said finally, clamping his hand on the bar-pump - 'But your too late for any grub.. kitchens closed and the chefs pissed'

Crane settled on a pint of Kronenbourg and strolled back to his seat pondering. Analysing what the Landlord had said. Then nearly downing his pint in one-go he resided to himself that he could now finally relax a little.

But for some reason he knew this feeling wouldn't last. In many ways this was a 'strange-land' albeit now home. With three-eyed-fish.

Lashing the boat at the harbour side Sam turned around and again stared at the grey lump that was sitting in the middle of the deck. Piercing his nose, he grabbed at his face and tried to hide from the smell.

'Smells like rotten eggs.. or meat' - Sam blurted as his Dad sauntered past him.

'Yeah.. god-knows what it is.. still it's not our problem .. Ole Nory will be here shortly.. then it's his'

No sooner had Sam's Dad mentioned him, then Nory the local village copper jumped off the jetty and into their boat - 'Talk of the Devil..!' - said Nory with a broad smile.

Old Nory had been a Cornwall-Bobbie man and boy. He knew the area well and all the locals. And apart from stolen farm machinery and the odd punch-up, this was the first time he'd dealt with mysterious items found at sea.

'God.. it don't haf-onk.. don't it.. !' - Blurted Nory, inspecting it with a grimace.

'Yeah.. but look we're off OK.. we'll leave it here on deck and you can deal with it how you want to ok.. it's been a long day and me and my boy are starving.. OK Nory..!'

'Yeah no-worries.. leave it to me.. I'll get it shifted but you'll have to come into the station later-on and make a statement'

'Right- O.. ' - And Sam and his Dad clambered up the small ladder and made off.

Taking out his trusty note-book Nory wandered around it and scribbled a few simple lines. Nothing too dramatic. Just a note of 'Lump found at sea' and today's date and who found it.

Then after taking his cap off and scratching his head he radioed through to his station and requested a van to come and collect it. Grabbing his nose too, Nory clambered back up the ladder and made for his car.

Crane still felt uncomfortable. But also relaxed in some small curious way. Then again four pints of strong lager on an empty stomach will do that at least. Of all the countries he'd travelled, now being back home felt odd and the land old, strange and somewhat alien.

But the air was mild and the sounds of gulls squawking over-head made his weird posture even easier to cope with. And sitting on the wall at the bus stop, just a long from the pub, he waited for the local hopper-bus to appear.

The journey seemed longer than he remembered. Bumpy and winding. But he enjoyed every minute of it. His head darted back and forth. Side to side. As he took in the old Cornish landscape. The thatched cottages. Coupled with the odd lonesome chimney of a long forgotten tin-mine perched on a hill. He was eager to take it all in once again. Keen to refresh his old memories.

Then finally, as they scaled the crest of a hill, the sight of Looe and its harbour came into view. To Crane it looked beautiful and serene. Just how he remembered it. Quiet, peaceful and now it would be his home.

Crane spied the bus stop. Still in the same place. Same as when he was a child. Just outside the little croft of houses and local store. These hadn't changed either. And getting off, he crossed the road and started on the old, cobbled lane.

And finally standing at the front gate to his grandmothers little thatched cottage, he placed his case down and allowed himself again to reminisce. Closing his eyes, he could see her. Sitting on the veranda. Big floppy hat and her reading glasses chained around her neck. With a cup and saucer perched on the little occasional table in front. It was Tea. Hot. Steamy and always earl grey.

Finally fishing the keys from his satchel, he pushed the gate and strolled up the path. His head gently glancing right and left as he went.

The garden was over-grown. And the bay-windows and veranda had seen better days. But the peeling paint and garden were jobs he could attend to later.

For now he was just content to be there and free of the 'Office'.

Placing the keys into the locks, he wrestled for a moment. Then with a loud clank the front door was open and Crane pushed his way inside.

Sauntering up the hallway, he allowed his hand to gently run along the wall. Something he always did as a child. Then finally he stood in the lounge. The smell of moth-balls and old musty hymn-books coupled with creaky floor-boards greeted him and his thoughts once again fell to his dear Grandmother. He couldn't help it.

The warm ghosts of childhood memories came sweeping back and again he broke into a broad loving smile. Coupled with a tear that slowly rolled down his cheek.

He glanced around. Dust sheets covered what little furniture there was and the light switch, after a few flicks, flatly refused to work. So dumping his bags Crane went in search of the fuse box.

And finally locating it in a cupboard, he threw the master-switch and the front room and kitchen sparkled into life.

The sudden swath of light cut the warm feeling dead and the place seemed sparse and somewhat cold from what he could remember.

It was bereft. He could see that. See that clearly now. It was empty. Empty of all the little things. The little knick-knacks that his Grandmother held so dear. No pictures. No ornaments. Even her walking-stick was missing from the corner of the room.

Just timeless old weather-worn furniture and a tatty thread-bare rug sitting in front of the fire was all that was left. The only indication that anyone had ever lived there.

Shaking his head in disgust, it was obvious. To the point of being painful.

He may have been left her cottage and her money, but his family had picked it clean of all they could take. And anything they thought perhaps had any worth. All the odds and ends his Grandmother had owned. The little touches that made the cottage hers. Made it a home. Had gone.

And with it, so had her warmth. And any real indication that it was once her home.

Crane strode into the kitchen. And glancing around, that too was somewhat thread-bare. Just a lone kettle. With a worn frayed lead, snaking along the worktop. He grabbed-up his leather satchel and fished out his new mobile phone. Brand new and not even registered yet.

He stared at it in his hand. Turning it over. He'd avoided powering it up. Knowing it would delay the 'Office' being able to triangulate him. But plugging it in and placing it on the side-board. He knew Matherson's final words would in the end ring true.

You don't ever truly leave British Intelligence. Not really. You just get let out on a lead for a while. A C27 form give pledge to 'Queen and Country' that in dire-need you can be recalled to active-service.

But Crane would ensure that his lead would be the longest of all. He was a patriot. That was never in question. But sometimes even patriots have a sell-buy date.

Briskly moving through the cottage Crane checked each room. They too were mostly empty. Again picked clean. Even the little bedroom that used to his, was now empty. Just his old single bed sitting there alone. Bare, apart from the old mattress. And his grandmothers was no different. Just her old double-bed and an empty wardrobe.

Even the rugs had been taken from the floor.

And pulling dust-laden curtains, he threw open every window he could find.

He wanted to be rid of the smell of damp. But the odour of musty hymn books and wardrobe moths. The things that made him feel so welcome and almost child-like again, he hoped would remain.

If only perhaps for a while.

He needed it. To help him adjust. It had been almost thirty years since he was last here. And even though the memories were there, the feeling wasn't.

The mood started to lighten in the cottage. And the air seemingly a little dryer. Crane came bustling out the front door and didn't even lock it. He waltz back through the front gate and started back down the cobbled lane towards the little croft of houses, the shop and some small signs of life.

His stomach was once again doing somersaults and this time his hunger was very real and he couldn't avoid it any longer. He never ate breakfast and had missed lunch and it was now taking its toll. And walking back up the cobbled lane, he knew the local shop wouldn't have much.

But it would have to do. And in his situation, he couldn't be choosy. And even the bare essentials would be good at the moment. And besides, he could do a proper shop when he got around to it.

'What the bloody-hell has ole-Nory got us moving now Johnny.. ?'

'Dunno. . but Pam's just called from the station.. we gotta collect something off Davy Parsons boat..

...he's hooked summit today and it ain't crab.. or fish.. for that matter!'

Getting into the driving seat Johnny looked over at his brother and smiled half-cocked - 'Come on Danny works work.. ain't it !'

Winding down the window Johnny crunched the van into reverse and careered backwards up the drive and onto the main road. Then slamming the van into gear he gobbed out the window, sped away and hawked again. Just for good measure.

'So what's Davy hooked this time Johnny.. Second World-War Bomb.. Bluebeard's Treasure.. ? '

Johnny placed a rolled-up fag into his mouth as he shrugged his shoulders - 'Dunno.. but Nory said it stinks.. bad!'

'Oh great.. we're in the darts match tonight remember.. and I don't wanna go to the pub smelling of dead fish.. or anything else that bloody matter..

Juicy-Josey's from the cafes gonna be there remember !
and I don't want Sammy Parson's getting first dibbs coz
I smell like shit..!'

Nearing the quayside Johnny shook his head -
'Cor blimey.. sniff that.. ! you can smell it from here..
Jesus what a pong.. that's gonna stink the whole bloody
harbour out.. !'

Negotiating a few parked cars, Johnny parked as
close to the harbour wall and jetty as he could. And
shoving another rolly into his mouth he jumped out of
the van and peered over the edge and onto the deck of
the small fishing boat.

Tapping the wall, he motioned with his head
and they moved round, scaled part of the ladder and
jumped down into it. Danny clamped a hand to his
face and turned away.

'Oh.. come-on.. come on.. candy-arse.. let's just
get on with it' - Johnny snapped.

Moving around the grey package, they made a
grab for it and lifting it shoulder high they moved to
the small ladder. And grappled with it back up and
onto the jetty.

Dropping it to the floor Danny turned, gripped
his knees and buckled over yakking - 'You all-rite.. ?'
called Johnny, spinning around.

After yakking for the third time and then finally
puking. Danny wiped his face and slowly straightens
himself up. Breathing hard.

'I never could stand bad smells.. Jesus.. not to mention its leaking some weird green shit.. look it's over me hands and me jeans.. oh.. for fuck's sake..!'

Throwing open the rear doors to their van they manhandled the package into the back and slammed the doors hard. And holding his head out of the window Danny motioned to his brother to get a move on.

'Let's get this thing over to Nory's.. then we can get home and have a shower.. and change me-jeans..! look I'm gonna glow in the fucking dark now.. that green shit is all over me..!'

And with Danny still hanging out of the window. Trying to stifle his desire to puke again. Johnny pulled away from the quayside and zoomed out of the harbour. But unbeknown to them. Their activities were being watched.

Hidden in the shadows of an old dockside warehouse. The occupant of a darkened BMW took a thin pencil like cigar from his mouth and breathed out a small plume of smoke. It wafted up almost ghost-like and gently pulled itself out of a cracked-open window in a passing breeze.

He had been watching them. Silent and still. Watching and studying their every move with an almost steel-like intensity.

And gently placing a small set of binoculars into the seat beside him the car quietly and powerfully skipped into life. He watched the van make off and slipping the BMW into gear he pulled slowly away after them.

Approaching the Police station Johnny raised Nory on his mobile and just as they pulled up outside the nick, he appeared and ushered them around the back.

Following just out of sight. The BMW kept pace. It never skipped a beat. The driver was an old, seasoned professional. And albeit someway up behind them. He slipped into a lay-by up the road.

And with a final faint blip of the engine, it fell silent.

Slamming the rear doors on their van the brothers were glad to be rid of their smelly load and waving to Nory as they left, they eagerly made off home.

Nory strolled back into the little station and took one last look at the mysterious package. Then he closed and locked the doors to the holding room. And shutting the door to the front desk he climbed the stairs and went back to his beer and the evenings game show.

Hoping that would be it for the day.

Back up the lane the driver of the BMW was still. He hadn't moved. He'd been watching their every move with the upmost of intensity. Flicking the stub of the cigar out of the window he gently reached inside his jacket and retrieved a mobile phone.

He raised it to his ear - 'We've got real problems' - he hissed.

Crane was right. The little shop didn't have much. But he made a final choice on the sauce he wanted with his chicken. It was curry.

He had no idea on how hot. The label gave nothing away. As it was 'Happy Shopper' and all it said on the label was 'Curry'. So curry it would be. He filled the rest of his basket with some PG tips. Crisps. Milk. Sugar and lastly some chocolate and several bottles of red wine.

Then he finally made for the till to pay for his groceries. Stopping momentarily on his way to grab a small bottle of Tabasco. Hoping this would make 'Happy Shopper Curry' more like a curry.

As he left the shop he stood for a moment and gazed-out over the harbour and suddenly felt an evil shiver crease his spine. And a cold breeze blew-up washing over him. Stinging his eyes.

Looking into the sky, no gulls were flying. And the sea out in the harbour seemed almost still.

This was a feeling that he'd had many times before. But never as cold and sharp. Then thinking perhaps he just needed time to adjust to a life of not looking over his shoulder. Or perhaps even, carrying a gun. He started back up the path and onto the cobbled lane that led home.

He was certainly no cook. Never was. He'd burnt the chicken and boiled the sauce but sitting out on the tatty weather-worn veranda. Watching the sea and the sun fade over the horizon. To him was sheer bliss and washing his poor effort-of-a-meal down with some of the West Countries finest cheap red-plonk. His relaxed feeling thankfully returned.

It wasn't long before he was asleep and the plate slid from his lap. Clattering to the floor.

The driver of the BMW was still. He'd sat motionless like a child's unloved doll for hours. The sun had gone down and the lane and houses were over-shadowed by a silvery full moon.

There were no real street lights. Only a few dimly lit in the village. Everything was clouded in a sombre darkness.

Then silently the car door opened and placing a foot onto the road. The driver slid effortlessly from the car like a Cobra stalking its prey.

Each movement was measured. Timed. Slow and calculated. And his eyes darted almost sniper-like studying his surroundings. Scanning each house. Each window and driveway for any signs of life.

Even his breathing was paced. Timed. And silent.

Moving in the shadows he finally stood at the front of the little Police station and looked up at the windows above.

A light was on and he could hear the muffled sound of a television. With an almost radar efficiency he scanned the front of the building. There was no burglar alarm or indeed any alarm of any kind.

He smiled to himself. Creased his eyes and turned and walked silently to the side of the station and stood in the shadows by the driveway.

With one final glance around he vanished.

Ghosting down the rear steps he peered up the window and then placed a leather gloved-hand on the door knob and twisted it gently.

It relented slightly then stopped. Raising himself on tip-toe. He peered through the window again.

It was dark but through the moon light he could make out the hallway and a door that lead to the front desk and stairs leading to the rooms above.

Suddenly lights pierced the darkness and a battered old Land Rover came crunching up the driveway and screeched to a halt on the gravel.

Suddenly the door flew open and clanged as it hit the cars door-stop. Clambering out. The driver gathered-up some shopping bags from the back and dumping them on the ground, fished for the keys. And finally shoving them in the door she fought with the lock. Nory's old Land Rover was always playing up and this evening was no different.

'Oh.. for Christ-sake.. you fucking-old-car'

Busily wrestling with the keys. She was oblivious to anything else and she didn't notice the dark figure now stealthy approaching her from behind. With its hands out-stretched.

Losing patience she tugged hard. And the key gave a ping and snapped. Letting the rest go in the process. They dropped to the floor with a jingle. And kicking the wheel furiously she bent down to retrieve them.

'Now look what you you've done Pam.. ! you've broken the bloody key!'

Pam shot up right and spun around with both fists clenched ready to lash-out - 'NORY.. DON'T FUCKING DO THAT.. you nearly gave me a fucking heart attack.. you dozy-bastard..!'

Laughing he grabbed up the shopping and together they walked over and into the station.

'God.. what's that smell ?' – Nory turned to look at Pam and shrugged all bag laden.

'Don't ask.. !' – and he closed the back door and turned-off the light.

Back. Just up the lane. The BMW's engine gently thumped as it pulled past the station. Disappearing down the lane and into the night.

The moon-light glinted on the boot badge at it vanished around a corner.

Looking at his watch it said 5 o'clock. The sun was low in the sky and it was getting in his eyes. He never could stand bright-light. Crane swivelled around in his chair and it was at that moment he saw a vision of death coming silently towards him.

They were messengers. Deaths messengers.

Their heads were bowed with distorted faces hidden behind long black crepe veils which almost seemed to almost touch the ground. Behind the black. He knew them. Knew them all. In spite of their funeral trappings. And their dark fabric-like armour.

His mother. Unmistakeable. Then moving behind her. The men.

Moving as though they were using her as a screen. A shield to hide their grief. Crane didn't go towards them. Didn't stir. How could he. His limbs felt like lead.

His heart had stopped. And his eyes stung as he wanted to weep and yet he couldn't muster a single tear. His breath was cold and every pull of air seemed poisonous.

They paused some ten yards from him. They seemed ashamed or rather afraid of him. The flirted movement of feet showed this. Crane knew it. He could feel it. Almost taste it in the stale cold air.

They would sooner be dead than face him and tell him what he already knew. Because without uttering a word their black clothes and garb spoke to him in more ways than they ever could.

'Your Grandmother's dead' - came the faint whisper in his ears. And yet no-one spoke.

Who had been with her ? Crane wanted to ask. Ask them all. Wanted to scream. Scream this loud at every one of them till his voice collapsed. But he knew only too well. Nobody. None of them. Nobody was with her. Since I, her greatest love. Her favourite was not there. She was gone. Dead and buried without me ever having seen her. To say goodbye. To say thank you. And in many ways tell her that I loved her with all my heart.

His mother was the first one forward. Moving and yet she seemed almost floating. Her poor face painted a picture of desperate suffering and regret.

Her tears fell without ceasing. But Crane remained still. Unable to move. As he felt what little life he had left in his body, drain away from him. Like the flame of a candle being snuffed-out.

Then finally she reached him and threw out her arms to embrace him. Crane looked into her eyes and what he saw made him wince and almost recoil from her touch.

They were black and lifeless. Almost shark-like - 'She died asking for you.. Peter'

Crane threw his head back and forth trying to break free from the grip that held him. Suddenly his arms shot out in a flapping motion and with a surge he sat bolt upright.

His eyes were as wide and saucers and in reaction he kicked out. And the plate at his feet shot forward and smashed against the wall.

Wildly Crane leapt bolt-upright from his chair and shook his head from side to side. He rarely dreamed. If ever. So why now !.

He rubbed his hands up and down his body. Still able to feel his mother's cold dead embrace. He breathed hard and stumbling forward from the veranda. And made for the kitchen.

There was a bottle of Scotch. Still un-opened. Sitting on the sideboard. And seeing it - Crane make a grab for it. He wrenched off the top and didn't even bother to search for a glass.

He raised it to his lips and snatched an almighty gulp. Then another and another.

The warm liquid scaled down his throat and filled his chest with an immense feeling of warm and powerful indigestion.

Placing the bottle down. Crane gritted his teeth and breathed in sharply. In an effort to push and force the acid-like liquid further to where it needed to go.

He raised it again to repeat the experience. But just as at it neared his lips. He stopped and slammed it back down onto the sideboard.

He'd recovered once from being an alcoholic. And being here in Cornwall and retired. He'd vowed to himself that he'd wouldn't start down that road again. It never solved anything and his Grandmother never drank.

Fishing for the switch Crane turned off the lights and made for a bedroom and hopefully a peaceful night's sleep. The Whiskey was kicking-in. Doing its job.

He could feel it starting to course through his veins. He hoped it would dispel his demons. Because at that moment they still felt very real.

And still felt very close.

Nory came trudging down the stairs. Clothed in his dressing-gown and slippers. It was only 6am and only just getting light and it was supposedly his day off - 'All-right.. all-right.. don't knock the bleeding door down for Christ-sake.. !'

Nory made a grab for the bolts and yanked them back and the front door to the station lurched open with a painful creak. Pullet. The area SOCO shuffled in man-handling his large, battered leather doctors-bag.

'I don't want to be at work on a Sunday either Nory.. but you got a strange package that wants looking at right.. !'

'Well I'm here now so let's take a look'

Nory stared blankly - 'There's no-one else around on a Sunday . . so I'll do it'

Nory slammed the door shut again and reaffirmed the bolts.

Pullet waited until he'd finished dealing with the door and made after him. Walking towards the holding area Pullet grimaced - 'Jesus.. you said it was smelly '

But as they neared the storage room Pullet's faced turn to concern. He was an old-hand and had experienced much in his profession but the smell that was coming from the room was unmistakeable.

'Well there it is.. it's all yours.. I'm gonna make some tea'

Pullet didn't answer. He waited for Nory to leave the room and he made a grab for his case.

Feverishly donning some rubber gloves. Pullet placed his hands on the grey package that lay on the examination table and ran them over it. Examining each line.

It was leaking a strange green fluid that seemed to react in the light and wafting his hand past his nose. It seemed to be the source of the horrific smell.

Stepping back Pullet took a deep breath and grabbed-up a scalpel. He mused for a moment then stepping forward he dug the blade hard into a seam. And with a firm drawing motion - ran it scythe-like from end to end.

More of the green substance seemed to ooze from the wound as he did so. Then with a final yank across the bottom the package split open with a blood curdling crack. Like the sound of a sternum being cut open for a heart transplant.

Nervously Pullet put the scalpel down and placed his hands either side of the opening and peered inside. With a gasp he spun around. Tearing off his gloves and dropping them to the floor.

He clasped his hands to his face and bit his lip as he fought his desire to wretch. And leaning on the door frame to steady himself Pullet breathed hard.

So hard in fact, he thought he'd pass-out.

'You al-right ?' - said Nory as he suddenly reappeared, all tea-laden. Pullet didn't answer he just stood for a moment his eyes fixed on the door.

Finally turning, he looked at him.

And returning his stare Nory raised his eyebrows. Prompting an answer

'L.. L.. L.. Look for yourself' - exclaimed Pullet. And passing him a mug of tea Nory strode forward and glanced into the package. Pullet stood in silence as Nory's head darted back and forth staring into the opening. Taking a huge gulp of his tea Pullet stepped forward and stood the other side of the table.

Nory was struck dumb. The colour had drained from his face like a plug being pulled from a bath.

Inside the package was the body of what seemed to be a man curled-up in the foetal position. He was completely naked and hair-less. The face appeared frozen in a scream and the lips were drawn back and shrivelled. The teeth were missing and the eyes looked melted in their sockets like two runny fried eggs. The body had a green-hue-like colour and a slimly substance oozed from its nose, mouth and ears and anus.

Nory looked up - 'W.. W.. What the fuck.. is it ?'

Pullet just shook his head and shrugged - 'I I I.. don't know.. I've never seen anything like this in my life.. but we've gotta report this !'

Nodding his head, Nory downed the last of his tea and made for the door

'I'll make some calls.. Fast!' - he said dribbling.

Out in the hallway Nory grabbed up an extension and dialled feverishly. But just before the line clicked through. Nory froze as he felt something hard and cold press against the side of his head. Mid temple.

His mug slipped from his grasp and shattered onto the floor. And slowly he turned.

Staring down the barrel of a suppressed-pistol. Nory was faced with a man dressed in black. His face and features hidden behind a thin black cotton balaclava.

Looking cross-eyed at the barrel of the pistol Nory's eyes slowly moved and he stared at the dark figure again. The armed man returned the stare unflinching. And glared in an ice-cold intention. No blinking and the eyes spoke a thousand words.

Raising a leather gloved hand he placed a finger across his hidden mouth. Motioning silence.

And with the same hand. He slowly took the now garbling handset from Nory's trembling fingers and hung it back on the wall. Measured and controlled the dark figure back-tracked slightly and pulled the gun down from Nory's head and motioned with it back into the room.

Nory turned and walked slowly and the figure closed-in behind. Jabbing the gun into his back. Giving note of his firmed and steeled intentions.

Pullet looked up and seeing the look on Nory's face realised something was wrong and tried to look round him. Nory was nudged slightly to one side and the dark figure now pointed the pistol at Pullet.

And with a wave he motioned them both back to the far wall.

Pullet raised his hands and turned to Nory - 'What the fucks going ?'.

Nory didn't look at him. Just shook his head. His eyes wide with fear.

The dark figure racked the slide. Drawing the hammer. And double-handed the pistol. In a classic weaver-like stance.

'On your knees.. both of you' - he hissed. Quiet and almost snake-like.

Looking at each other they did as ordered and instinctively placed their hands on their heads. But Pullet seemed to be made of sterner stuff than Nory. And sensing something bad was about happen he took his hands off his head and opened his mouth to shout at the figure in black.

But he never got the chance.

The hammer slammed home and a 9mm hollow-point tore into Pullet's head. Just above his right eye. The impact threw him back against the wall like he'd been shoved. Then he slowly sank to the floor leaving part of his head and brains on the wall behind him.

A tell-tale hole. Painted in blood. Was left in the wall where the bullet had gone right through him.

Pullets arms were still in the air as he crumpled. And he sank to the floor like a child's inflatable toy being un-plugged. His face forever frozen in surprise and his eyes locked in stare at his killer.

A last exhale of air squeaked as it left his body. And his nerves stuttered and stomped as he finally succumbing to the head wound. And the sound was coupled with the clatter of the spent 9mm casing as it landed and rattled on the tiled floor.

Nory only got one chance to look at Pullet's lifeless body and glimpse back at the Assassin. When a second 9mm hollow-point hit him mid-temple.

The bullet disappeared into the wall close to the other and the force of entry and exit threw him sideways and he landed over Pullet's lifeless body. His eyes were now fixed in death and the pupils slowly grew to the size of coat buttons. He lay there over his colleague. Staring at the floor just over Pullet's waist.

The blood and brain matter mingled on the side and collar of Nory's dressing gown and the spray slid down the wall like a macabre Jackson Pollock. Finally forming puddle-like beside him.

Slowly moving forward the assassin retrieved the two spent casings from the floor and carefully slid them into his fatigue pocket.

And bending down he placed a hand on each man's jaw-line. Checking for a pulse.

Then finally, he raised a hand to his ear and gently pressed a hidden switch and hushed - 'Area Secure'.

3

CRANE TRIED TO OPEN his mouth but his lips flatly-refused. And searching with his tongue he forced at them and finally yawned as wide as he could. Flexing his mouth. He stuttered his jaw from side to side. Then again for good measure.

Finally opening his eyes he stared at the ceiling. Frowning. Searching his thoughts. Then suddenly realising where he was he grasped his head. And ran his hands over his face breathing hard.

Gingerly he sat up and slowly swung his legs round and steadied himself. He was in his Grandmothers room. In his Grandmothers old rickety bed. With a faded old pillow and bare dusty mattress for company. The blanket that was covering him was now on the floor. But he couldn't remember where he'd got it from.

He'd slept in his clothes and felt sweaty but at least he was warm. And his shirt and trousers felt comfortable and soft as he shuffled in them.

The whiskey had done the trick. He'd slept well and the enemy ghost's thankfully hadn't bothered him any further.

He'd shut them out. They didn't get back inside and haunt his dreams.

Stumbling to the bathroom Crane wasn't sure if the shower would work. But feeling confident that nothing would spoil his first real day of retirement. He threw off his clothes and bravely stepped into the enormous enamel bath.

He bashed it several times and finally the shower sprang to life. But the water remained tepid and a seemed a little rusty but steeling himself just long enough to wash himself and wash off the soap, he snatched at the tap and jumped out with a sharp intake of breath.

And gathering-up an old moth-eaten towel Crane stomped back up the hallway. Back to his Grandmothers bedroom and hurriedly padded himself dry.

It's Sunday. Fishing. I'm going fishing. I think. As he threw on his shirt and jeans.

Crane mused over this as he strolled into the kitchen setting the kettle in motion. The last time he fished. Fished for anything. Was when he was a boy and the most was grabs from the quayside.

But again it was a warm childhood memory.

After a breakfast of double eggs. Smothered in brown sauce. Bacon and several rounds of burnt toast.

Crane searched in his shoulder bag for his box of Cuban's. And after clipping the end and snatching up some matches he wandered into the back garden and made for his Grandmothers old shed.

He could clearly see. As he approached. It wasn't locked.

The rusty old padlock was just hanging there. Limp and redundant and pulling the door free he peered inside.

Apart from some old sacks and a pile of old box-wood it was empty.

'Fucking family' - Crane muttered to himself as the cigar fidgeted back and forth.

Not only had they picked the cottage clean but the damn shed too. There was never much in there anyway. As he could vaguely recall. But what little was there had gone.

Checking his watch. It was eight. And back in the cottage he grabbed-up his satchel and keys and made for the lane outside.

Maybe there's a shop down in the harbour he thought. But who cares. Crane was just content to have a wander and take in the sights and sounds of his new home.

Strolling up the cobbled lane he neared the cross roads and stopping he looked out over the harbour and cove.

It was a beautiful sight. Peaceful and calm. With the sun dancing on the sea.

Then glancing back at his little thatched cottage his mind wandered and past memories of long summer holidays came to pass. When he was home from boarding school, his dear grandmother always insisted that he came to stay.

He now truly relished those bygone times. Swimming in the sea. Cricket on the beach. Searching among the rocks and then finally as the sun set, waiting near the harbour for the bus. And bumping out of town with the cottage slowly coming into view.

It was the only place that Crane had ever really known as home.

He smiled to himself and gently shook his head. Recalling how his grandmother would always accompany him every day down to the beach.

She'd sit there quite content. Allowing him to do the things that young boys do.

Resplendent in her flowing dress and floppy hat. Reading a book. Or doing the Times crossword.

She never once complained. She was just content to be there in one of life's most simple of riches.

Trudging on Crane took a long drag on his Cuban and paused for a moment as he neared the main road.

Cuban cigar smoke is not meant to be inhaled but just as he stepped onto the road a black BMW shot across his path. Closely tailed by a large black van.

Crane whirled backwards, swallowing hard. He choked and gagged on his forced inhale. And the cigar shot from his mouth like a bullet. Hitting the ground.

He bent forward, hands on his knees, trying to breath. And peering through watery eyes at the fleeing cars he swore several times under his breath. Realising his cigar had hit the deck and half landed in a pile of fresh horse shit.

Stamping on it in anger. Crane composed himself and this time looking both ways, he crossed the road and made for the first line of houses that lead down the hill. Towards the bus stop.

Just then a strange sensation gripped his feet and legs and suddenly an almighty gust of wind hit him from behind like a runaway train. Sending him sprawling to the ground.

A crack of thunder shook the air and a wave of intense heat rolled over him like a blanket. A fierce hum now echoed in Cranes ears and slowly rolling over to one side he pushed himself up and sat on the path.

The sounds of silence were deafening - 'Christ.. what was that' - he mouthed..

Peering through the dust and smoke Crane looked back up the hill and saw a large plume of smoke rising almost mushroom-like into the air.

Opening his mouth. He flicked his jaw back and forth. And tried to clear the incessant ringing in his ears.

Looking around, bewildered people suddenly started appearing from their houses. Scurrying around like ants. Pointing and waving their arms.

Feeling a hand on his shoulder Crane glanced up and an old lady in a tea-cosy hat looked at him and mouthed something he couldn't quite make-out.

Smiling half-heartedly he nodded and mumbled - ' I'm alright.. I'm alright' - and breathing hard he took a deep breath and flexed his chest.

Crane hawked in an effort to clear his nose and suddenly his eyes went as wide as saucers !

He smelt something !

A strange aroma. But totally unmistakeable ! Once you've smelt it. It never leaves you ! Worryingly Craned looked around and slowly climbed back to his feet.

'Somebody gonna call the Police !' - he squawked.

Seeing that his statement was completely ignored Crane upped the ante.

'OI ! ! . . SOMBODY GONNA CALL THE POLICE ?'

The old lady in the tea-cosy turned and faced him wearing a horrified expression.

Crane looked at her dumb-founded - 'What ? ?'

'That was the Police station son!' - she replied clasping her hands to her face.

Crane looked at her in astonishment. Then curiosity took hold and gathering up his satchel from the grass verge. He took one final look at them all then started hurriedly up the hill towards the billowing smoke.

No-one tried to stop him. They only seemed too happy to have someone to investigate.

Just as he rounded the crest of the hill, Crane came face to face with a scene of utter chaos. The remains of what was once a simple house was now a smouldering shell with no roof.

He stood surveying the carnage.

Bricks and shattered roof tiles lay everywhere and to the left the remains of a land rover seemed just visible under a pile of wooden beams and broken glass.

And behind him in the distance he heard the distant wail of a siren slowly getting louder. Hopefully it was the Police or Fire Brigade. But he wasn't concerned with that.

What still struck Crane was the familiar pungent smell. Now even stronger. Stinging his nose with every breath he took.

A screech of tyres and hiss of air-brakes still didn't prompt him to move. Crane was almost in a state of shock.

How could this happen here !

Crane had seen countless explosions and houses blown-up and destroyed during assignments in Libya. Angola and the Congo. But this was Cornwall.

Things like this just don't happen here.

'Move-Back Please.. !' - ordered the rather burly fireman as he pushed past hose laden.

Craned turned to face back down the hill. Back towards town.

And slowly walking away he glanced again back at the ruin. Watching the firemen scurrying-around spraying water at anything charred and smoking.

Trudging past two other fireman working on a hose Crane heard the words - 'Gas leak.. ?'.

But he didn't stop. Didn't offer conjecture. He just carried on walking.

Back at his cottage Crane made a grab for the bottle of whiskey that he'd started the night before and this time grabbed a glass from the cupboard. And he poured himself a measure that was almost half a pint.

Golloping It down. It stung with the after-bite of a raw tooth being yanked.

Slouched on the kitchen side and with watery-eyes he glared at the brand new mobile sitting there resplendent in its charger. The little green light wasn't flashing anymore. It was now fully charged.

If I switch that on Matherson's gonna know where I am.. ! Exactly where I am ! - he pondered.

Palming it Crane ran his fingers gingerly over the smooth glass. And with a squeeze it flashed and bleeped into life.

Placing it down he knew it would be a matter of seconds before it rang but nothing happened.

Craned pulled a surprised puzzled face.

No call. No buzz of an email. Or text message.

Perhaps Matherson had had a change of heart. Or realised that retirement meant retirement.

But in all that time in his career. This was the one time that he truly wished that he would call.

Suddenly Crane's knees felt relaxed and twitched.

He put his hands on the side-board and steadied himself. The whiskey was gripping his legs and he could feel it moving. Pulsing through him. Towards his head.

Cranes mind started to race - 'Gotta sit down.. before I fall-down'

Sinking into the old leather armchair. He again felt warm and incredibly relaxed. His eyes fluttered then it all went black.

Crane didn't dream. Not really dream but at that moment he felt like he was standing alone in the dark. With someone unseen pummelling his head with a hard rubber-mallet.

Thump after thump after thump. Each one getting harder and louder in his head and ears.

Crane snatched his eyes open and the thumping now turned to a humming. Piercing his ears. He grit his teeth hard till they almost creaked. And he cursed himself for drinking again so hard and so soon.

Slowly regaining his senses Crane realised the thumping was real but it was in his head. And a hard tone for his gross over indulgence to block things out.

Where the hell 's that buzzing come from ?

With blurred precision Crane surveyed the room and ceiling like the spy he was. Nope. No flies no honey bee. Busily looking for an exit.

Crane shifted his scan and finally his eyes settled on the small occasional table. And low-and-behold there was the buzzing insect. Small black and shiny.

Grabbing it up the buzzing abruptly stopped and the insect spoke - '*Crane.. I know its Sunday and early.. ! but how's the retirement and your beloved Grannies old chicken-coop.. Ha.. ?*'

Taking the phone down from his ear. He stared at it. Biting his lip. Knowing he shouldn't have switched it on.

'Miles..! for the first time ever.. I'm glad you've called.. something bad has happened down here.. !'

Crane could almost sense the look on Matherson's face at his statement.

'*What.. ? hang-on.. Crane you wanker.. you rang my secure line and then rang-off.. remember ?.. but don't tell me Crane !.. there's a dirty-great hole in your thatched roof.. !*'

Crane breathed in hard - 'No Miles.. it's the local Police station.. someone's just blown up the police station.. for fuck-sake !

Again a vision of Matherson's fat podgy face. Looking all red and confused shuttered into his mind.

'Eh.. what the fuck you talking about ?.. blown-up ?.. it was probably a gas leak or something.. you've been retired for 5 minutes and already started World War 3 in Cornwall !!!'

Crane pulled the phone down from his ear again in frustration and stared at it closely for a moment.

Then slamming it back to his ear - 'It was no damn gas-leak Miles.. !.. MILES.. IT WAS C4.. !'

The fireman danced his way over the debris and sprayed water everywhere. As he'd been ordered to. But there was little point. Everything had been blown to bits or already burnt to a crisp. But the fire had long since died out. But spotted areas still smouldered here and there.

The Police had cordoned-off what remained of the station but the locals still stood and watched. It was probably the most excitement they've had in years. But even they started to thin-out after a while.

'Guv.. there's not much left to water-down.. nothings alight !'

'Yeah all-right.. turn it off'- replied the Fire Marshal as he walked back towards him.

'Shit.. what a mess !' – he motioned further.

Looking around they surveyed the burnt-out shell of the house.

'Beat-over some of the ash and remains nearer the rear wall to make sure nothings smouldering.. and then we'll call it a day.. we'll have to section it off.. the whole buildings not safe now'

Placing the hose down the fireman grabbed a large rake and started to pull and sift through the burnt timbers.

Moving forward he slammed the rake into what looked like a door laying almost flat and just as he flipped it over he fell back with complete surprise.

'GUV.. GUV.. OVER HERE !'

The Marshal came running over from the side of the fire engine and stumbled to a halt.

'Oh Crikey.. I'll get on the radio.. !'

The Paramedic pulled the stethoscope from his ears and checked his patients pulse. It was Faint. Very faint. But there. But only just.

With a hard slam of the rear doors the ambulance sped off down the hill. It's siren wailing. All lights flashing and pulsating.

'Anybody else in there?.. what about old Nory?' - Asked the Paramedic.

The Fire Marshal turned ashen-faced and looked at the floor. And took a deep breath.

'Yeah he was in there alright.. got caught downstairs.. with Pullet.. but there not much left of them.. the blast blew them all over the place.. !'

'The Regional SOCO guy's found what was left of Nory's head outside in the back yard.. and one of Pullets legs under Nory's old Land Rover.. the rest of them was mashed-up.. pulped-up and burnt to a crisp.. but they bagged what they could find and removed them'

The other Paramedic stood beside the Marshal -
'Cheez what a mess!.. gas-leak ?'

'Yeah looks that way.. I think it started in the
back storage room.. Nory's cottage needed new central
heating and electrics.. he knew that !.. the whole place
was on the fritz.. just a time bomb waiting to go off I
suppose.. but god-knows how Pam survived.. the door
must have shielded her from the blast.. ?'

The Paramedic smiled half-heartedly and nodded.
And the Marshal returned his look.

'Right I'm all done here'- and stepping over what
was once the front door the Paramedic made for his
4x4.

The Marshal made one last check of the scene
and barked instructions to his lads to hose-up. And
scurrying like ants. The firemen cleared them away.
Eager to leave the scene.

A clink of glass made Crane snap his eyes open.
Looking around he'd slept in the arm chair again.
With nothing more but an empty whiskey bottle
for company sitting one side and an up-turned glass
tumbler the other.

He sighed and breathed hard. Realising he'd done
it again.

Crane was used to sleeping in his clothes. It was
almost second nature. As at times on assignment he had
no choice. But he was home and retired. And wanted
to get back into a homely routine of sleeping in a bed.
And not hiding a loaded pistol under his pillow.

Running his hand up and down the empty bottle. He frowned. Annoyed with himself. Then with a side-swing he launched it into the kitchen like a hand grenade.

The noise of the glass shattering splintered through his head and Crane leaped suddenly to his feet.

'Cold shower?' - Then again he realised had no real choice. The central heating in his Grandmothers cottage was always temperamental.

Crane spent the rest of the day at home. Constantly pondering on what had happened. There was no TV in the lounge. So book reading made sense. And grabbed one from his satchel in the kitchen.

But he couldn't concentrate on anything other than what had just happened.

But no matter how hard he tried. His mind kept playing over the scenario.

'C4.. plastic explosive..!' – I know what it sounds like. How it blows. What it smells like. He knew all this. Knew it all.

But could he be wrong this time?. Crane kept shuffling things through his mind like a croupier dealing cards and he always turned over the joker.

No. he wasn't wrong. C4 leaves a distinct smell. Almost vinegary. A burnt pungent acrid vinegary smell. And once you've smelt it. It stays with you. Locked into the membrane of your nose and brain. To anyone else. The people down here. They would never have known.

It's rather like the legendary clack of an AK47 being cocked. When you hear the breech being lifted and then dropped on an AK. It makes a certain sound. A sound that stays with you. A loud metallic clack.

This was no different. Same scenario. Once you've smelt C4 after it's blown. It's there forever.

'No fuck it.. I gotta get back to that Police station.. something just doesn't feel right' – Crane muttered to himself.

It was late and already getting dark outside. So arming himself with a small Maglite Crane made for the lane and back up the hill.

Standing once more outside the burnt-out wreck of the Police station Crane lifted the cordon tape and slid under. He knew instinctively where he had to go. The building had blown out from the back and taken part of the front with it in the fall-out.

Stumbling over the rubble and past the remains of what was once a wooden staircase, Crane stood in what seemed to be a back room of the building.

The rear door was lying flat but not far from the doorway itself. Indicating that it caved-in before blowing out. A tell-tale sign of the percussion of C4. When C4 blows it pulls the immediate air inwards before pushing outwards. Then you get the bang and the incendiary of the blast.

Instantaneous. But that's how it works with horrific effect.

Leaning on the doorway Crane shined the torch into the room.

Two of the walls had vaporised but part of the rear brick wall was still intact.

The floor was marked with little white flags. Indicating where the remains of the bodies were found. And black burnt patches showed where the blood had boiled with the heat then vaporized.

Painting the floor in the process.

The aroma of C4 and burnt flesh hung in the air, coupled with charred wood. It filled his nose.

It was a smell that you would never forget. And never get used too.

And Crane had known it for far too long.

Bending down he studied the floor and the position of the bodies. And their outlines.

They seemed very close together. Almost as if on top of each other. And he noticed that one was missing the outline of a head. And they also appeared to be positioned at the far side of the room.

If they had been caught mid-blast they would gone in different directions. In pieces for sure. But certainly different.

Crane shone the torch back and forth and then lined up the wall were the indications of the bodies were and then suddenly something caught his eye.

He was very superstitious. And didn't want to step over where they fell. It would invite bad luck. But he had no choice.

Crane pushed the torch close to the mark on the wall and then ran a finger around it. Then pushed his finger inside. Whatever was inside it was cold and felt metallic.

Taking a small pocket knife. He dug around in the hole and then finally worked free what was lodged there. It fell to the floor with a clatter.

Searching he finally grabbed it up and ran it through his fingers. He knew it. Knew what it was and realised there must be another.

Sure enough it didn't take him long to locate another hole and retrieved what was hidden within it.

Suddenly he heard some rubble move behind him and instinctively he flicked off the light.

His muscles tensed and the adrenaline surged through him with every heartbeat.

He crouched and pulled the Maglite back truncheon-fashion.

The noise grew closer. And suddenly a meow pierced the dark and a cat sprang passed. Almost as surprised as he was.

Crane rapidly shone his torch after it. And then relaxed slightly. It was ginger.

Back at his cottage he ran the small metal objects over in his hand. This was bad. Real black-bag stuff. They were bullets-heads. 'Hollow-Points'. And in the UK they are only ever issued to special squads and 'Black-Ops'. And the last time Crane had seen them was in Belfast.

The tips were mushroomed and splayed-out. A tell-tale sign. But nine times out of ten 9milly hollow-points mangle themselves as they go in. To create the maximum amount of damage on exit. And only shards remain. But these apart from the tips were almost whole.

Crane realised they must have been low-velocity rounds. And shot through a suppressed pistol. Only used by hit-squads. For when things are up-close-and-personal. Saves any ricochets. And any blue-on-blue casualties.

9mm hollow-points at close range. With close target recognition. Single-tap was all that was needed.

Forever cautious Crane went through the cottage making sure that all windows were secure. Locked and curtains pulled. And then locking each door in turn he placed an old kitchen chair just in front of them.

An old trick he'd learnt a long time ago in Sierra Leone. If anyone comes through the chair would slow them down and make a racket. Giving just enough time for him to respond.

Then finally taking something very personal from his suit case. He ejected the mag and tapped it to make sure all the rounds were seated. Then gently pushed it home and racked the slide.

Then performing a brass-check he de-cocked and dropped the hammer. Then gently slid it under his pillow.

Crane then laid on the bed. Again fully clothed.

Something major was going on here ! - This was real 'Black-Bag Shit !' - he mused.

Of all places. Here in a quiet part of Cornwall. Where all the peopled cared about was the weather and getting their veg to grow bigger than last year. Or catching enough fish.

Little-else mattered to these mild mannered gentle-folk.

There was not much else Crane could do. Just sit and wait and see if Matherson took him seriously.

Crane knew that Miles would think along the same lines eventually. That he wouldn't have called him unless there was something seriously wrong.

They had only spoken twice in almost 20 years during overseas operations. And that was only when something had gone 'Rat-Shit' in a big way.

Glancing at his watch. It was witching hour.

Between 2 and 4am was the best time to launch a surprise attack. Standard SOP for any take-down or hostage-grab. Everybody would be asleep and one on guard. In and out in 3 minutes. In one clean sweep.

Something was missing. Crane got up and retrieving his pistol from under the pillow he shoved it into his waistband and slowly moved into the kitchen.

Grabbing-up his mobile he spied it. No calls or txt's. No flashing lights to indicate he'd missed anything.

Then just as he turned to leave his hand shot-out and grabbed the other bottle of whiskey. It was a knee-jerk reaction and he didn't even look. Just snatched it from the sideboard.

Crane sat on the bed and suddenly his training kicked in. If he laid back and relaxed he'd go into a deep sleep. Undoubtedly helped along the way with the whiskey.

They'd be in and he'd be tapped in the head with a low-velocity hollow-point. Before his eyes would even be open.

Training dictates that if you have to sleep. Sleep in a chair. At least that way your still subconsciously tense. And your mind still but active.

Walking back into the lounge Crane moved the leather chesterfield armchair to the furthest far wall. And moved the small occasional table to the right side of it.

Placing the bottle down, Crane though at least he could be civilized. And rather than drinking from the bottle like a common lager-lout. He went back to the kitchen and retrieved a glass and this time, some ice.

Plonking himself down, puffs of dust bloomed from the old armchair and Crane watched them rise and shimmer in the air. Clinking the neck of the bottle on the glass. He poured a large measure. The ice swirled and floated to the top.

Crane pulled the pistol from his waist-band and palmed it for a moment.

It was his service pistol from his time in Belfast. A Browning Hi-Power 9mm. No serial numbers. No indication of where it had come from.

Clean side-arm issue was SOP. If he'd been captured by the IRA and the weapon taken from him and then used. At least if it was recovered there would be no connection to MI6. And therefore no-one to portion blame to.

No blame associated. No finger pointed.

But Crane smiled slyly to himself. When the Belfast assignment was over. Crane handed back in a Hi-Power he'd taken from an IRA informant and kept the one he was issued.

An operational souvenir. As he saw it. And certainly not his first.

Crane snatched-up the whiskey and clinked the pistol and the glass together.

'I'm ready' – he said to himself out-loud! – 'Whiskey and bullets.. come and get me.. motherfuckers.. I've got whiskey and bullets.. '!'

And with a single gulp, drained the whole glass. The large lump of ice smacked his top lip and he rolled them over. Savouring the last few drops.

Crane performed another brass-check and placed his Browning on the small table. And leaning back into the chair he stretched his arm. It reached. He could snatch-up his pistol in less than a second.

And sitting there. His mind started to wander again on the day's activities.

The Police station had blown-up. That much was sure and it was C4. Unmistakable. I've used that shit and I know what it smells like and how it blows. Crane mused to himself.

And I've pulled two 9-milly bullets from a wall in the Police station. Right near where the two bodies were. Not ordinary 9-millys. Hollow-points.

So a cover-up ? but for what ? This is Cornwall. Not Belfast. Nor Africa.

Crane drank more whiskey until again his legs felt numb. He reached out to make a grab for the pistol but all he did was succeed in knocking it to the floor.

Crane breathed hard. And it all went black.

And luckily he didn't dream.

The night wore on and was uneventful. In that small, thatched Cornish-cottage, perched on a small hill, nothing changed. And the solitary figure in the arm-chair for some reason slept a peaceful untroubled sleep.

The early morning sun shone through the old curtains and Crane felt odd. Felt damp and wet. He squirmed and opened his eyes. He squirmed again then realised he'd pissed himself.

His training had kicked-in. In his sleep.

Training dictates that it's better to wet yourself. Then move and give away your position.

Crane scanned the room. No change. Nothing. With a measured movement, he reached down and grabbed-up the pistol from the floor. Again through instinct he performed a brass-check.

Now standing, Crane double-palmed his Browning and moved in a classic weaver-stance through the cottage and checked very room and every closet. Always pointing the Browning wherever he looked.

Nothing. No broken windows. No doors forced and the chairs hadn't moved.

He breathed out a sign of relief. Then looking down at himself. A shower and change of clothes was now in order.

Feeling human again at least. Crane still didn't trust what was going on. His Browning was now securely tucked into his waist band again and he moved through the cottage on a mission.

There was no radio or TV in the lounge and he knew his late Grandmother didn't really watch TV that much. But he knew she did have one. Somewhere. Albeit small and ancient as he could remember.

Crane finally located the old set in the cupboard under the stairs. It was covered in cob-webs. But who knew, it may still work.

Dragging it out. Crane wheeled it into the lounge. Plugged it in and attached the aerial coaxial to the small socket in the wall.

He flicked the switch and the little green light came on. 'Happy-days' - he thought. – 'Here we go'.

The screen finally shimmered and then settled on a picture of a cooking program of some sort. But Crane wasn't looking for tips on his culinary skills. He wanted the local news.

The set was old and in black'n white. Clad in wood. With sticky-out trumpet-like buttons.

But flicking through he finally found what we wanted. The channel stated that the next program was the local news.

And turning-up the volume, Crane went into the kitchen and set the kettle in motion. He needed coffee and lots of it.

And the frying-pan. Still covered in chicken remnants. Was now bubbling. And Crane cracked a couple of eggs into it. Along with several rashers of bacon. His hunger matched his need for coffee.

And throwing it all together in a make-shift door-step. He covered it with copious amounts of brown-sauce, slid it onto a plate and made back to the lounge.

He sat on the sofa rather than the pissy-chair and gobbled at his breakfast-sandwich. Eagerly waiting for the news to make a screen appearance.

'Local area news now and yesterday.. mid-afternoon.. the local area Police station just outside Looe village exploded in what was believed a gas-explosion..'

Crane didn't avert his gaze. He was just intent on listening and concentrating on his brunch. He'd loved brown sauce since he was a kid.

Finally, the news elaborated – *"The local village Policeman Keith Nory died in the explosion long with the regional SOCO officer James Pullet.. the building.. whilst been cleared by the Fire Brigade found one survivor in the rubble.. !'*

Crane head snapped up – *'The local Policeman's wife Pam Nory had survived and appeared to be in the hallway when the explosion happened.. she's in intensive care and has yet to regain consciousness.. but she's stable'*

The coppers wife. The local hospital. Crane now had a potential lead.

The he suddenly stopped, mid-chomp on his sandwich – *'Christ.. !'* – what was he thinking ! He was retired. But now he was going to investigate an explosion and 2 deaths.

Crane shook his head and swallowed. No they were murders. And the local flat-foots would think this was nothing more than a gas-leak. A tragic accident.

Crane's still couldn't stifle his curiosity. 9-milly hollow-points and C4. This was black-bag stuff. No doubt about it. And he knew it. And both were shot-dead and the station blown-up with hi-explosive to cover their tracks. No-one looks for bullet-wounds in an explosion.

There was still no word from Mattherson. And the news report wouldn't say anything more than a gas-leak. So Crane would need more evidence. More proof. If he was going to get the office involved.

Let alone get 'Fat-Git' Mattherson out from behind his blasted desk

Leaving the cottage Crane slowly strolled up the cobbled lane. Towards the main road. He crossed and walked down the hill and towards the bus-stop.

He had no car or means of transport. But public transport was always a good way to see if he was being tailed. Plus being out in the public meant that no-one could make a move on him. If some-one was planning it.

And making that call to Matherson would have been recorded and logged.

Standard SOP at the office. Not to mention that his mobile would have been triangulated.

Now on the bus Crane saw they were approaching Looe main town and harbour. Several people got up to leave the bus and he did the same. To mingle-in.

Stepping off the bus, he stood for a moment. It was beautiful and picturesque. Looe was a lovely Cornish town with a small working harbour. Crane hadn't been here since he was 12. But it had changed a lot. A little more modern than he remembered. But the warm feel of the place was still there.

Snapping back into operational-mode, Crane walked up the high-street and made for a paper shop and bought the local rag. The words 'Gas-Leak' emblazoned across the front. Folding it, he placed it under his arm.

And looking around he saw a sign for tourist information and made a b-line for it.

Posing as a tourist was good cover. Buying a map in the paper shop would have possibly raised eyebrows and people would ask questions.

As a tourist he was one of many and walking around he picked up various leaflets on day trips etc. But finally he saw what he needed.

Sitting on a bench near the square. Crane read through the local paper and saw pictures of Nory. The local copper. He vaguely remembered him from when he was a boy. But couldn't really place him.

But in some small way he's seemed a little familiar. And the paper painted the same picture as before. And he learnt nothing more than what he'd heard on the news. But luckily for him there was a picture of Pam. The coppers wife. So at least he could ID her when he got to hospital.

Then standing once again at a bus stop. Crane stepped on to the No4 bus that apparently did a round-the-houses trip to the district hospital.

He strolled to the back once more. Again SOP. This way he could keep an eye on who got on and off.

And just as he sat down, he tapped his right side. And readjusted his belt slightly in his waist-band.

He'd forgotten how heavy his Browning was.

4

THE COUNTRYSIDE WAS GREEN and lush. Picturesque and totally Cornish and Crane smiled inwardly to himself as he looked out of the window. But his smile waned. He was on a bus and hurtling on his way to a hospital. To try and speak to a woman who had been blown-up and lost her husband and home in the process.

She was in a coma. She might never speak again. It was lame. But all he had to go on.

If that was the case. A coma. Then Crane decided there and then he would leave it. Leave the whole damn thing alone and stay retired.

Forget it ever happened. And let the local yo-yo's sort it out.

But Crane knew that he wasn't that lucky. For some reason he just knew. And an icy hand gripped his heart. His hands started to tingle and his feet felt like pins n' needles. This was a now a chain of events.

That would grow and fester as they went along. A bit like lighting a fuse and watching it burn along until it reached the end.

Then a bang. And he'd be in the fall-out. Nothing more than 'collateral damage' as Matherson would label it. A damage statistic. Nothing more. It was a hell of a way to end a 'glittering career' in her majesty's security services.

The small houses and ploughed fields started to thin-out and gave-way to a long winding road. And finally the bus did a gravel-grinding semi-circle in front of a hospital. Crane stared at it. He'd never been here before. It was old. And appeared some-what Victorian in style. But had recently been done-up to make it look more modern. And appear up-to-date.

The words 'Looe District Hospital' adorned a small road sign. And indications for A & E and admissions. Coupled with main-entrance showed the way.

Crane was still sitting at the back. As he always did on public transport. Then slowly, he got up and left the bus and followed the other passengers into the hospital. Safety in numbers he thought as he mingled. And with any luck this was visiting day, he pondered and good cover.

The Hospital only had a couple of main wards. That was clearly evident from the front desk. But Crane paid an unseen attention to his fellow bus passengers. And realised that one of the wards was for children. So he'd make for the other.

Making his way down the corridor Crane tapped his right hip. His trusty Browning was tucked away just inside his waist band and it made him feel confident. But god knows why he should need a side-arm.

Here, in England of all places. Not to mention a hospital. But the smell of C4 was still lingering in his nose and the bullets. The spent 9mm hollow-points. Were still in his pocket. Jangling together as a constant reminder. He needed them. To spur him on that this was very real.

A painful reminder. That whatever or whomever was behind this. The threat was here and now. And certainly real enough to do what they have done with the most chilling precision.

His 9mm Hi-Power gave him assurance. In this game it was paramount. Also he could at least defend himself If he had too. And he certainly hadn't hesitated in the past to fire-first and ask questions later.

Having a gun pointed at you was sobering. Specially if the person on the trigger-end was willing and eager to pull it. In the end leaves you with no choice. If its them or you. Send flowers.

Crane had something of a photographic memory and the picture of Nory's wife Pam. Gleaned from the local paper, kept flashing constantly into his mind.

Flowers were a good cover. So Crane grabbed a bunch from a stall in the main corridor and swishing them as he went, he scanned left and right with an almost bat-like radar.

There wouldn't be any Police watching over Pam. Armed or otherwise. As she was involved in a gas-leak not a terrorist bombing. So no guards. Only an over-zealous doctor perhaps. And the odd nosey-parker nurse.

Finally he saw her in a side room. Not in the main ward. And she was hooked-up to a heart monitor and a drip. Several in fact were taped to her right arm. She was slightly elevated and appeared to be asleep.

Crane decided to be *'overt'* rather than *'covert'*. So he strolled past and made for the main desk.

An old elderly nurse. Possibly the ward sister. Looked up through rather thick national-health glasses and surveyed Crane in a rather nonchalant way.

'Can I help you ?' – she said fingering her glasses back up her nose and finally braking into a loose-limp half-hearted smile.

'Er Yes.. I'm an old friend of Nory.. and I've heard about what happened.. how's Pam ?' - said Crane. Motioning with his head back up the ward. His eyebrows up as far as he could muster. And trying to paint a stupid melancholy but sad look on his face.

The sister looked down at her papers briefly and then back at him.

'It's hard to say.. early days at the moment.. but there has been some blips and she has opened her eyes now and spoke albeit briefly.. so she's out of the coma .. but not the woods.. so-to-speak.

Crane returned the sisters stare. She seemed very matter-of-fact to the point of been rude.

'Oh.. OK.. but I've got some flowers I'd like to leave her.. so is it ok if I stick my head in..?'

'Sure' - came the sister retort without looking-up.

Crane assumed that the sister had more pressing issues. Or she'd already had a long day. So didn't seem too bothered. But letting her know he was there would pay dividends if someone started asking questions.

'Ok thanks' - and Crane sauntered back up the corridor towards Pam's room.

Fortunately Pam was awake and looking out the window when he strolled in. She turned to look at him. Her face blank. And showed no emotion at all.

Crane felt a little uneasy but it was too late to back out. He needed to get into 'Actor-Mode' and play this out as best he could.

'Hi Pam.. how you feeling ?' – he motioned with a weak limp side-smile.

Pam didn't answer. Just stared. Like a soldier who had been in combat too long. The thousand yard stare they call it in the army. He's seen this before. The shock was gone. But the inner mental shock always lingered.

Crane raised the flowers and now smiled as best he could. Trying to fain concern. And Pam's face broke into a weak one. But at least it was a small sign of recognition.

Placing them down on the bed-side table. Crane decided to make his play.

'I'm an old friend of Nory's.. I was down here traveling around with some friends and I heard on the news what happened.. !'

Pam's face didn't change. No register. So Crane decided to play the soulful idiot. It was worth a try he pondered.

'.. they.. they said it was a gas leak ?' – and finally Pam's face lit-up slightly.

'Yeah that's what they say' – she murmured in a quiet soft tone – 'The old station was one-step away from being derelict.. it needed pulling down anyway.. but I can't remember much.. !'

Crane gave a little laugh - 'Yeah.. but that was a bit extreme.. !'

'I'm so sorry for what's happened.. Pam.. I meant to come down here years ago and see him.. talk about old school times.. you know.. the old days.. !'

'Old Nory wasn't playing around with fireworks was he ?' - said Crane braking into a big smile.

'I wish it was that simple' - said Pam with a stunted snigger.

Then moving her head forward a little - 'I think it was that thing.. that horrible smelly thing.. that Nory had brought to the station'

Crane suddenly switched from playing and his senses twitched !

'Thing.. what thing.. what do you mean Pam?'

'Oh it was Davy Parsons and his son… out fishing and they caught some large package-thing in their net.. it had a green ooze.. !'.

Cranes mind raced. He now had another lead.

Pam shifted slightly in the bed to get a better look at Crane - 'I know you.. from way back'

'Your old gran lived in Thimble cottage.. just up the cobbled lane from the village.. your Peter.. aren't you.. ?'

Crane breathed out hard and his nerves went from amber to green. She knew him. There was some small glint of common ground. This would only affirm his cover further. An old childhood friend would speak volumes if anyone else started asking questions, especially the local yo-yo's, about her visitors.

'Yeah.. I thought I recognised you too Pam.. it's all coming back to me now.. and yeah that was my dear old Gran.. gone now though.. bless her'

He needed to make a move. Follow-up what Pam had said as this was hot-of-the-press. And need following-up before anybody else did.

'Look I'll be off now.. let you get some rest OK.. but I'll pop back later in the week.. we can talk about the old times.. kids' stuff.. if you like.. ?'.

'Yeah' - said Pam - 'I'd really like that.. your old Gran was a lovely lady.. !'

Before Crane knew it he was marching back up the corridor and making for the exit. 'Davy Parson's' and his son Sam. The names didn't ring any bells thought Crane. But they would be his next port-of-call. The next rung on the ladder.

Breezing through the main entrance to the hospital. Crane looked either way and then made for the bus stop. A sweet little old lady in a baggy woolly hat and moth-eaten carpet-slippers gazed his way as he approached.

'Bus should be along soon son' - she said though puffs on her rolled-up cigarette and a somewhat toothless-grin.

'Thanks' - said Crane with a warm smile and a nod.

Boarding the bus. Crane instinctively sat at the back again. But as he strolled down to take his seat, something caught his eye.

The carpark was sparse but littered with the odd car. Mainly old 4x4's and a couple of small vans. But sitting in the far corner was a large black BMW. And to Crane. It looked very out of place. But to everyone else, just another car perhaps.

The number plate flashed into Crane head. Several times. And staring hard, he could just make out there was an occupant. Enforced even more by the plume of smoke leaking from the driver's window.

I've seen that car before – but where ? ' he mused.

Crane kept his gaze as the old bus shuddered and stuttered out of the carpark and wound along the road. There was no movement. The occupant stayed where he was. Probably watching him as much as he was watching back.

Crane took out his trusty notebook from his inner pocket and scribbled a few notes. Even having a memory like his did fail at the odd times. So this was a simple case of 'belt and braces'.

If Crane was still on active service he'd simply call the office and run a-make on the BMW's number plate. Then again if Matherson ever calls. He'd get him to do it. If he ever did show any interest with what was going on down here. In 'Darkest Cornwall'. As he'd put it.

Stepping off back in Looe. Crane made for a café. The one that sat purposely right on the harbour side.

The door tinkled as he walked in. And taking a window table Crane surveyed the harbour and scanned the billboards for fishing-trips and sight-seeing.

He was pondering on Davey Parsons when suddenly cod and chips was slammed-down in front of him. He couldn't remember ordering anything. But he was hungry. So grabbing up his knife and fork he eagerly got stuck in. Lashings of salt and vinegar and brown-sauce drown the dish. But he loved it and whist tucking-in. Reminisced once more about his younger days again. Whilst feverishly chewing on a dark pickled-egg.

Cod and chips was a stable food down here. And he enjoyed it. Just as much now and he did back then.

Finishing his meal he pushed the plate aside and then took out the leaflets he got from the little tourist info office. Thumbing through he found what he was looking for. He'd taken a handful along with the area map. He did that for cover. But it may pay dividends now

Finally finishing on a flyer for 'fishing-trips and coastal adventures' and Crane thumbed through it searching for the name Pam had given him. But there was no sign of it.

Noting that perhaps this chap didn't partake in tourist activities. Crane would have to make inquiries and ask around. And gathering up his note-book and papers he sauntered to the counter to pay his bill.

The young girl behind the counter smiled and noticed the flyers in this hand.

'Holidaying ?' - she said, as she passed him his change.

Breaking his line of thought. Crane looked at her and smiled and then looked down.

'Er yeah.. just looking at the fishing and coastal trips available' - he said fumbling with the flyer again.

'A friend of mine mentioned a Davey Parson's.. but he's not in the leaflet'

The young girl leaned on the counter towards him and glanced at it - 'Oh Davey Parson's.. he's just a local fisherman now.. him and his son Sam.. they don't do the trips.. they just fish and that's it'

'To be honest.. he's a bit of a misery-guts' – she continued looking up.

'But your find him further up the harbour-side.. a yellow boat.. if he's there.. but all the fishing been done today.. so your probably catch him tomorrow.. early'

And Crane glanced around and briefly looked out the café window - 'Oh.. thanks.. I'll look him up tomorrow then'

Leaving the café he decided to wander up the quay side anyway. Just to get his bearings and he may get lucky.

Sure enough the small yellow trawler was there. Right at the furthest end. Probably to ensure he wouldn't get bothered by the holiday-makers and would-be shark fishermen. Crane stood a while and scanned the boat. There was a reg number on the bow.

He scribbled a note of this. But doubted it would be needed. But as before. This was habit.

Sitting on the bus once again and bumping his way back out of town. Crane didn't think. Just dozed, still jet-lagged perhaps.

Getting off. Just at the top of the hill. He gazed back towards Looe and the sweet Tranquille picture it painted. But it did nothing to warm his heart or his composure. He had a feeling gnawing away at him. He had to prepare himself. After all those years in the field, you slip into an almost combat-like mode. Instinctively. And for some reason this was with him now.

Leaving the little village shop. Wine-laden and yet more curry mixes. Crane crossed the road and started on the cobbled lane towards his cottage.

Standing at the front gate, Crane shuffled the bags into one hand and fished for his keys.

The lock would need some oil to loosen it up he pondered as he aimed the keys at it. But the front door wasn't locked !

Crane dropped his shopping bags and snatched his Browning into hand. He dropped to one knee and performed a brass-check. One-round in the chamber and a full-mag.

And slowly he pushed the door open with his left hand. Pointing the Hi-Power everywhere he looked.

Then he moved. Crane stanced his way through the door and moved silently down the hallway. He checked each bedroom. Nothing. And then made back along the hallway for the lounge. The door was a jar and straining to hear. There was someone in there. Beathing quite heavily coupled with a faint whiff of brandy.

Crane lowered the Hi-Power and pushed the door open.

'MILES.. what the fuck are you doing here ?'

'Oh.. nice to see you too Crane' – Matherson said as he looked up.

Matherson was sitting on the sofa. Almost sprawled in fact. With a bottle of Hines Brandy on the floor beside his feet and a glass in his hand. That looked almost drained.

Crane had to smile. For once he was glad to see his old controller. Jerking his head forward Matherson motioned to Crane and Crane's right hand.

'Oh.. some other operational souvenir you didn't inform me about.. eh Crane.. ?.

Crane bent his wrist and waved the Hi-Power -'Better to have a side-arm and not need it.. then need it and not have it Miles'

Matherson sat back and smiled rather slyly. Then opened his jacket just enough to give clear indication of a shoulder-holster. And that he too was armed.

'No doubts there Crane.. operational prudence'

Crane hooked his mouth to one-side and laughed quietly to himself - 'Hungry Miles?'

Matherson didn't answer. Just raised his glass and nodded in silent agreement.

Crane wandered back to the front door and grabbed-up his shopping. Then placing them down on the kitchen side. He shouted-out to Matherson.

'Curry.. chicken curry ? .. that's about all I've got Miles..!'

Matherson was busily quaffing yet more of his Hines - 'Sure.. I'm famished' - he blurted. Dribbling the expensive brandy down his chin in the process.

Passing a plate to Matherson. Crane dragged the little coffee table over and placed his own down and palmed his fork.

The old leather chesterfield chair groaned as Crane perched on it. And happy in the knowledge that his earlier pissing-episode had now dried.

They munched away in unison and the occasional - 'Mmm' - from Matherson indicated that perhaps Cranes cooking skills where improving.

Matherson relaxed further into the sofa and placed the empty plate to his side - 'OK.. talk to me.. you've only ever called me twice in almost twenty five years.. so this is serious.. I know that much'

Crane didn't answer. He reached into his pocket and threw the two spent hollow-point slugs into his lap.

Matherson looked down and grabbed them-up. Thumbing them through his fingers. His eyes suddenly widened and his brow became furrowed.

'Shit.. Oh shit' – said Matherson and he stared at Crane. His face in a shallow-look of shock and wonderment.

'I dug them out of the far wall in what was left of that local Police station.. no doubt where the C4 was planted and detonated as well.. !'

'This is serious Crane.. fucking hollow-points.. hollow-points for Christ-sake !.. what the fuck is going on down here.. ?' - said Matherson as he looked at the spent slugs again. Turning them over in his fingers.

Crane decided that the best course of action was a full rendition of all he knew.

'A few days ago a local fisherman found something at sea.. caught in his net.. he then brought it ashore and reported it to the local flatfoot.. it had a horrific smell and a funny colour liquid leaking from it apparently.. !'

'They collected it and the local yo-yo officer was informed and then the day after I arrived.. the Police station.. the one up on the hill from my Grandma's cottage.. it blew-up and I was caught in the blast.. !'

Crane shuffled in his chair – 'That's when I smelt the C4'

'It was well planted Miles.. and it took out most of the down-stairs.. later that evening I went for a bimble and dug those two slugs out of the wall.. right where they found the two bodies.. or what was left of the two bodies.. they were supposedly both caught in the blast.. !'

'And you're not going to look for bullet-wounds.. in a supposed gas-leak.. are you Miles !' – smirked Crane.

Matherson listened intently as he continued – 'This supposedly sea-package was gone !.. no sign of it in the wreckage.. or at least the locals never found it.. or any evidence'.

Crane leaned forward – 'That Police station was blown-up to cover two things Miles !'

'The package found at sea.. and the two coppers who were taken-out.. !.. C4 cleans the slate Miles.. you know that coz we've used that shit.. remember.. for just that very purpose.. !'

Crane leant back into his chair - 'There was one survivor though !.. the village coppers wife.. caught in the blast as she was upstairs or coming down the stairs.. but she's alive'.

'Has she said anything ?' - said Matherson inquiringly, leaning forward.

'Already done.. I've been to see her and she mentioned about this package.. and the fisherman who found it.. but that was all she could remember.. !'

'Next port-of-call then Crane' - came Matherson's retort.

'Already tried Miles.. they have a birth down on the harbour.. far end of the quay.. little yellow trawler but they fish early in the morning apparently.. so I missed my window'.

'So now what ?' - said Matherson. Downing yet more of his brandy.

'Well I'm gonna hit the sack Miles.. you can please yourself'

Crane got up and grabbed his plate and made for the kitchen - 'Crash where you want.. there's beds' in the other rooms.. and blankets and pillows in the wardrobes.. but I suggest a good night's sleep and then we'll pay this fisherman-chap a visit.. early tomorrow'.

Standing back in the lounge, Crane stared hard at Matherson - 'Still like the Hines ?.. eh Miles'

Matherson looked up and smiled widely. Palming the Brandy bottle and twirling it in his hands.

'Yeah.. numbs the pain of the things we've done Crane'

Crane bent down and picked up his Browning from the side of the little table – 'Nothing will do that Miles.. not even drinking.. just gotta live with it.. or at least try too.. for Queen and country and all that patriotic shit and bollox.. remember..?'

Crane once more sat on the squeaky old bed in his Grandmothers bedroom and gripped his side-arm. Brass-Check. And he half-racked the slide and spied momentarily at the shiny 9mm Luger round. Perfectly seated in the chamber. He released and it snapped-shut.

Jesus. That would be a hard habit to break. Being armed was a way-of-life.

He slid the Browning under his pillow and threw his jacket over a chair. Followed by his trousers.

Settling-down Crane made a grab for the small bed-side lamp and the room went dark. Only the faint shadow of the moon shone through the old thread-bare curtains and danced spider-like on the wall.

He closed his eyes. He hadn't drunk anything. None of his wine. So had a feeling that sleeping would be hard. Being alone in the dark old memories would creep back and haunt him. They always did.

Suddenly his eyes snapped open. Sleepily and on instinct. He snatched-up his Browning. Cocked the hammer and aimed it at the door.

Then realised it was Miles. Trundling down the passageway to one of the other bedrooms. Crane breathed-out hard and thumbed the hammer. De-cocking the Browning.

He'd obviously finished his Brandy.

He slid the weapon back under his pillow and laid back on the old bed. It creaked and groaned. Like it always did.

5

'CRANE !.. GET YOUR ARSE-UP' – Crane snapped awake and strained to see what was going on. All he could make-out through blurred watery eyes was the shape of Matherson beating a hasty retreat from the bedroom. In his un-tucked wrinkled blue Oxford shirt and flat podgy feet slapping on the bare wooden floor. Like a fat water-logged penguin.

'Coffee..' - blurted Matherson as he disappeared out of the door.

Crane turned to his left. And there on the bedside table was a steaming mug. The strong smell of coffee came wafting over and at least smelt inviting.

Sitting-up with the mug in hand Crane was taken completely by surprise.

'You're up early Miles !' - as Crane took a gulp. It was black, hot and very strong. And no sugar.

'And your coffee's makings shit ! … nah scratch-that.. worse than shit.. !'

'Not my fault Crane.. you've bought Happy-Shopper crap.. what did you expect eh ?' – came a garbled reply from the lounge.

Crane shifted in the bed and the Browning slid down from under the pillow and tapped him on the lower back. Reaching round he grabbed it and placed it onto the bedside table.

Grimacing. Crane gulped down more of the rancid coffee. And slamming the mug down he lurched forward and pulled his clothes on.

Standing back in the lounge he peered around. The remains of last night's dinner and drinking were still evident. Matherson's empty plate was still sitting on the sofa. And the now empty Hines Brandy bottle was still sitting sentry-like on the floor. Paired with the empty glass.

Crane was glancing at his watch when Matherson came bustling into the lounge. More coffee in hand and what looked like a very rough bacon sandwich.

'I didn't make you one.. as I know you don't eat breakfast or eat early in the morning.. for that matter' - said Matherson. As once again he took his place and sprawled onto the sofa. Taking a hungry bite.

'Nah.. there's a nice café down at the harbour.. I'll grab something there' - said Crane shrugging to himself.

And striding into the kitchen, he set the kettle in motion again. As two cups of coffee in the morning for him, was always the way to go.

'None for me.. I'll be pissing too-much..' - said Matherson. Before he was even asked.

Crane stirred his coffee and this time it looked a lot healthier than the last effort he had and sitting back in the lounge, he looked at Matherson. Who was still greedily munching away.

'Plan of action' - said Crane.

Matherson didn't look-up, just acknowledged with a grunt.

'We'll head into town and tie-up with this fisherman and get him to take us to the stretch where he found the package.. we'll get our bearings from there.. OK ?'

Crane shot a glance at Matherson - 'I bet there's more of those things down there Miles !'

This caught Matherson's attention as he fumbled with his sandwich – 'What makes you think that Crane.. ?' - wiping brown sauce from his fat stubbly chin.

'Dunno.. something just tells me that response was too quick.. too-damn-good for this to be isolated.. whatever it was.. it was covered-up too fast.. and too-well.. so that tells me that there's more to this.. not to mention 9 milly hollow-points Miles..!'

'Well it's not the 'Office' Crane.. I can tell you that' - replied Matherson.

'There's no OPS in the area.. nothing' - he continued.

'I've checked.. the last - was years ago.. operation from 2 section in Penzance.. using a new type of sonar system.. remember ? ..you obtained it.. on that Polish OP.. but the office shut that OP down'

Crane gently nodded - 'Yeah I remember.. but somethings going on down here Miles'

Walking up the cobbled lane Matherson stood for a moment and looked out over the bay. It was just starting to get light and the sun was breaking over the water - 'It's beautiful here Crane.. truly beautiful and peaceful.. I can see that for certain..!'

Crane stopped and looked back - 'Yeah.. but evil can hide behind beauty.. Miles'

Standing at the end of the lane Crane made a move to cross the road - 'No.. Crane..' - and he motioned up the hill towards the Police station - 'I Just want to flex my curiosity.. as I'm here'

Together they eclipsed the brow of the hill. And the burnt-out ruin of the little Police station came into view.

They stalked around to the rear of the building. Crunching on broken-glass, shattered roof-tiles and side-stepping charred wooden remains. And glancing around Matherson limboed under the police cordon tape.

'Wow.. they certainly cleaned house Crane' - said Matherson, as he stood in the remains of a doorway.

'Yeah.. a like a bad-day-in-Bosnia' - and Crane pointed - 'That's where the two bodies where and here's the two bullet holes'

Matherson looked down and then stared at the supporting wall. He ran his hand down it and then made a fist. Wriggled his fingers and sniffed it - 'Yeah.. C4 alright' - and Matherson rubbed his hands together to get rid of the smell.

'The local Yo-Yo's wouldn't have been able to tell Crane.. no way.. plus your right ! .. no-one's going to look for bullet wounds.. or bullet holes in an explosion..'

Crane shot Matherson a surprised glance and raised his eyebrows sarcastically – 'Hate to say I told you so Miles.. but I told you so..!'

'Come on' - said Matherson – 'Let's get to that town and see what the fisherman's-friend has got to say about all this..!'

Jumping-off the bus Crane briskly made for the harbour with Matherson slowly tailing behind - 'Very quaint Crane.. I can see why you want to retire here.. I can certainly think of worse places..!'.

Crane glanced back and smiled – 'Yeah my Grandmother loved it here.. as did I'.

The sudden squawk of gulls over-head gave Crane some childish comfort.

Reaching the end of the quay Crane could see the little yellow trawler was still there. Same birth. But no sign of life so he turned back to face Matherson.

'Doesn't appear to be here.. let's sit in the café.. we can keep an easy eye-out on the quay'

'Yeah.. nice' - said Matherson – 'Another bacon sarnie.. I think'

Sitting once again by the window their vantage-point gave a clear view. They could survey the whole quay side. Most of the other fishing boats had already gone. But the little yellow one was still moored. Which seemed a little odd to him.

But glancing at his watch Crane saw it was only 6.30 in the morning. Still early in some respects but I suppose fisherman knew when to start. He mused to himself.

'Davey Parsons hasn't shown yet.. probably still sleeping off a hangover'

Crane snapped round and yesterday's waitress was standing there. All tea laden and smiling.

'Oh.. er right.. thanks' – replied Crane looking back out the café window.

Matherson took the tea and passed a cup to Crane – 'How did you know we wanted tea ?' - mused Crane as he looked back at her.

'Educated-guess !.. anything else ?' - she continued.

'Er yes.. my friend here will have a bacon sandwich.. well-done.. in fact make it two' – smiled Crane.

Crane returned his gaze to the window and finally Matherson turned around to join him – 'Nice girl.. pitch-your-tent Crane.. might do you some good..

110

some female company' - and he gently nudged him with his elbow.

Crane laughed inwardly. As in many ways he was right. Crane had been on his own too-long. And had almost forgotten what the warm company of a woman was like.

'What's this guy look like ?.. all sou'wester and wellies ?.. fishing-rod over his arm ?' - blurted Matherson through gulps of his strong West country tea.

'Oh Shit !' - thought Crane.

Crane sprang to his feet and approached the counter. And just as he was about to speak two rather large and burnt bacon sandwiches where plonked down in front of him.

'Oh.. right.. uhm.. Davey Parson's.. what's he look like..?'

'You can't miss him' - said the waitress - 'He drives an old black Vauxhall Frontera 4x4.. more rust than black.. and your hear it before seeing it.. and he parks it right down there on the quay.. beside his boat'

'Your see him.. or rather hear him when he drives past' – she continued.

'Great thanks.. everybody else seems to have already gone out.. but him ?' - replied Crane in a querying tone.

'Oh.. he's probably hung-over' - said the waitress, shaking her head – 'His wife ran off a few years ago supposedly.. and he's never really got over it'

'Thanks again' - and Crane took the sandwiches.

Re-taking his seat beside Matherson he slid the most burnt of the two across to him. And looking down Matherson didn't even frown. Just slid the top slice of bread from the sandwich and smothered it in brown sauce.

Through a messy mouthful - 'Well.. ?'

'Keep an eye out for an old black Frontera.. that's him and he parks down there.. right beside his boat' - replied Crane.

Matherson with a full slurping mouth just nodded in acknowledgement.

Crane followed suit. And lashings of brown sauce hit his bacon sandwich. And snatching a big bite he chewed with vigour. Surprisingly he was hungry and soon finished it and washed it down with the rest of the tepid tea. That seemed to sting his tongue more than the brown sauce did.

'Now what.. ?' - said Matherson looking at Crane.

'We sit and wait Miles.. I'm sure you can remember what that like.. !'

Time drags on observations and this was no exception. Crane glanced at his watch and it was just after eight.

Matherson now had his head buried in a local paper but blurted over the top in a worrying sarcastic tone - 'This is a loss-leader.. he's not going to show'

But no-sooner had Matherson spoke but an old, battered Vauxhall Frontera came spluttering onto the quay and chugged along to the far end.

Both Crane and Matherson watched in unison as the blue smoke cleared and the Frontera came to a juddering halt with a high-pitched squeal of brakes.

Matherson dropped his paper and made a move to stand. But Crane grabbed his arm and motioned with his head to stop in his tracks.

'Let him settle for a moment.. don't want to pounce just as he gets here' – and they both sat and stared. Silently monitoring the fisherman's every move.

Finally a young man appeared from the Frontera and was shouting. And he gestured towards the café and after finally hearing a muffled reply, started to walk towards them.

Cranes agile mind saw this as an opportunity.

Matherson looked at Crane and Crane hooked an eyebrow in reply. There seemed to be an invisible agreement between them and they returned to their table and tried to look busy.

The door to the café opened and watching in Cranes minds-eye the young man ventured in and straight past them.

'Two coffees and a fried egg sandwich.. please Josey.. and loads of brown sauce..!'

Crane snatched a brief glance at the counter.

'Coming-up.. Oh Sam.. those two guys over there.. have been waiting for you and your Dad' - and the waitress pointed towards Crane and Matherson.

Sam turned around - 'Oh aye ?' - he blurted with a frown.

Crane again slipped into under-cover mode. And wearing a dazzling smile he sprang to his feet and approached.

'Hi Sam.. is it ?' - and Crane warmly out-stretched his hand.

'Yeah' - and was greeted with a firm shake.

'What do you want ?.. not a fishing trip I hope.. me and Dad don't do that anymore' – he continued as he turned and grabbed his coffees and sandwich.

'No.. nothing like that.. we understand that you guys found a package at sea.. the other day' - said Crane with an open curious look.

'Oh that' - said Sam as he gulped at his coffee.

'Oh Yeah.. that !.. damn thing got caught in our net and we brought it in and old Nory took it.. not our normal fishing route but hey-ho.. Bastard-thing stunk like rotting meat though.. horrible.. !'

'Talking of which' – he continued – 'Fucking terrible what happened to him.. Ole Nory.. Bless-Him.. I remember as a kid.. when he used to catch me scrumping.. I used to get a clip round the ear-ole.. but damn lucky that Pam survived.. !'

Sam stood momentarily prompting an answer and Crane nodded. Then took a note book from his pocket and pretended to scribble some notes.

'Do you think that you and your Dad could take us out to where you found it ?' - said Crane as he looked up. With an inquiring but warm smiling look on his face.

Sam frowned and looked puzzled.

'We'll pay.. cash no problem.. I assure you' - continued Crane upping the ante.

This seemed to do the trick - 'Oh.. Ok.. why are you guys so interested ? .. but I'll have to ask me Dad first.. it's his boat.. !'

'Oh.. my colleague and I are writing a book on Cornwall and her coastline and the old mysteries and pirates.. we're interested in anything unusual that happens at sea'

'Huh.. hardly edge of your seat stuff.. is it..!' - sniggered Sam sarcastically as he made for the door.

Crane nodded at Matherson. And he got up and waited for Crane to pass and they both followed at pace.

'Dad.. coffee' - shouted Sam as he stood near the stern of the little boat.

Sam's Dad appeared and clambered back onto the quay. And looking at Sam he eagerly took the coffee, prized-off the lid and took a gulp.

Sam's Dad stared at both Crane and Matherson and took another gulp. Then he motioned with his hand. Prompting Sam to explain.

'Oh Dad.. these guys are interested in our catch the other day.. that large grey smelly lump thing.. they want us to take them out and show them were we found it.. !'

Sam's Dad just stared and creased his brow angrily at them - 'Oh we ain't got time that load of ole-bollox.. we've got work to do.. fishing been shit round here.. so we ain't got time to waste..!'

Sam motioned back at his dad – 'They said they'll pay.. cash.. !' – as he took a final bite of his egg-sarnie.

Sam's dad broke into a loose smile - 'Oh.. OK then.. if your pay for the diesel and the mornings catch.. you've got a deal..'

Crane looked at Matherson and then motioned forwards.

Matherson didn't say a word. Just walked past Davey Parson's and jumped haphazardly into the little boat.

Crane approached – 'How much we talking about ?' - he gestured openly. Taking his silver money clip from his pocket.

'Call it £500 !' - and Davey Parson's shot out his hand.

'Phew.. Blimey.. ! – 'Er.. OK then deal' - and Crane prised the silver clip off his roll of notes and handed him ten fifty pound notes.

Davey Parson's eyes went wide and he raised the notes to the sky - 'Ooo nice !.. and brand-new !'

'I'll take you guys where-ever you want to go' - said Davey Parson's waving the notes and now wearing a wide beaming smile.

'Just where you found that funny package.. or the stretch it's in' - said Crane matching his wide grin.

As he too sauntered past and jumped down into the boat. And wandered over towards Matherson.

The day was calm. The wind was low. And the sea was smooth and seemed mild. The waves were kind and gentle as the little trawler slowly chugged out of the harbour.

And with little resistance headed West-ward out into the open swath of sea and beyond.

The sun was starting to climb over-head and Crane stood in front of the wheel-house and closed his eyes. Embracing the on-coming salty breeze.

He breathed-in hard. Filling his lungs and holding it for a moment. Savouring the feeling.

'It's amazing how things like this can set the mind turning.. eh Miles ?'

Matherson was lumped to one-side and holding his head - 'God Crane.. I've got a right bastard behind the eyes.. feels like a pig shat in my head.. !!'

Crane shot him a brief glance and smiled - 'Too-much of that Hines Brandy Miles.. that Brandy may be the best you can buy.. but it has a hell of an effect on you if you over indulge.. and you necked the whole damn bottle.. !'

Crane stared again into the sky – 'The sea air is just what you need.. it'll wake you up'

Matherson didn't reply. Just groaned.

'We're not far now' - came a call from the wheel-house. And Crane turned to see Davey Parson's pointing roughly. With an out-stretched arm through a crocked-window.

Still wearing his sunny wide smile and 500-quid richer.

Then briefly glancing back at Matherson Crane smiled to himself. He'd never had a taste for Brandy. Too heavy. Too fierce. And it muddles the mind the day after.

'You Ok Miles.. ?' - looking at Matherson again. Crane kept his gaze, hoping for a reply.

There was another muffled groan through clenched fingers and Matherson raised his head - 'Where are we..?'

'Close.. very close.. apparently' - replied Crane.

Matherson looked up and then slowly got to his feet. Wrapping himself in his over-coat. At what little breeze there was.

Suddenly the engine was cut and both Matherson and Crane turned around.

Davey Parson's clambered around the wheel-house and stood at the far end of the bow - 'Here we are guy's..' - looking down at the water and the waves lapping at the side of the boat.

'This is the stretch.. right here in this current..' – he pointed - 'It's quite gentle today.. as normally this current is pretty-strong and most things here get carried-out'

'Carried out..?' - called Crane in response.

'Yeah.. no-one fishes here.. not for years as anyone who lays pots - gets them lost.. carried out in the current or covered in the drift and sand-bank.. and then lost forever I suppose.. until someone gets lucky.. '

'Like you guys did the other day' – furthered Crane.

'Oh yeah.. right' - said Davey Parson in a sarcastic-tone.

'I thought we might have.. got lucky I mean.. but it was a just something dumped at sea.. that's all I suppose'

Crane came over and stood next to Davey Parsons and peered over the side into the surf. He scanned - 'The sea seems very calm and you can see clearly.. almost to the bottom.. !'

'Yeah.. calm today' - replied Davey Parsons as he joined Crane and looked over the side.

'It's not too deep here either..' - he said further.

'How deep.. ? diveable..? - queried Crane.

'Yeah you could.. we're about 5 miles off the point and here.. as there's tidal drifts.. so I'd say 50.. or 60 meters down.. but that's on a good day.. like today though.. if it's a calm day.. your good..!'

Crane pulled his mobile from his pocket and checked the longs and lats for their position. Took a screen-shot and noted the time.

Crane turned and Matherson was standing right behind him. Looking worse for wear but attentive.

'You're not thinking.. what I'm thinking are you Crane..? – he mumbled.

'Yeah.. pressure-suit and a floor walk.. you could do that Miles.. you're a trained diver as I recall'

Matherson suddenly straightened himself soldier-like and re-affirmed his tie. He hooked his head back and raised one eyebrow.

'Been a while.. but I'll do it.. I'm still as fit as I was - when I was 30 Crane !'

Crane looked Matherson up and down. Smiled and tapped him on the shoulder.

'Of course Miles.. a walk in the park for someone like you'

Crane turned - 'Hey Davey could you give us a sweep of the area.. and the bay.. we'd like to take some photos etc.'

'Sure.. no problem' - and he scrambled back to the wheel-house.

The engine gave a strangled-like burble and they chugged on. And Davey Parsons shouted-out above the din.

'We'll go out past the point and then back round OK' – And Crane glanced over and nodded in agreement.

'What the hells that.. ?' - and Crane pointed to the cliff-top. Matherson squinted and bent forward.

'Looks like an aerial-tower' - replied Matherson and he turned to face Crane with a surprised look on his face.

Craned motioned to Davey Parsons with his arm and pointed upwards towards the cliff-top - 'What's that.. ?'

Davey Parsons looked at Crane and then bent down slightly and peered through the wheel-house window. And upwards in the direction he'd indicated.

He nodded – 'That's the old Naval base from the second world war.. submarines or divers.. something secret.. my old dad told me about it when I was a kid'

'It's derelict now.. but there's an opening further round.. I'll show you' - and the little trawler chugged on.

Confused Crane looked at Matherson – 'An opening..?'

Sure enough. Just around the cove. It came into view. And both Crane and Matherson stood in silence and just stared.

It was an opening. Certainly man-made and looked crudely carved into the cliff-face. Small and cave-like but certainly big enough for some sea-fairing traffic. To the right of it was a small quay and a place to moor. But it looked years old and certainly weathered and sea-worn.

'Didn't know about this Miles..?' - said Crane as he peered forward – 'Didn't know about it as a kid.. either' - and Crane moved to the far end of the bow.

'Nor did I' - replied Matherson. 'It's not on the books at the office.. so it's probably been moth-balled.. !'

They both stared in wonder and bewilderment.

'Can we get closer' - Crane shouted without looking around. Then upping the ante Crane shot back a hard stare. Prompting an answer.

Davey Parsons looked at Crane and shrugged – 'Sorry this ain't a speed boat.. the currents too strong.. you need something with a bit of power'n speed to get you in there and out again.. there's rip-tides and your end-up on the rocks.. !'

Crane looked back at the opening and saw for himself. The sea was rough and breaking hard around the entrance.

'I'll get a close as I can though.. if you like' – he blurted with a thumbs-up.

Crane and Matherson again stood in silence and eagerly surveyed their new find. The sun was high in the sky now and it was a clear day. But inside, the hidden-cove remained dark and somewhat eerie. And for some unknown reason to Crane it seemed menacing. And he had an instinctive feeling they were now being watched.

Chugging past they stayed rooted to the spot and took-in every angle.

'Hmm.. this is very interesting Miles' - blurted Crane – 'I had no idea this place was here.. but it may be worth a look perhaps'

'I've got an idea Crane..' - and he turned and looked at Matherson, prompting further.

'Let's get back to the harbour and then go and get your plane and do a fly over.. we can then land at Penzance and I'll grab some diving gear and a boat.. and we'll get inside it.. what you recon.. ?'

Crane gave Matherson a surprised look but smiled and nodded in happy agreement – 'Sounds like a plan Miles.. let's do it'.

Sam jumped off the boat as it neared the quay-side and tied the bow to a mooring gleet. Then strolling back to the stern. He did the same and then waved at Crane and Matherson as he scrambled up the quay ladder and made for the Frontera.

'Thanks for the trip Davey.. much appreciated' - as Crane eagerly shook his hand.

'No problem.. anytime.. at the rate your willing to pay' - he said with a snigger – ''Let me know if you want to go out again..'

Crane and Matherson made their way back up the quay - 'What do you think Crane..?' - pulling his overcoat around himself again. Then Matherson stopped in his tracks and stood staring like a regimental sergeant major. Waiting for his order to be carried-out.

Crane stopped. Sighed hard and slowly turned.

'Miles.. let's get this straight.. we've two police officers shot dead and then the station was blown-up with C4 to cover their murder.. all over a strange package that was found at sea.. and now we've seen an old Naval Intelligence base that's not on the books.. supposedly abandoned.. that may have something to do with all this.. as that aerial tower certainly isn't from the 1940's.. it's got a bouncer-beacon at the top..'

'AND Miles.. I've got a nasty feeling that we were being watched..!'

'Watched..?.. Jesus Crane ! .. your still as bloody paranoid as you've always been.. !'

A little angry Crane slowly sauntered backwards - 'Maybe Miles.. but that instinct.. that paranoia as you so easily call it.. has kept me alive.. ! not to mention I've only been down here and retired five fucking minutes and already I've been blown-up.. we've found a potentially live OPS base that's probably been since I was a kid and I'm carrying my sidearm on home-soil.. damn Miles.. we need to know what's going on.. so don't call me paranoid OK.. !'.

'Some fucking retirement Miles..!'

Matherson looked down at his feet – 'Yeah.. I can't argue with you there.. and that tower.. I saw that.. the locals wouldn't know any different would they.. even if some of them have seen it over the years'

'Common Miles.. let's get airborne' - Matherson slowly nodded.

The cab ride to the little airfield was shorter than Crane remembered. But standing once again next to his Cesna Skymaster, he clambered in the right-side and Miles followed suit.

They both placed on their headsets. Wrapped on their harnesses. And Crane turned the key to position one and checked the dials. All was in the green and then he flicked the key. And once more and the engines burst into life and settled into the steady humming rhythm.

Crane didn't play for protocol and could see the sky was clear. So a brief taxi over to the main strip and he gunned the engine and they were streaking skyward in moments.

Looe village and harbour soon came into view and through the small wisps of cloud cover, Crane flew lower and made his way directly out and across from the harbour.

The cove point came into view and Crane banked right and slowly round. And then descended even lower.

'There it is.. that's the aerial tower and part of that old base.. by the look of it' - Crane squawked over the comms to Matherson.

'Go past and then come back round for another sweep.. try and get lower' – said Matherson craning his neck against the window.

Crane flew out to sea and then gunned the engines to swing round for a further pass. But just as he came over the point again a bouncer signal ringed in his ears and a red light flashed on the planes control-dash.

Matherson heard it too and stared in disbelief at Crane. And then at the controls.

Scratchy static pierced Cranes ears - 'We're being tracked Crane' - said Matherson. The worrying tone in his voice was clearly evident.

Crane banked around again hard and flew back passed the point. They both looked out the far-left windows - 'Yeah.. it could be an old safety bouncer.. for air traffic..'

Matherson shook his head – 'Not there.. too remote.. and too low.. the only traffic around here is little private stuff.. that's an early warning system.. somethings going on down there Crane'.

'Yeah.. this shits getting even more real Miles.. what the fuck is going on down here.. ?' – and Crane stared back out and gunned the little plane again to get some altitude and then flicked the inertial nav and the plane pulled further Westward. Penzance bound.

The airfield just outside the town at Gulval was a little bigger than the one in Looe. Not much bigger. But at least the runway was tarmac and not manicured lawns. Crane feathered the engines and planted the Cesna down smoothly.

He taxied over and came to a stop at a pull-by and they both got out.

They didn't check-in. Just made a swift exit to the main road and the nearest bus stop.

Public transport was still the order of the day and both Crane and Matherson boarded a bus that stated, 'Penzance Town Centre'.

Neither of them commented about the scenery. Neither of them uttered a single word. They sat apart. All seemed 'Operational' now. Operational means that when on a job, you only speak when you need to. Unless you know your being watched and then small-talk and disguised small-talk can sometimes diffuse.

Crane was first up. Again operational procedure. And the bus stopped just off the end of the main high street. He got off and headed towards the harbour. He didn't look behind. Didn't need to. He knew Matherson was trailing behind him.

He headed towards the offices highlighted for 'Coastguard' and walked along a side pathway towards the rear of the building and a large, galvanised gate loomed. Above was a globe-type CCTV and to the side of the gate was a small silver intercom and keypad.

Crane stopped and leant against the wall. Hands in his pockets. And with a shuffle of his arm, near his elbow. He felt once again his trusty Browning tucked away on his hip.

Ten minutes later Matherson came shuffling into view carrying a large Costa.

'Couldn't get you one Crane' - as he waved the coffee-cup – 'Operational prudence..!'

'Just open the fucking door Miles.. I'm cold and tired' - came Crane's reply.

Matherson pressed the buzzer and looked up at the round CCTV. There was a clang and the door opened slightly.

He didn't move. Just stood and continued to greedily slurp on his now tepid coffee.

Crane pushed the gate and walked forward and then descended down a galvanized iron stair-case.

Matherson followed suit and pulled the gate shut behind him.

At the bottom Matherson pulled a code-key from his inner pocket and shoved it into a small card-reader. There was a buzz then the metal blast-type door popped to one side with a whir.

They stepped into a room that was all clinical and white. A few chairs and large table where set to one side. And in the far corner, a lone computer terminal.

'I suppose you'd better check in Miles.. let the office know what you're doing and give a sit-rep.. just in case this all goes South' - said Crane.

Matherson didn't answer. He was already making his way towards the desk.

'I'm on it' - replied Matherson. Through final gulps. And emptying his Costa.

'Then put in a rec-order for the boat and diving gear.. and we'll get some sleep till morning I suppose' - said Crane as he sat down.

Matherson waved his hand in acknowledgment. That for once he was one-step a-head.

With a final hard tap on the computer keyboard, Matherson pushed himself away from the desk and spun round on the office chair. He smiled at Crane and then folded his arms.

'What the fuck am I doing here Miles ?.. I'm supposed to be retired' - blurted Crane as he sat slouched at the table. His elbows perched and his head in his hands.

Matherson sniggered – 'Well what can I say.. shit happens and it's nice to be out of the office for a change.. and on operational's again.. !'

Crane looked up at his old controller – 'Is this an operation Miles ?.. I've stumbled into this and now you've come along for the ride.. hardly an operation.. !'

'C4 Crane.. remember ?' – squawked Matherson.

'C4 !.. yeah.. that ain't normal Miles.. there's no-way we could have been wrong about that.. that's for sure.. !'- continued Crane – 'And I'm carrying my side-arm.. on home soil.. that ain't normal either.. !'

'Normal or not' - replied Matherson - 'it's an operation now.. I've just logged it and the gears been allocated.. tomorrow we'll take a look'

'Hungry..?' – he said with an inquiring look.

'Yeah.. starving' replied Crane.

A short while later a buzzer sounded and young girl of around 20 appeared at the far entrance. She was dressed formally and in uniform and looked coast-guard. But more-so, under-cover coast-guard.

British Intelligence had eyes and ears everywhere and here was no exception.

'Your take-aways here.. Commander Matherson'

And the young girl disappeared from view momentarily and then re-appeared and passed Matherson a small white bag and a large Domino's box.

'Excellent' - and taking the items, Matherson shut the door with a kick and made for the table.

'Your pizza Crane' - handing him the warm red and blue square box.

Crane re-took his seat and pulled the lid-up. The smell of cheese and jalapeno-peppers filled his nose and he hungrily grabbed a slice.

Matherson retrieved some plates and serviettes from a cupboard and started to spoon out his Chinese.

Crane stared at him as he ate. Matherson had always been a greedy-bastard and a Chinese meal for two was soon being decanted. Spoon after spoon onto his plate.

They sat and ate their respective meals in silence.

Tomorrow was going to be a busy day and Crane had a feeling that something was going to go wrong. Terribly wrong. He just couldn't shake it. And worst still, he'd never been wrong before.

Every mouthful of his pizza now chocked him a little. As for some horrible reason. He thought it could be his last.

6

CRANE STIRRED IN HIS bunk. It was uncomfortable and he felt hot and sweaty. No matter what he did. No matter how he tossed n' turned. He couldn't get settled.

MOD bases. Particularly those for surveillance ops where rudimentary at best. They weren't designed for comfort. Just the basics in living quarters. Latrine. Cooking area. Table and chairs. And a comms desk. Coupled with bunk mattresses as thick as a slice of toast. And felt the same when you laid on them. Their only saving grace was that they had heating. But the air was piped-in through the floor. And it smelt old and musty. Not to mentioned the bedding gave off the same aroma.

Crane swung his legs out of the bunk and slapped his naked feet onto the floor. It was bare polished concrete. But at least It was warm. And he shuffled his toes to relieve the numbness.

Peering through the darkness he could just make-out Matherson. Laying sprawled on his back in the other bunk and snoring like a wild boar in the mating season. There was a faint glint of shiny metal on the floor. And leaning forward Crane could see that Matherson had obviously drained the last of the hip-flask he was carrying. The infamous Hines Brandy had once again done the trick

He stared at his watch. It was still early. A little after 2am. So way too early in fact.

So leaning back he pondered on the day's operation. Up at 4. First check the diving suit.

Pressure suits could be temperamental. So Crane would make sure that the equalizer valves would be working. Not to mention the helmet seals. These where the first-port-of-call. And paramount. If the suit had not been used for some time, then these had better be changed.

Then the boat.

Matherson had requisitioned a twin engine jet-turbine pursuit boat called a 'Patriot'. Not very big but it had the power of a souped-up V8. Fast and very manoeuvrable. British Intelligence uses them for off-shore big-ups and agent intercepts.

So ideal for this type of job. As getting into that little sea cave in the cliff-face would be tricky to say the least. Let alone make our way out.

Crane took to his feet once again and ventured for the small canteen area. After throwing open the various cupboards, he finally settled on a jar of Mellowbirds coffee.

Ha palmed it and turned it over in his hand. It was old and it only reminded him further of his days with his Grandmother. It seemed funny to him as now in Cornwall. So many things did. And looking at the jar. He frowned and pondered as to its age. Or since when perhaps that this small coastal intelligence base Op had last been used.

Still with a click of the kettle he poured the water into his mug and gave it a stir.

Crane smiled in surprise. As the coffee tasted better that it had looked and he made for the door opposite. He thought to himself that as he couldn't sleep he'd make an early start on the equipment check.

Anything was better than sitting around. Watching the clock and listening to Matherson honking like a pig in his deep slumber.

In the prep-room, a large metal inspection desk ran the whole of one side. And laying upon it was the diving suit. And far to the other side was the closed-dock and in it sat the Patriot.

It bobbed and swayed up and down in the gentle undulations of the current.

Crane placed his coffee down. Grabbed-up the helmet and made a start.

Turning it over. He could see that it had new seals to the collar and neck-brace. Then placing it back on the desk, Crane attached the air-lines for the helmet and then turned them on.

A powerful stream of air came through each side terminal.

All seemed fine so-far. The re-breather would work once all was connected. And expel the spent air.

Then picking-up the diving suit, Crane slid the helmet on to it. And with a hard turning left motion, it clacked into place.

He then hung the suit onto a crook hanger and then re-attached the air-lines.

Turning on the air, he stood back and waited for it to inflate like a balloon. This would take some time as the suit needed to pressurize and then finally equalize.

Crane sniggered to himself. The diving suit had finally finished inflating and looked like the 'Michelin-Man' and he sniggered even more as it bobbed up and down in front of him. This would come in handy as Matherson, although fit, was a little portly and would at least need the extra room for his Brandy filled belly.

Crane grabbed the suit and ran it through his hands and checked every seam. Expansion joint and seal. Then he ran his hands over the suit's valves for ingress and return.

All seemed fine and he switched off the air from the supply aqua-lung. But left the suit inflated.

Continued pressure would be a good way to see if any issues where hidden. Or delayed.

Turning away Cranes attention fell to the boat. And he stared at it. The 'Silver Bullet'. As they were called in the service.

He walked around it slowly. Up and down both sides. Admiring it.

Then he jumped into it and leaned over the dash-board. There was no key. No key-start. As this would cause a problem out in the field. All operational vehicles. Either cars. Boats. Planes and even helicopters had secret immobilisers.

You merely flicked the switch or pressed the button and then hit the ignition. In the field, you can't be hunting for keys. Or indeed the person who had them. If they were killed in action then you'd be seriously fucked.

Craned looked under the dash. Nothing.

Then he looked at the dash. Somewhat intently. But still nothing.

Then suddenly realising. He clicked his fingers in conclusion and with a flick of his thumb removed the small plastic cap on the end of the throttle lever and there it was.

He pressed it and a small green light lit-up on the dash.

Then pressing the small button beside it. The little silver boat roared into life.

Crane turned around and looked at the stern and gave the engine a rev. It sounded like water-born formula-one.

The boat gently rocked from side-to-side with each rev. As little plumes of white smoked spat and flared from the exhaust tails that poked out just above the rear engine cover.

'WOW..' - said Crane. But he couldn't even hear himself speak.

He gave the engine a final rev and then cut the ignition.

And glancing at the dash. The fuel tank was full.

Crane didn't bother with the immobilizer again. Just jumped back on the dry-dock side.

The pressure suit needed further inspection and Crane walked back towards it and just as he made a grab for one of the arms Matherson appeared. Looking much the worse-for-wear.

'what the hell you doing up.. ? You shit the bed Crane..?'

'Nope just operational prudence Miles.. not to mentioned that I couldn't sleep.. those damn MOD cots don't get any better with age.. not to mention you snoring like a stuck-pig.. didn't damn-well help either..!'

Matherson didn't acknowledge anything. He turned and walked away.

'There's coffee.. and it's not bad Miles.. Maxwell House of all damn things.. would you believe..!'

The finally Matherson just waved an arm in acknowledgement.

Crane was once again checking the suit when a thought occurred – 'Miles' - he called out – 'What

136

about a transponder.. ? I didn't see one on the dash.. or under it for that matter.. !'

The kettle clicked off again. And echoed down the corridor.

'Don't worry.. this little mission is off the office books.. so we won't or at least.. shouldn't need one Crane.. as we're only going for a look.. !' – Matherson called out in reply.

Crane didn't like the sound of that. They didn't know anything about what they were about to step into. Or indeed what they were up against.

Matherson knew that too. But seemed less concerned. And almost oblivious to it.

At least if it all went 'Tits-Up' the cavalry would come looking. Black-ops to the rescue. And the thought of that did give Crane some small measure of comfort. Without it. They were up on offer and Crane knew that no-one goes on an operation without back-up of some-sort.

Even with himself. Out in the field. In some foreign land. Locating a piece of tech to buy. Barter. Or steal. He knew he had back-up. He'd make a call and it would be there. Land extraction or air-extraction.

Crane finished his checks on the diving suit and finally un-clipped the air hoses.

Striding back up the corridor and stepping back into the little kitchen. Crane gave Matherson a hard concerned look. Prompting a further answer. The look on his face said it all. Crane wasn't happy.

Matherson didn't return his look. Didn't even avert his gaze other than to place a fourth spoonful of sugar into his coffee.

He stirred it once then threw the spoon onto the side.

'Your retired.. remember Crane' - blurted Matherson. Without looking up.

'What the fuck has that got to do it with Miles.. C4 and 9 milly hollow-points.. remember.. no back-up is not operational Miles.. we could be getting way over our heads with this.. with no-one to throw us a rope.. !'

Matherson didn't answer. That seemed very odd to Crane as he was never short words in the past. And he wondered if his old controller knew more about what was going on than what he'd let-on.

'Truth is Crane.. I'm up for retirement too.. but not by choice.. I've had the red-letter.. the office thinks I'm now too old and I should be put out to pasture.. training wet-nosed Oxford grads..

no longer on active intelligence service.. no longer at the sharp-end giving the orders.. just a child minder.. !'

Matherson finally turned – 'I've taken this little holiday and in the process I'm gonna prove them wrong.. !'

He moved closer – 'I know there's something going on down here Crane.. you wouldn't have called otherwise.. you've only ever called me twice in over twenty years active service.. I know your right.. I know your instincts are right.. they always have been..!'.

Crane stared Matherson straight in the eye. He held his gaze for a moment and then he realised. He seemed strangely sincere – 'OK.. you're on.. Miles.. let's go take a look.. and re-shine those medals of yours yeah'

Crane paused. Stepped back. And drew his Browning. Did a brass check and then slipped it back into his waist-band.

Matherson noticed this and he did the same with his side-arm.

'Operational prudence.. eh Crane.. !'

'Yeah Miles.. old habits.. and they die-hard' – Crane blurted as he zipped up his flight jacket. Just as Matherson threw him a protein-bar for breakfast.

Back in the dock Matherson stepped into the boat first. And Crane passed him the diving suit and helmet and the feeder-pipes for the air-supply.

The Patriot was already fitted with a diving compressor and although Crane hadn't tested it, he was sure it would be fine. In many ways using an air-line was safer than an aqualung. If you got into trouble you could ditch your weights and then use the airline to ascend and pull yourself back to the surface.

Matherson switched on the little boat and the engine roared into life. Crane untied the mooring lines and Matherson pulled a little black remote from the side of the dash and aimed it at the swept-way doors.

With a hum they swung open like stables doors. It was still quite dark as the Patriot manoeuvred backwards and out into the harbour.

There seemed to be a stealth mode. As the Patriot made hardly any noise as Matherson spun it round and then pulled it forward and cruised it round the other moored yachts and dinghy's. Only the faintest of ripples in the gentle calm sea could be heard in the early morning air.

The harbour was now some way behind them and still the Patriot was running silent. Then Matherson snapped the throttle back and the silver bullet took-off across the sea and way out into the horizon and the rising sun.

Crane was thrown backwards and stumbled against the stern. Then feeling his knees creak. He sat down on the small perch-seat and held onto the rail-side.

He looked up and felt the salty wind in his face again and the cool breeze made him shudder slightly. Then opening his eyes. They stung and he clenched them even tighter.

He felt un-easy. It was a gut feeling. An instinct. That things were going to go wrong. In a big way.

The feeling of no back-up plan plagued his thoughts. And no back-up was not SOP (Standard-Operating-Procedure).

No variables. So he had to make sure that nothing went wrong. There was no room for error.

Crane looked at Matherson. And he was in control. No doubts there. Just like Captain Ahab standing at the wheel of the Pequod. Searching for Moby-Dick. So in other-words. All was wrong from the get-go. The last time Matherson was out in the field was some fifteen to twenty years ago. Crane knew he hadn't had any refresher training. So for all his years. He was green.

Crane shrugged it off. He had to. This was now an Op. An Operation. A fact find. And his retirement would have to wait. And perhaps when all this was over Matherson would let him keep the Patriot. It would be great for fishing he mused.

He stared at the horizon and the silver bullet started to bank to the left and round the hooking coast-line. It skimmed the calm sea like a child throwing a smooth flat stone across a lake. And looking behind. There were hardly any ripples. No tell-tale wake. So anyone keeping them under surveillance wouldn't be able to keep pace. And certainly not from the air. Or even by spy satellite.

Time wore-on quick and before he knew it the cove leading to Looe and Looe harbour slowly but surely started to come into view. And faintly to one side the hidden cave entrance.

Crane moved forward and stood next to Matherson at the helm. He looked at his mobile and snap-shot from their recent trip. Then flicked on the app that recorded the longs and lats of yesterday's position with Davey Parsons.

Crane tapped these into the small navmaster on the dash and Matherson looked down and made the course adjustments needed to get into line with the required vector.

A small red light flashed a steady heart-beat. Giving rise to their course and it rose in tempo as they locked on. Neared their target.

Matherson slowed the Patriot – ' Looks like we're here..' - And he glanced at Crane.

Crane looked all around and then down at the sea. It was calm. Very calm and ideal for their purpose. And flicking a switch on the dash, deployed an anchor-line.

'OK.. over to you Miles.. costume-time.. suit-up'

Crane picked-up the diving helmet and spun it in his hands like a basketball. Then passing it to Matherson. He placed it to the right over his head and then giving a sharp left turn it snapped and locked down into place. The face-plate was clear and positioned right over Matherson's podgy-red face.

He stared him right in the eye – 'You still good for this ?.. been a while since your last op.. let alone a pressure-dive Miles.. you sure your good.. ?'

Matherson shot Crane a smile and gave him a thumbs up. And grabbed the large search-torch. And lopped the lanyard around his left wrist.

Crane smirked at him and cocked an eyebrow and winked. All seemed good.

Matherson perched himself on the side of the Patriot and Crane switched on the compressor. And it started with a low beating hum. He then attached the air-pipes. And gave them a final reaffirming tug just to make sure. Thirty seconds and he'd be good to go.

With the pipes attached the air-compressor now had a faint heart-beat and the pipes jigged with the flow of air. He watched intently as it pulsed through and built in pressure. Slowly Inflating the suit.

Matherson watched too and ran his suited hands up and down his legs.

Crane placed a radio-headset on and flicked the mic round to his meet his lips – 'Still feels strange Miles.. ?'

He looked at Crane and gave a thumbs up again – 'Yeah.. it's still strange.. done this so many times though.. legs feel a bit pins and needles and my hands are throbbing.. !' - came Matherson's crackled voice over the comms.

Crane gave the pipes a jiggle. In an effort to move the air further. He wanted this to be over as soon as possible. His uneasy feeling was still there. But now with a vengeance.

With every move. Cranes spine twanged like guitar-strings being viciously plucked. But he hid it. He had too. Matherson said he was never wrong. But this time he wished with all his soul that he was wrong.

143

Matherson lifted his left arm. And glanced at the pressure-suits management dials on his forearm – 'Another 10 seconds and we're good to go.. !'- crackled his voice again over the comms.

Crane lifted the weight-belt and checked the buckle. And then checked the lead-blocks. Again all looked good.

Finally Matherson stood up and a static - 'Green-light.. we're good' - muffled in Cranes ears.

Crane grabbed the belt from the floor of the Patriot. And struggled as he pulled it around Matherson's waist and fastened it. With a final re-fold of the belts end clasp Crane tapped him on the leg in a note of affirmation.

Matherson sat back on the side of the Patriot again and then swung his legs over the side and dipped them gently into the calm water.

Crane pulled the air-pipes and then fed them over the side and into the surf next to him. And then continued to feed them further into the sea.

Crane didn't get a chance to look. Just a sudden splash as Matherson allowed himself to slip from the side of the boat without warning and to disappear under the soft waves.

Crane stared into the surf and broken water - 'Miles.. Miles.. we good ?' – nothing but static.

'MILES.. FOR FUCK SAKE.. REPORT.. NOW.. !' - and Crane scanned the broken and white foamy surf again where Matherson had jumped in.

There was a sudden burst of static. Then another - 'Yeah all good Crane.. ! Wow been a while since I last did a pressure dive.. feels wonderful.. !'.

Crane almost collapsed against the side of the boat. Then he slumped down on the seat in front of the helm.

Finally breathing hard – 'Fuck sake Miles.. don't do that.. I want a sit-rep every 5 minutes OK.. no arguments.. and let me know when you've bottomed-out.. OK'

'Roger-that..' - came a static reply from Matherson.

Crane kept a watchful eye on the compressors dials. All seemed good. Equal pressure. And all read five-by-five.

Retrieving the power-bar from his pocket. Crane tore the wrapper with his teeth and took a sniff of the crushed raisin and oats. And so-called glucose.

It had no smell. And looked dry as a bone. And totally inedible. And turning the packet over to take a closer look. The date read July 1975. Again this was standard MOD rations and designed to last a life-time.

Crane snatched a looked at the date again. Crikey ! He thought. He was only five years old then and still at junior school. When suddenly a blinding white light flashed in front on his eyes. And his neck felt detached from the rest of his body.

Cranes arms and legs went limp and the power-bar slipped from his hand. Then a hard shooting searing pain shot across the back of his head and streaked down back his neck. His eyes blurred and then his vision wavered and stuttered.

He went cross-eyed. Then everything went black.

Crane slumped forward and his face struck the control-panel with a solid bone crunching thud. And behind him a figure dressed in black. A frogman. Slowly rose-up and lowered his stun-cosh.

Pulling up his face-mask. The frogman surveyed the Patriot and looked at the air compressor.

Then he roughly snatched the head-set from Crane and placed the head sets ear-piece to his left ear.

'Crane.. Crane.. touch-down.. and Jesus the sea beds littered with strange looking lumps.. or packages.. I can just about see them.. but there's loads.. gotta be almost 30.. 40.. that I can see.. !'

'Christ what the fuck has been going on down here.. ?'

The Frogman dropped the head-set and let it dangle from the dashboard. Then he moved over to the compressor and switched-off the main return valve. And then took a firm grip of the air-pipes.

Seconds later the redundant head-set started to garble – 'CRANE.. FOR CHRIST SAKE.. TOO MUCH AIR.. MY EYES ARE GOING RED.. CRANE.. EQUALIZE DAMN IT'

Then frogman pulled a knife from his boot and cut through both pipes. And he watched as he let them go and trail snake-like over the side of the Patriot.

The head-set went quiet. Just some muffled static. Then a click.

The frogman turned and grabbed Crane round the scruff of his neck and yanked him hard to one side. And unconscious he slid from the helm to land on the floor of the Patriot. And he took his place at the wheel.

With a flick of a switch the anchor-line silently wound in. Then he made a quick scan of the dials.

He tapped his ear - 'One target eliminated.. other target secure.. coming in..' - and he pressed the immobiliser button on the side of the throttle and fired the engine.

The frogman threw the wheel to the left and slammed the throttle back and the Patriot lurched to one side then straightened-up. Heading towards the hidden cave.

And some way far below them. A small two-man submersibles motor whirred and bubbled and sprang into life. And the lone occupant steered the rudder on the same trajectory.

And even further below his craft. Laying on the sea bed. The now lifeless body of Matherson remained still. Just a small whisp of current moved his arm in an almost waving goodbye motion.

And blood slowly started to leak from the ruptured air pipes. To gently mingle with the sea.

The torch. Now redundant. Sat beside him. Slowly sinking into the muddy-sand. Its light slowly diminishing as it disappeared. Then it moved. Pushed in the gentle current. And it shone in the glass face plate of Matherson's diving helmet.

It wasn't clear anymore.

It was stained. Spattered red. Matching Matherson's eyes and mouth. His mouth forever open in a scream that will be never heard.

7

IT WAS A WARM day. The sun was high and the gulls were squawking relentlessly. The beach was empty. Not a soul to be seen. And the sea was still. No movement. Nor tide or waves. Crane stared hard at the horizon then back at the sea. He frowned. The tide was normally quite strong and the breeze would be blowing for most of the day.

There was nothing no sound. Just a plain sunny picture. A warm feeling. But nothing else. Only gulls high in the sky.

The sand felt cold on his feet as Crane looked down at his buried toes. Then he glanced up at his Grandmother who was standing above him. Her large floppy-hat shaded him from the suns glare.

Hands on her hips she returned his gaze - 'Come-on Petie.. time to go..' -

'Time to go.. my beautiful-boy' - and she ruffled his curly hair.

Crane tried to move. Tried to get up but he couldn't. He looked down in horror and saw his feet and legs start to sink into the sand. He pulled at his knees. Tugged and tugged. Then Fear gripped him and he looked back up at his Grandmother.

She stared at him. She seemed unconcerned. Then suddenly her mouth turned into an angry wolf-like snarl and she slapped him.

Crane recoiled. His Grandmother had never hit him before. Never lifted a finger to him. Ever.

He looked down at his legs. But couldn't really see them. Then tried to raise his arms to shield his head. But couldn't. Then a further blow struck him.

He clenched his eyes tightly. And they started to burn and throb as another slap glanced off his head.

He flung himself forward. And tried to slowly open his eyes. There was a humming. It was all around him. Shimmering in the air. He could feel it. And now he could almost feel his feet. He realised they were bare and on a cold icy floor. He squinted hard again as now a bright light pierced his shuttered eyelids.

As battered and bruised as he was. Cranes instinct slowly started to kick-in. And he could just make out the feel and presence of someone walking past him. Trailing smoke. Thick cigar smoke. It was unmistakeable. Then a loud hollow-clang rang out as a metallic door was slammed shut.

He couldn't move. His whole body ached. Pain powered and streaked through his joints. And his legs from the knees-down where numb. His mouth and tongue felt sticky and swollen. His teeth ached and creaked as he ground them.

And the left side of his face felt liked he'd been kicked by a horse.

He gently shook his head to one side. The blows had woken him. But the blow he'd got earlier that day still rattled in his skull.

After several hard blinks Crane managed to open his eyes and looked down. There were cable-ties around his wrists and forearms. And juggling his legs. His ankles too.

'Congratulations.. you found us !' – an elderly voice. Heavily amplified. Boomed all around him. And Crane stared straight ahead.

He was in a small white room. That smelt bleached and disinfected. And in front was a large mirror that almost covered the entire wall. The light was coming from thin powerful strobes that encircled it. Like a square halo.

Crane could clearly see himself now. And he'd looked better. There was a deep purple bruise to the left of his face. And his left eye was slightly swollen.

He looked ashen. As if he'd slept in his clothes. He was cold. And his flight jacket. His prized Northern Ireland flight jacket. From his Belfast days was gone. And so was the tell-tale lump and feel of his trusty Browning.

He shuffled again. Pulling at his bines. And in doing so he glanced down. And his left wrist felt light. His Rolex was gone too. Cranes blood now started to boil.

'WHO THE FUCK ARE YOU..? - bellowed Crane. Staring straight at the large mirror.

'SHOW YOURSELF..!'

This did the trick and the mirror started to shimmer. Then it turned clear and was opaque no longer.

Crane concentrated his stare.

Behind the glass sat a man in a wheelchair. Some 80-plus in years. He was dressed in a smart grey three-piece suit. With a crisp white shirt. Open at the neck and was adorned with a pale pink silk cravat.

Pipes appeared to run from his right wrist up into an IV that hung above him. Gently swaying in a chrome hooked-cradle. That seemed to be attached to the back of his wheelchair. Along with another small device.

Then Crane scanned his face. He was old and weathered. With a neat grey tash. Coupled with greying stubble to his chin. He had a Mr Punch hooked nose and chin. And eyes that had the depth and evil darkness of a great white shark.

He returned Crane's stare with a subtle but x-ray-like intensity. And he carried an air and look of old aristocracy. Crane knew the type. Pompous. Arrogant. And an inbred sense of so-called superiority.

Crane leant back in his chair – 'Well.. who the fuck are you.. ? Ironside ?'

His feeble attempt at humour seemed to give rise – 'I'm impressed.. the locals have never come across anything.. ever in all these years.. ! what recently happened was a mere fluke as you English say.. but now you're here.. you're a problem!'

The wheelchair man didn't change his demeanour.

'A burnt-out ex-MI6 agent.. hoping to retire.. but now hoping to uncover the truth to something that's.. well.. not happening !' - the grey-man continued.

And raising his left hand, he pointed – 'You're not happening.. Mr Crane.. Mr Peter Crane'

Crane leaned forward slightly. The look on his face could kill – 'How the fuck do you know who I am.. ?' - he snarled back.

The grey-man lent back into his chair and gave a little chuckle – 'We know everything.. and yet you know nothing about us.. we're the best kept secret.. !'.

Then the grey-man gently pushed a lever on the arm of his wheel-chair and he silently moved out of view.

Crane watched in silence as he disappeared. Then stared at the door. Expecting it to open and the next stage of his interrogation to take place.

But nothing. Then the light in the room went dim. The mirror returned to opaque. And a hissing noise started to emanate from the floor.

Crane struggled. But he knew it was futile. So leaning back into the chair he relaxed his shoulders.

There was no use in trying anything yet. It was time to wait. If they'd wanted him dead they would have done it already. He was sure of that.

No watch. So he couldn't keep track of time. The sounds of hissing were now deafening.

Crane got up from the sofa and walked towards the mantle. He glanced back and forth at the little silver framed pictures that adorned it - 'That's your uncle John.. my brother.. long time ago.. we were just kids then.. !'.

Crane looked at the next photo on the mantlepiece – 'Is that you.. when you were young.. Nanny.. and a soldier.. ?' - said Crane pointing.

His Grandmother stuck her head around the archway and looked at him and then looked at the mantle - 'Yes Petie.. I was very young there.. I was in army intelligence.. that was taken just after the end of the war.. !'

Crane looked closer at the photo and his Grandmother continued – 'Taken in East Berlin.. just before the Russians took control.. I was there on government business.. !'

Then Crane felt his Grandmothers hand on his shoulder – 'A long time ago.. it was all just an adventure back then.. but that's a story for another day my dear sweet boy'.

Then Crane felt another hand on his shoulder. And the sudden feeling of being shoved forward made him recoil. He stared at the mantle and it was now swaying and moving backwards and forwards.

Then the mantle started to shimmer and fade. And the photos fell onto the floor and slowly vanished.

He shook his head. And in the distance he could make-out a light. It started to blink and come into view. It painted a corridor and the walls started to form. White. Clean. And they loomed and stretched towards the on-coming light.

Crane looked at his arms. Then his shoulders. He was being held tightly. Between two men in black and their faces hidden under balaclava's. The sound of their combat boots echoed down the corridor and thumped in his ears.

There was a chink of metal and he realised that he was hand-cuffed. His feet were free. But he couldn't walk. And he couldn't really feel them. He was just being dragged.

Then they stopped abruptly by a large door. And one of the dark-men punched a keypad and it shooshed open.

Crane was dragged inside and dumped unceremoniously into a chair. His handcuffs were checked for a final time and then they left.

Crane was groggy and still coming to terms with all that had happened. When suddenly Matherson popped into his mind. The last he could remember was seeing his old friend and controller smile through the glass plate on his diving helmet. And giving him the thumbs-up.

Then came the strange feeling of a knock-out blow to the back of his head. And having the dash of the Patriot coming up and hitting him in the face.

He shook his head. Hard. And took a few deep breaths.

The mirrored room and the grey-man in the wheelchair now entered his thoughts. And they stayed there. Centre vision. Centre place. Who was he? What the fuck was really going on here?

Crane was determined to get the answers. But his specialist training was now punching through hard his brain. In interrogation if your caught. Then you play the grey-man. The broken-man. That way, hopefully they will go easy on you.

But they knew exactly who he was. He was MI6. They would know full well the training that he'd had and how he would react to this situation.

Operational prudence – he'd have to improvise and level the playing field. Some-how.

Crane glanced around the room. It looked like an office. Sparce and yet plush in what trappings were there. A large antique oak desk sat somewhat-middle and looking at the floor. It was plain painted concrete. Old and worn in areas. The centrepiece was a large burgundy Arab-style rug. And the desk sat squarely on it.

No other chairs and no feeling of warmth was there. No pictures. No ornament's. And above a long strip-light hung-down that gave the room a sort of shadowy but luminescent glow.

Crane tried to look over his shoulder as a whirring noise broke the silence. Then he watched as the grey-man came slowly buzzing hover-like into the room. He didn't look at Crane. Just continued until he was positioned behind the desk.

Crane followed his movements. Studying them intently. The grey-man gave nothing away apart from being dependent on the motorised wheelchair he was sat in.

He raised his hand and pressed a button on an unseen keyboard and small screen pulled up out of the desk. The light from it shone on his old, tattered face. Then the grey-man pressed another and a screen came down out of the ceiling. It whirled around until it faced Crane and it blinked on.

Crane looked at him. Then at the screen. Puzzled he went to speak just as the screen blinked and then blinked again. And suddenly a picture buzzed into view.

Crane stared hard at the screen. It was a room. And the view came from above and in the centre was a single chair.

He looked back at the grey-man. Still no-notion of intent.

Crane tried to get a rise again – 'What's this.. dinner and a show..?'

Once again this prompted a response – 'Oh yes.. a show.. a show indeed' - replied the grey-man without looking up.

There was movement and Crane returned and stared intently at the screen. Then Cranes mouth fell open. As both Davey Parsons and his son Sam were bundled into the room'

They were both bound and tied. Hands behind their backs and appeared to be barely moving.

Then a man appeared dressed like a doctor. He pushed the chair to one side and then bent and administered an injection to them both.

Completing this he turned and disappeared from view. The clang of a door echoed in the back-ground.

Crane watched intently. As they both started to regain consciousness. Davey Parsons was laying on his side and then rolled onto his back. His son Sam seemed a little more awake and he managed to get to his knees and was looking all around him.

They seemed to be speaking. Talking to each other but Crane heard nothing.

Crane looked back at the grey-man. He seemed non-plussed. No interest at all at the activity on the screen.

'What the fuck is going on.. ? why have you got them here..? Oi.. I'm talking to you – you old bastard !'

The grey-man shot Crane a glance that almost made his blood run cold. His eyes were dead and he seemed to have a quiet anger written on his face – 'They are here because of you Mr Crane.. you involved them.. now we are merely cleaning-up.. no loose ends.. !' - and he pressed a button on the keyboard.

'Dad.. what the fuck is going on.. ? where the fuck are we.. ?'

'Dad.. DAD' – Cranes head darted back to the screen.

He watched as Sam managed to shuffle his way over to where his Dad lay. There was no movement from him. No indication he was awake. Almost falling over Sam tried to kneel on him. And suddenly Davey Parsons opened his eyes.

'Whoaaah.. Sam..fuck.. whoaa !' and he turned and looked at him – 'Dad.. what the fuck ?' and Sam motioned to him prompting a reply of sorts.

Davey Parsons wiggled around on his side and then shuffled into a sort of crouch. Then fell onto his knees. Both he and Sam stared at each other.

'Dad.. what's happened ?.. where are we..' - and Sam's voice had a tremble to its tone. He was scared. Very scared.

Davey Parsons just shook his head. And looked at Sam in complete bewilderment.

Crane tore his head from the screen – 'What the fuck are you going to do ? eh.. answer me you old bastard' – but this time no reaction from the grey-man. He failed to see any reason to respond to Crane's insults.

Crane's head felt like it was full of stones and with each movement they rattled. The pain was almost unbearable.

In a millisecond he leapt to his feet. And although cuffed he knew he'd have to try something but in that brief moment of stupid bravado. He forgot that his legs where numb from the from the knees down.

All he did was merely crumple into a heap on the floor. And smack the back of his head on the chair on the way down

Black leather gloved hands grabbed his shoulders. As once again and he was hauled to his numb feet and thrown hard back into the chair.

Crane pushed with his shoulders. Giving rise to his assailants they should take their hands off him. All he saw was the angry glare of pale blue eyes from under a black silken balaclava.

'I admire your spirt Mr Crane.. I truly do' - the grey-man squawked as Crane composed himself.

'I'll show you my spirt.. I'll kill you with my bare hands.. cuffs or not !.. wouldn't be the first time I assure you of that.. !'.

The grey-man gave a shrill guttural laugh. That sounded something like a goose with shredded vocal chords. And then looked Crane straight in the eyes – 'Oh I'm sure.. we've both killed for a purpose Mr Crane.. both for queen and country..' - he said with a sneer.

Crane leant forward. Almost falling again from his chair – 'You know nothing of me.. or the things that I have done.. nothing.. so let's get that straight right now OK..!'

The grey-man gave a warm but smarmy smile. Then looked down. He seemed to be studying something. Or reading from the small computer screen in front of him. His mouth moved. And jittered. Indicating he was in fact reading. Then he looked up.

'Well Peter Crane.. or should I call you Lieutenant ?.. your almost 50 and you've spent the last 25 in British Intelligence.. man and boy as you English say.. you've been well-trained throughout your career.. an expert in weapons explosives tactics.. time served in Belfast.. seems you had some fun there as well.. an intelligence operative with a free hand to obtain what you needed too.. lived your life from continent to continent with zero accountability.. as long as you got your hands on the tech and brought it home.. to the British Empire.. !'

Then the grey-man leant forward and once again out stretched his weather gnarled finger – 'All in the name of Queen & Country ! .. and now you've retired and left your docklands flat and come to Cornwall.. to your late Grandmothers cottage.. Thimble Cottage.. !'

He looked down again – 'And the ink isn't even dry on your C27.. and not even filed for that matter'

Crane raised his eyebrows. He seemed confused by this statement – 'My controller filed that.. the day I signed it.. I'm retired you old bastard.. I'm not on active service anymore.. and it's obvious your Government.. otherwise how would you know.. !'

Again the grey-man gave a shrill laugh – ' Oh yes.. and to re-cap.. Matherson.. he never filed it.. never filed your C27 and now he's sleeping with the fishes.. as the Italians used to say' - and smugly he continued - 'As far as The Office is concerned your still on active service and if you disappear.. your nothing more than collateral damage and your be filed as such'.

Crane knew he was speaking the truth. And this scared him. If Matherson hadn't filed it then the Office would think he was still on assignment. If he never calls in. Never reported. Then they would think that he'd been taken out on an operation.

To The Office he'd probably turn-up somewhere. In a ditch perhaps or an old cellar floor. Two bullets in his head. Paid in full. And they'd close the file and merely write him a simple obituary.

Crane played an ace. The only one he now had – 'There's a transponder on our boat.. if the boat doesn't come back.. they will come looking..'

The grey-man shook his head – 'Wrong.. we know full well that when you left Penzance.. there was no activation code entered.. plus we swept the Patriot.. there's nothing there.. no transponder.. no cavalry coming to the rescue I'm afraid.. !'

'Your alone.. dead in the water.. abandoned by your Government' - the grey-man finished. Wringing his hands in a smug contempt.

Crane looked at the ceiling then the floor and breathed out hard - 'Alright you old bastard.. now what ?'.

The grey-man responded in kind – 'Now you get to watch.. and take note !' and he motioned back to the screen hanging from the ceiling.

Crane looked back. To him there was no change. But he knew something bad was about to happen. He could sense it.

Suddenly the light in the room turned green and flashed several times. And both Davey Parson's and his son jerked with each blink of the light.

Sam threw himself sideways to the floor and pulled his knees up to his chest. His dad was laying on his back and he too pulled his knees up towards his stomach and then threw himself on his side.

Crane frowned but kept his gaze. Then the screaming started. The sound was excruciating. Both Davey Parson's and his son both started to convulse uncontrollably. Their legs started to kick back and forth. Their heads started to spin and shake from side-to-side. They kicked. Jerked and writhed like giant fish caught on a hook.

Their relentless screams went on and on until finally they both shredded their vocal-chords. And the sound resonated through the room like geese having their necks rung.

Then suddenly they stopped. No more screaming. No movement. And they became still. Then by strange reaction they both drew their legs up into their chests again. And their heads became bowed. They looked almost foetal.

Then Sam's head jerked back. As-if being struck by an unseen force. Then his mouth popped open like a garden pea being burst from its pod. And a green slimy liquid started to pour out. And it collected pool-like on the floor. And their hair. Both he and his Dad. Dissolved into the floor.

Crane kept staring. Then he shot a glance at the grey-man. Then he looked back at the screen. Crane could see that Sam had no eyes. They were gone. Now just blacken-holes.

'What the fuck.. what the fuck was that ?.. their dead !! .. you've fucked killed them !!'"

The grey-man was completely unfazed by what had just happened. By what had just taken place on the screens. He seemed unconcerned.

Crane was now glaring at him. His blood was burning with a desire to kill him. By any means possible and he shuffled his legs. Hoping that he could now use them. But still. From the knee down. He was numb and they wouldn't move.

Crane's agile mind searched for a solution. He had to play for time.

'Hey.. OK you've got my attention.. what's going on here'

The grey-man looked up and warmly smiled. This only angered Crane even more.

'Weapons test.. !'

Cranes mouth fell open – 'What the fuck do you mean.. weapons test.. !'

The grey-man leant back and continued - 'I feel a touch of kindred spirt in you Mr Crane.. so I'll tell you.. as you've probably noticed from my accent I'm not English.. I'm German.. and from an old revered titled family called Von Heben.. during the war I was working for Hitler's secret weapons department - developing new technology to help fight the cause but sadly.. when Berlin finally fell.. I was smuggled out to England before the Russians took control of East Berlin.. and I was to continue my work for a new master.. the British Government and I've been here ever since.

He leant forward. His eyes glared and Crane recoiled – 'A most secret of secrets.. Mr Crane'.

'I've read quite a lot of your file.. your Grandmother was in Berlin just after it fell.. Army intelligence by all accounts.. who knows I may have met her in my younger years.. I was a bit of a ladies-man in my day.. wealthy.. good-looking.. dashing even.. your Grandmother does seem familiar shall we say.. yes come to think of it..

YES.. I do remember her now.. how interesting !' – then the professor paused and seem to ponder. And look past Crane and into the air.

'Yeah !! .. my Grandmother would have put two in your head as look at you.. you.. you evil bastard' - blurted Crane – 'She would have got the measure of you from the get-go.. make no mistake.. !'.

Crane had to keep momentum. Keep him talking – 'So what weapon was that ?.. nothing I've ever seen before and I've seen most I can assure you'.

The professor now seemed interested in Cranes curiosity and swung back to look at him – 'Amplified iridium and gamma radiation.. when amplified in a certain-way it reacts with the bodies electrical field.. when concentrated and fired at specific targets.. organic targets that is.. it causes the body's internal organs to melt.. literally.. but the green colour is still a mystery at the moment but I'm sure we'll get to the bottom of that one day.. but for the moment it's most effective.. as you've just seen on your friends'

The utter shock on Cranes face prompted the professor to continue further. He seemed proud to explain more of his creation – 'At the moment it can be mounted on a small vehicle.. taken to the battle field and aimed at an advancing army.. to melt them.. the true purpose would be to create a small hand-held version.. but we're working on that at the moment'

Then the professor pressed a button on the keypad and pointed back to the screen with a gnarled finger – 'There see.. that's the prototype.. but we are experiencing an over-heating issue.

The picture on the screen was of a hand-held weapon that resembled a large fat sub-machine gun. It had an expansion-tank situated to the rear, near the stock. The barrel was bulbous and almost trumpet-like. But it looked fearsome and deadly.

'It works.. but the most is one applied concentrated shot.. then the barrel over-heats.. and if you don't release the trigger - bang..! the explosion is considerable but localised and not totally nuclear.. more EMP in its final throws.. but still deadly !'

Crane nodded. Showing a degree of horror. Interest and warped appreciation.

'We call it the Pulse Rifle.. because it fires a pulse-like energy-beam' - said the professor.

'Apt name.. very apt.. more like a fucking ray-gun.. from Star Wars !' - said Crane.

Just then he felt a sharp pain in the back of his neck. And he slumped forward. And the last thing he saw was the tassels on the rug.

All was black and he was laying down. The first thing Crane did was wiggle his toes. Then he flexed his knees. His legs. He could feel them at last. He was relieved and he also felt warm.

Crane breathed out slowly and controllably and opened his eyes.

There was a faint light above him and he squinted.

He moved his head and looked around. He was in a small room. More like a prison cell.

The bed was an old wrought iron type. And it was rusty. The mattress was thin. Stained and thread-bare.

He swung his legs out of the bed and tried to sit-up. He was dizzy and his chest hurt. He tensed and flexed his muscles. First his arms then his back and neck. And remembering the jab. He ran his hands over his neck to sooth the cut-like pain that was still there.

His crotch felt damp. His stomach hurt and his bowels ached. And struggling to his feet he trundled over to the small toilet-pan that was in the corner. He yanked down his trousers and sat on it. It was small and he wobbled.

Steadying himself he let go. And took a long-needed crap and piss. The feeling was some-what liberating. And comforting in a small way.

But looking around there was no paper. So Cranes Commando training again kicked-in. As he emptied himself he pulled his arse-cheeks apart. Hard apart. To open his anus as far as he could. The mess he'd leave on himself would be minimal. As training had taught him. That personal hygiene was paramount in the field.

He strained. Then strained hard again. Then pushed his right hand through his legs and scratched and itched at the opening to his anus. He could feel the mess. It was warm and wet.

Then he reached around with his left and flushed the toilet. As the water ran he pushed his dirty fingers into the water. Rubbing them together. Then he pulled his hand free. It was wet but at least clean.

He stood up. With his trousers and pants still around his ankles. Then he turned and flushed again. And shoved his hand into the flow of water one final time. Just to make sure.

He looked at his hand. His fingers. They appeared clean. He raised them and sniffed. But his nails weren't and he winced. At the slight smell. But there wasn't much more he could do.

Crane pulled his trousers back up and sat back down on the bed. He looked at himself. Nothing had changed. He was still bare-footed and dressed in only his jeans and stained ripped shirt.

He glanced around the room again to get a feel of his surroundings. This was definitely a cell. A holding cell in fact. Just a concrete box. No window. A simple bed and toilet. Nothing more. Even the light above was the bare minimum. But at least there was no camera.

Crane pulled himself further onto the bed and placed his back against the cell wall.

'Now what..?' - he mouthed silently.

There was no sound. Nothing. And the time would pass excruciatingly slow. Crane mused to himself. This was like interrogation training. Sensory deprivation. No sense of time. No sound to break the silence or monotony.

Remembering that time. And that training. He recalled being cable-cuffed. With his hands behind his back. And a canvas bag being roughly placed over his head. And being made stand in a prone position. With his head bowed and against a wall.

Then suddenly being grabbed and forced in a crouch. And made stay like that for several hours.

The assault on the senses was horrific.

But seeing as he wasn't on show. Crane got up and decided to get some feeling back into his legs and thighs. Now that he could move them at least.

He did some squat-thrusts. Then started jogging on the spot. His feet and calf muscles stung but they felt good.

Crane controlled his breathing and his heart gained a steady-pace.

Then finally stopping he stood straight and flexed his arms and back again. The heat and adrenaline ran through him. Although controlled. He felt better and his muscles felt strong and tense.

Suddenly Crane heard foot-steps. They were approaching. And they were getting louder.

Quickly he re-took his place on the bed. And slumped. Look the 'Broken-Man' reverberated through his head.

The foot-steps stopped outside the door. And Crane's mind raced. He'd have to think on his feet. Improvise. Adapt. Over-come screamed through his head and the face of his old drill-instructor snapped into view.

There was a scraping coming from the door. Like keys being used. Then the door creaked opened inwards.

'Broken-Man.. Broken-Man.. Play the Broken-Man..' – this screamed through his head.

Leaning to one side. He opened his mouth open in a kind of drool. And he very slowly looked up. Making sure his eyes looked tired. Dark and weary.

His mind flashed as in walked one of his previous assailants. All in black. Black combats fatigues. Black combat boots and a silk balaclava covering his head. A webbing-belt loosely slung around his waist and on his hip sat a holstered pistol.

The black figure didn't move. He seemed to be surveying Crane. Seeing if he was more awake. More conscious than he was letting on. In his right gloved hand he held a plate.

Crane slowly moved his head back to face the floor. The black figure still didn't move.

There was four feet of cold concrete between them. Crane knew he'd have to reduce that before he made any move.

Crane let out a whispered strangled groan and shuttered his head slowly from side-to-side. But inside his muscles tensed. His joints creaked with the tension. And his mind was as sharp as a razor.

This did the trick. And Crane watched from the very corner of his eye as the black figure dropped his guard slightly and walked forwards and bent to put the plate on the bed.

Crane sprang into action with an almost inhuman speed and ferocity. And in one lightning move slid his hand right under it. And then brought it up and smashed it squarely straight in the dark figures balaclava'd face.

It shattered instantly. And there was a muffled groan and a satisfying crunch and the feel of a nose breaking. Then Crane whipped his left arm up and around his neck. Joined and locked it with his right and spun him round. Brining him backwards. And making him lay prone to the left of Cranes hip.

Crane bent forwards. Harder and further in one swift smooth movement. Almost like giving a one-sided piggy-back in reverse. Then with a sharp pull to the right. The dark-figures feet left the floor momentarily. And almost seemed to toe-tap the concrete floor.

There was a snap. He felt his neck snap in the crux of his elbow. But Crane didn't let go.

He waited and waited. It was mere seconds. But seemed like minutes. Then with a final tug. Crane mirrored his deadly movements again and a short exhale of warm air left the black figures body. Crane winced as it brushed pass his cheek. His victim went limp and his gloved hands fell from gripping Cranes arms in a useless defence to his assault.

Training dictates that when you have to kill up-close and personal. You have to compensate for the adrenaline-rush.

But to Crane this was personal. This dark dressed figure could have killed his controller. Could have killed Nory. But time was not on his side and he knew this. His mind raced.

Crane gently lowered the limp jittering corpse to the floor. And then stepped forward and slowly closed the cell door. He made a grab for the combat boots and quickly unlaced them. Removed the belt and holstered pistol and made for the trousers. The same with the jacket. Finally he pulled the balaclava off and looked at the dark-figures face.

Oh shit.. !. He was just a kid. Fresh-faced. And no more than twenty five years old.

His nose looked completely flattened. And blood seeped from his nostrils and mouth. His eyes were now crossed and almost rolled back. But Crane continued his search. No id tags. No insignia. So he was now nothing more than collateral damage during this operation.

Crane sat back on his haunches. And for a moment. Regret started to stomp through his brain. But then his in-ward horror at his actions now turned to sheer anger. And he grabbed back his prized Rolex that was on the dead kids left wrist.

Crane quickly dressed himself. And luck was on his side as the combats fitted him well. Even the boots were good. Then Crane hurriedly dressed the dead kid in his clothes and laid him face down on the bed. If discovered. This may bide him some time.

He pulled the silk mask on. It was still warm and had the smell of his dead victim. And warm blood brushed his cheek. Still there was no time to loose. No time for false sorrows at what he'd done. Crane adjusted the belt and pulled the pistol from the holster and recognised it instantly. It was his Browning. He felt even more confident now and he snarled happily to himself.

He did a brass-check and re-holstered. Then tapped it reassuringly. It was time for pay-back !

But one thing dawned. He didn't know the layout of this subterranean hide-out. So he'd have to play everything by ear. And again the sentiment of -'adapt improvise and overcome' - sang through his ears. Coupled with 'operational prudence'.

Crane searched the pockets of the combats. Nothing. No written instructions or anything to indicate the base or a name of the operation. But one thing was sure. This was a black cell. Black Ops as they say at the office and certainly above his pay-grade.

Crane slowly opened the cell door. The corridor that lay beyond was silent and dimly lit. Closing the door behind him. He locked it with the keys that he had retrieved.

To the right. The corridor stretched far beyond showed doors. The same as his cell. Crane made a snap-decision that these must be more of the same. So going left was the only logical option.

There was still no sound. No indication of any activity. No voices. Not even a whiff of a breeze.

And there were no cameras either. This gave Crane an advantage and he walked briskly up the corridor towards a large pressure door.

His stolen combat boots gave a hard rubbery clatter on the metal floor.

The door had no catch. No handle to turn. Just a button keypad with two buttons. Both red and green. This indicated to Crane that the moment the door opened he'd be in no-man-land. What lay beyond was a complete unknown.

He took out his Browning and again performed a brass-check. Then re-holstered.

His hand wandered out towards the green button and suddenly he started to shake. The adrenaline that was fuelling him was starting to wear off. And this was dangerous. He hadn't eaten or drunk anything and was running on empty.

Situations like this could cause shock. And he could faint.

Crane inflated his chest several times. And then breathed out hard. Then back in through gritted teeth. In a vain attempt to whirl and push the air back into his lungs. His eyes bulged and the green button blinked on.

There was a muffled electronic click and a shooshing sound. As the pressure door popped open and swung inwards a little.

Crane pushed it and stepped through. There was no stopping now. The adrenaline had returned with a vengeance. And he was out for blood. Blood and answers.

8

CRANE TURNED. HE WAS on a gantry. Just above head-height. He stood for a moment and surveyed the room below him. It was a lab. A large lab and there were several people. Lab-tech's. Running around and looking busy. They paid him no attention. Much to Crane relief. And near a far wall. Sitting on a raised plinth was the 'Pulse-Rifle'.

He stood above for a moment. And watched curiously as one of the tech's walked towards it and attached a lead. And a small light on the side now started to slowly blink green. Coupled with a very low hum.

One of the tech's wrote on a clip-board and turned to look at the other – 'About an hour before full charge' – the other tech looked up and nodded in acknowledgement.

At the far end of the gantry. There was a further pressure door. Crane, spurred on by his new found luck. Strode boldly towards it. Full of bravado.

The clattering of his boots on the grating made a staccato as he walked. But again. This noise gave no rise in his presence to the tech's below.

Much to Cranes relief. It was the same deal as before. A simple red and green button layout sat to the left of it.

Crane punched the green and the door shushed open and sat ajar. He pushed it and again stepped through into the unknown. Gently closing it behind him.

Another dark dimly lit corridor loomed out before him.

He stopped halfway at a spiral staircase that lead down. Crane looked around but knew he was covered. He was armed and the black combats hid the real him. So standing at the top step he strained his ears and could hear a faint splashing noise. He ventured down and after four flights, yet another pressure door stopped him.

Cranes confidence was gaining with every step. There was no hesitation. The green button blinked and the door opened and he stepped through. As bold as brass.

He was in a small ante room. That looked almost like a prep-room. There were some long over-coats hanging from the walls and a rack that held large powerful torches. And what looked like distress-flares.

Crane breezed through and opened the proceeding door and stepped out onto a small dock. The sea was washing in and out quite hard and was splashing up the side onto the walkway. He was inside the cavern. It was dark with only a faint light emanating from the left. The opening out to sea appeared to hook to the left.

It was then he noticed the Patriot. It was moored. Further down the quayside. And behind sat another but larger speed boat and also what looked like a 'Sea-Lion'.

Crane mused. That's how they got onto the Patriot and knocked him out. They came at them under the water. The Sea-Lion was a two-man small sea-submersible. Designed for covert underwater ops. He'd seen them being used in Spain, sometime ago.

Crane spied a CCTV above the door to the ante room. But he had to play-out the part he was now in. So he strolled towards the Sea-Lion and checked the mooring ties. Then did the same to the other speed boat and then the Patriot.

Then ducked back into the ante-room.

Crane paused, he could have made an escape. He knew that. He could have took the Patriot and got away. But no. The professor was conducting weapon experiments on innocent people. People he had met. And inadvertently got mixed up in his mess. They were dead. And the professor was going to be stopped. He was going to pay.

He didn't care who was in charge of this operation. Or how far this went up the food-chain at the office.

Innocent people were being killed. In the name of science.

'Not on my watch' – Crane mumbled to himself – *'No.. this ain't happening.. this stops now'*.

Crane almost galloped up the spiral stair case. Back at the pressure door it shushed open and he was once more back in the main access corridor.

If he turned left he'd be back in the lab. Turning right. A further corridor with multiple doors loomed. Crane knew he had the upper hand. But only while he kept one step a-head. So his next target would be the other dark combat-clad operative.

He hadn't seen anymore. Just the two so far. But taking out the last one would again tip the odds in his favour.

Crane felt like his luck was starting to gain in momentum. As the next door he came to was slightly open. And he gently pushed it and peered inside. It appeared to be a billet. With lockers. A shower-room and two beds.

The bed on the furthest side of the billet wasn't empty.

Crane looked around and saw the combat boots at the foot of the bed. And crumpled black fatigues hanging over the end. The occupant was on their back. Hissing in their sleep.

There was no hesitation. And again with lightning speed Crane was at the side of the bed. His muscles and breathing were tense.

He stared for the merest moment. And with a quick scan up and down. He struck.

And with a hard single righted-handed scissor-blow. Hit the sleeper right across the throat. Mid-thorax. The sleepers eyes snapped open in sheer horror.

The mouth jerked. But no sound. Just a limp gurgle. He drew back and struck again with the same ferocity. Then placed his gloved hand over his victims mouth.

There was another gurgle. But stifled through Cranes glove. A slight kick of feet followed and a limp flailing of arms under the covers. Then nothing. The eyes blinked. Stuttered and then stayed still. Staring blankly.

Crane stared into the now bulging eyes. But kept his hand tightly over the mouth. Then reaffirming his grip. He pushed the head backwards into the pillow. There was no change in expression.

Crane relented and stood for a second. And surveyed the now lifeless corpse in the bed in front of him. He slid the leather glove off and placed his hand just inside bed-clothes. Touching the edge of its chin.

No pulse. A simple executed movement. He ran his fingers down the dead man face and the eye-lids flicked shut. Now it was two down. Two-one to Crane.

Crane spun and grabbed up the webbing belt laying just under the bed. He retrieved the pistol from the holster. It was a Sig-Sauer P226. He ejected the mag. Cycled the action. Performing a brass-check. Then slid the mag back in and tucked it into his belt.

It was black and with any luck. No-one would notice it tucked-in there. Searching further he found a suppressor in a side pouch. A sound-moderator. Crane raised his eyebrows. Thinking that this may be of use later. He placed it in his fatigue pocket.

Operational prudence. Never leave weapons behind that could be used against you. And Crane did a quick assessment in his head. Two armed guards down. And he was armed in a double two. They didn't know he was free and he was dressed as one of them.

'We're good to go' – mumbled Crane under his breath.

Then he spun on his heels. Checked the billet again and counted the lockers. There was four. Hopefully these didn't belong to any further guards, but Crane would deal with them as he went along.

He made his exit and closed the door. Then opened it again and took one last look at the dead guard. He looked asleep. And hopefully this would fool others if they looked in.

Right. Next room. Crane was still full of bravado and his heart was beating strong. And any hesitation had gone. And he grabbed the door handle. Turned it and went straight in.

This room was medical and he stopped dead in his tracks. In the bed in front of him was Pam. She was slightly raised and hooked up to a drip and god-knows what. He silently approached and raised a hand to cover her mouth if she screamed.

Then Crane saw the heart monitor. He watched the steady blip blip blip. Pam was either in a coma or she was drugged.

Crane back tracked towards the door. He could deal with her later. And as he stepped back into the corridor. He pondered and truly hoped that Pam was merely drugged. But he was sure of one thing. If she was here. Then they were going to use her someway. It was a horrifying thought.

'No.. *Not on my watch !*' tumbled through Cranes mind again.

A quick reccy of the next door further up showed this to be an exit to above. To above ground and probably to the old derelict base above. Crane knew this would be heavily secured. Just in case any wayward kids decided to break in and have some fun.

The less-guarded way-out was from below. Via the docks and out into the sea. His only real option to make a hasty retreat.

But there had to be a comms-room. And this must be it. So Crane flew up the stairs two at a time. And as he neared the top there was yet another pressure door. Same deal as before. The green button blinked. The door popped and Crane strode in.

He was right. A comms-room. In front of him were two chairs and an array of computer screens. One showing the camera footage of the underground base. The other the ground outside. And a side one showing the stretch of sea just out from the cliff opening.

One of the chairs spun round. And a young chap dressed as regular army looked at him and smiled – 'Hi Johnna.. how goes it ?.. having a wander ?'

Crane just grunted and nodded an acknowledgment.

'Take your mask off.. for fuck sake.. that nosey government bastard's in the cells now..' – the soldier continued.

Crane moved like lightning. With sheer aggression pulsing through him like a burst water-pipe. He sprang forward drawing the Sig from his belt and pistol-whipped him straight across the left-side of his temple.

He was old cold in a millisecond. And the soldier slumped to one side and then slid slowly from the chair.

Fortunately there was little sound as he slumped to the floor.

Crane gently spun the other chair. And the other soldier was fast asleep. Completely unaware that his comrade had just been rendered unconscious.

To Cranes agile mind. This was an opportunity to gain some intel.

He placed the muzzle-end of the Sig square on the sleeping soldiers right eye. And then pressed hard.

The soldier stirred. And Crane pressed his pistol even harder into his eye-socket.

Then his other eye. The one that was visible. Snapped open and Crane raised a finger across his mouth. Noting quite clear that he should be silent.

The soldier didn't move. Just gave a very slight nod. The look on his face. Mirrored through the expression in his free eye. That total fear gripped him tightly.

Crane stared. Almost evil in intent. Then in a hushed voice - 'I'm gonna ask you some questions.. all you do is nod OK.. anything else and I'll pulled the trigger..'

And Crane cocked the hammer-back on the Sig. With a solid resounding double click. Affirming his full intentions not to fuck with him.

This had a resounding effect. As there was a sound of water dripping from the chair. And Crane glanced down momentarily. Realising that the young soldier had wet himself.

'There's only four soldiers here.. you included ?' – the soldier managed a slight nod – 'There's the professor.. two labs-tech.. making three more.. correct ? - again a short solemn nod.

Crane pondered – 'The only way out is through the cavern below.. ?' – he nodded – 'This is the main

185

comms room for the whole base..?' - again a stunted confirmation.

Crane pulled the pistol away from the scared soldier. And with a swift move. Pistol-whipped him too. Hard. Right across the side of his head. And he slumped down into his chair.

Crane stood back and admired his handy-work. He now had the brief intelligence he needed.

He pulled several power cable flexes from the computer screens and tied them both. Hands behind their backs. Ankles together. And laid them prone-position. Then reaching under the backs of their combats. Crane tore several strips of cloth from their tee-shirts and gagged them both.

Then finally re-affirming their bonds. He looked around the comms-room.

The transmission array was clearly centre stage. And making a quick scan. Crane could see that they ghosted their transmissions behind the aerial bouncer signal. So anyone flying nearby would merely hear the warning signal. Not their transmissions.

Crane switched off the bouncer and revved-up their transmission signal and hit the mayday. They were live now and every MOD receiver from here to London would hear them. And hopefully come to investigate.

Crane again checked the soldiers. And satisfied that they would be out-for-the-count for some time. He back-tracked. Smashed their walky-talkies under his boot. And left the coms-room.

As the pressure door slid shut behind him. He caved-in the red button. Then the green with the muzzle of his Sig. Knowing this would delay the door being open again from the outside. And when they woke-up. They wouldn't be able to raise the alarm. Or even get out.

Then grabbing the hand-rail on the spiral staircase. He sprang-down every step like a scolded cat.

At the bottom Crane made on further and at the next door he hesitated for a moment. He took a deep breath. But now knowing the odds were firmly in his favour he turned the handle and shoved it open. To his relief it was empty. But he recognised it instantly.

It was the professors office. The tell-tale rug. The large Oak desk.

Crane shut the door and made his way around the desk. His eyes darted back and forth. He needed something. Something to prove what was going on down here. Anything.

He pulled open the desk-draws. But there appeared nothing of any real note. Save for retrieving his personal mobile phone. But in the large top desk-draw. A photograph fell out from a pile of papers he was rustling through.

Crane picked it up. It was old and black and white. And faded. But for some reason it felt strangely familiar. But he had no time to ponder. He stuffed it into a pocket on his fatigues along with his mobile and continued.

Crane gritted his teeth. And lent on the desk in frustration. As so far his searched had revealed nothing. Then to his surprise there was slight humming noise and he stepped back. A panel opened and a small computer screen rose slowly from the desk.

Once in position. A further small panel opened on the desk and a keyboard appeared.

Crane stared for a moment. Then lifted the keyboard and to his surprise there appeared to be a small hard-drive hidden underneath. He grabbed it. Snapped off the cables and unzipped his combat jacket and slid it inside.

It was all he had. But now was the time to end this.

Crane ran a quick assessment. Physical threat. Dealt with. Mayday. Active.

Now only three targets left. The professor and two lab-rats. Escape route. Through the cove in the Patriot. And out into the sea.

Then he stopped. Pam. Deal with them. Collect Pam. And escape.

Crane performed a brass check on the Sig. Then shoved it back in his belt. Then he drew his trusty Browning and did the same. He was well armed and was buzzing with energy. And sheer vengeance coursing through his veins.

Crane knew he was making up his plan of attack as he went along. But his next move had to be decisive.

Just as he neared the office door. There were voices. He stopped and stared through the gap. The two lab-rats came up the corridor and were busily talking about tests and the next data-rotor. Then his heart skipped a beat and he felt a lump grow in his throat.

One of the techs was carrying the pulse rifle. Trailing the leads behind as he walked.

They walked straight past the professors office and towards door at the far end. Crane was just about to make his move when he heard a faint whirring noise. He closed the door again and reduced the gap just enough to see.

The professor came jockeying past in his wheelchair. Making after the techs. Crane listen intently and had to think fast to make his next move. The end room must have been the test area. As Crane could tell the door hadn't been shut. And he could still hear their voices echoing around inside it.

Just then he heard the professors voice. It was raised. And he appeared angry – 'No.. we will test on the woman.. the agent we'll use for something else.. I have something special in mind for him.. now go and get her.. NOW.. !'

Crane wanted to burst out of the professors office. Both guns blazing and kill them all where they stood. But he had to keep control. Keep his composure and plan his attack.

Crane placed his head against the door frame and butted it gently in frustration. '*Come-on .. think damn-it.. think !*'.

Just then the two lab-rats came walking past and made back down the corridor. Watching them go by. He knew they were going for Pam. He had to act.

He couldn't just leave the professors office as he'd be seen. All Crane could do was wait and see what unfolds. Just then the lab-rats reappeared and in between them was a wheelchair. Crane could clearly see it was Pam. But she was still drugged and was sitting to one side.

They were pushing it in tandem. Talking as they went back up the corridor back towards the testing area.

Crane didn't think. Just reacted. He slipped out of the professors office and ghosted up the corridor after them. He sprinted on tip-toe. Knowing that his combat boots clanged as he walked.

He needed the element of surprise.

As he neared the test-room door he stopped. The voices were now raised. They seemed excited. Crane counted down and then peered round the pressure door.

Pam was sitting prone. In the centre of the room. Still slumped in the wheelchair. The professor was a little way back looking at her. And watching intently at the lab-rats setting-up the weapon.

Crane snatched the Sig from his belt. Quick brass-check. Then stepped boldly into the room. He drew the hammer back on the Sig with a double-clack. Just as his boots clattered on the floor and suddenly all eyes were on him.

Crane snatched a glance at Pam. She was centre-stage. No change.

'Johnna.. what the fuck are you doing !' – blurted the female lab-rat. Lowering and looking over the top of her glasses.

Crane didn't move. Just kept them covered. The Sig firm in his grip. Then raising a hand. He pulled the balaclava off and let it fall to the floor.

The look of surprise and terror moulded into one as both the lab-rats stared at each other. Then back at Crane.

'Who.. who are you..?' – she stammered.

'He's Peter Crane.. former MI6..' - and both lab-rats looked at the professor in amazement.

Crane peered round and looked at the professor – 'Well no introduction needed them.. and none need from any of you either.. professor !'

Crane then side stepped and took a closer look at Pam – 'What the fuck have you done to her.. ? is she drugged ?' – the female lab-rat spoke first.

'Yes.. she's in a deep sleep.. other than that she's.. she's fine !'

Crane waved his Sig at the Pulse Rifle – 'What's the score with that thing.. you were going to test it on her.. weren't you ?.

He took a few steps towards it – 'Still charging the protons in the expansion-tank.. I take it ?'

'How did you know that.. ?' said the male lab-rat. Finally gearing-up enough courage to speak.

Crane spun round and waved the Sig a foot from his face – 'I was walking over the gantry above you.. I heard you.. heard it all !'

'That was you.. ?.. where's Johnna ?' - said the male lab-rat in an almost defiant tone.

'Dead.. both your black-ops guys are dead.. ! along with your two army bods..!' - and Crane took a couple of steps back. In quick succession. Making sure he had good clear distance between them.

'So what now Mr Crane ?.. you're going to kill us and save your friend here..?' – piped-up the professor.

'Yeah.. fucking-A..!' - and Crane pulled the suppressor from his fatigue pocket. Ran his tongue over the threaded-end. And screwed it gently on to the end of the Sig. He performed one last brass-check and then fired.

There was a hollow-sounding thud. Just as the male lab-rat sank clutching his knee. He screamed like a banshee as he collapsed onto the floor. Blood pooling from his shattered knee. A chinking sound echoed as the spent 9mm casing spun into the air and hit the wall. And then bounced onto the floor.

Then Crane stepped forward and grabbed the female lab-rat by her long dark hair and dragged her forcibly towards the Pulse Rifle.

He then thrust the Sig into the side of her head. He jabbed it several times and she winced. As the suppressor sizzled as it touched her skin. Still hot from its last shot.

Crane was sure she knew he meant business. As she raised her hands in a surrendering submission.

'Right Bitch.. questions.. and unless you want a hole in your leg like your friend or indeed the side of your fucking head.. don't lie to me.. OK !' - and Crane gave her a final jab with the Sig.

'This weapons charging right.. ?' – she nodded – 'The cut-off is there' - and Crane indicated to a small slide switch – 'The green button.. it blinks when the weapon is charging.. stays a solid green when charged.. showing it's ready to fire..? – again she confirmed with a weak nod.

'What happens if you don't switch it off.. ?' – she didn't answer. The look on her face said it all. Crane saw this and smiled.

'So let me get this right.. you have to switch-off the charge when green.. if you don't.. the red one there starts blinking and gets faster and faster till the expansion tank explodes.. !.. does that sound right..?

Finally the female lab-rat nodded.

Crane threw her against the lab wall and another hollow-thud echoed around the lab.

She doubled-up. Screaming, clutching her right foot. As the second spent bullet casing rolled across the floor towards her.

Then Crane turned to face the Professor. His face was blank and ashen. And Crane saw no fear in his eyes.

'Now it's just you and me.. you evil old bastard.. pay-back.. Khama.. E-Ching.. whatever the fuck you wanna call it !'

The professor raised his head and gazed at Crane – straight into his eyes. But Crane wasn't concerned by any evil look the professor gave him. It was his time now and he was out for revenge.

'You don't think that I knew this would happen one day.. ! I knew that this.. my work would come to an end.. but my achievements will remain.. even if I die Mr Crane.. but you will look back and regret this.. I promise you.. but you'll have to live with it.. just like everything else you've done'.

'Glad we're on the same page Professor.. but as for your work.. it's not gonna see the fucking light of day.. that I can assure you' – Crane snarled back.

Then he stepped forward to the professor. And slowly maneuvered around behind him and slammed two bullets into the little motor and control-module.

The professor heard the thuds from the suppressed Sig and grabbed the wheelchairs small control lever. It was dead. He flicked is several times. Nothing. No power. No movement

The professor tried to look around – 'Don't strain yourself.. your dead in the water.. !' - and Crane re-took his place standing in front.

Reaching down. He gathered-up the two spent 9mm casings and juggled them in his hand. Then stuffed then in the hanky pocket on the professors suit. Then gave it a reassuring tap.

'There you go.. two bullets.. these have killed you .. and you never felt a thing.. !'

Then Crane walked over to the Pulse Rifle. The green button on the side was still blinking. But he could tell that it was now speeding-up. Gathering momentum. And blinking faster with each beat.

Crane looked at the shut-off switch. Then raising the Sig he brought it down butt-first. Right across the switch. Then he hit it again.

Crane surveyed momentarily. The small button-type lever had visibly crushed in-wards. Happy with his work he shoved the Sig back into his belt

'YOUR KILL US ALL.. !' - screamed the woman lab-rat.

Crane turned to face her. She had moved closer to her colleague. They were now both sitting with their backs to the lab wall. Both in shock with their hands on their wounds.

Their blood was pooling on the floor in front of them. It glowed in the florescent-light.

Crane ignored them and the professor. And he slowly walked over and grabbed the back of Pam's wheelchair. Flicked off the brake and pushed her out of the test-lab.

He made a grab for the pressure door and the professor looked up – 'I'll give your regards to your Grandmother..!'

Crane ignored his statement and pulled the large door shut. Applied the mag-lock and once more slid the Sig from his belt. He palmed-it momentarily. The hammer was still drawn. Then he placed the suppressor against the digital lock pad and pulled the trigger.

There was a muffled thud. Then a flickering of lights and the mag-lock went dead. Crane grabbed the main lock handle and gave a tug. It wouldn't move. It wouldn't cycle. They were in there until the weapon blew.

Crane stared through the small peep-hole in the door. And gave the professor a middle-finger salute.

There was no sound. Just the vison of the two lab-rats trying to crawl across the floor. Their arms waving at the CCTV. They were screaming but there wasn't any sound. And they trailed blood behind them like injured snails. The professor just sat there. No movement. No indication that he was in fear of his life.

Crane turned and started to push Pam down the corridor – '*Pay-Back Mutha-fuckers..!*'

He stopped at the top of the spiral staircase. There was no lift. So he no option but to carry Pam down the stairs. Crane was still pumped-up on adrenaline.

So he had to make use of it. The clock was ticking and he no idea how long it would be before that weapon exploded. And possibly took the base with it.

He hadn't performed a fireman's-carry for years and as he neared the bottom of the stairs. He placed Pam down on the small seating area in the ante-room. And placed his hands on his knees and breathed hard.

'*Gotta stop smoking cigars..!*' - mused Crane.

Crane watched as the green-button blinked. And leaning on the doorway. Still trying to catch his breath. He reached over and gathered up his passenger just as it shushed open. And heavy-laden he stepped hard onto the small dockside.

His knees felt weak. And with every step his body was crying out for him to stop. But the sea-breeze was still blowing hard. And it hit him and rudely snapped him back to attention.

Staggering to the Patriot. Crane had no option but to haphazardly dump Pam into it. He didn't have the strength for anything softer. And as he bent forward. He toppled and fell straight into it. Pam landed just a-head of him. And uncoiling himself from her arms and legs. He stepped back onto the quayside and undid the mooring ropes.

The tide was still quite high. And the Patriot now free started to bob quite high on the surf.

Crane stood back and watched dazed for a moment. As the Patriot bobbed up and down. His head was fuzzy and his ears were ringing. His limbs started to feel loose and weak. Then snatching what energy he had he jumped back into it and pulled himself into the driving seat.

He breathed in hard through his nose and placed his hand on the throttle housing. And flicked open the little end cap. Pressed the immobiliser and then the starter.

There was a roar and the Patriot thundered into life.

Crane yanked the throttle back. And the twin turbine engines gave a high-pitched scream and the little silver speed boat lunged forward with a spray of foam.

Just then there was an almighty crack of thunder that echoed through the cavern. Crane shot a glance behind him. There was nothing. Then suddenly dust and debris started to rain down from above.

Crane glanced upwards. There was a massive crack in the Cavern roof. And it was spreading and getting deeper with every second.

'*Oh – SHIT..!*' – Crane blurted to himself.

Suddenly the debris from the cavern roof started to accelerate. The lumps were now getting bigger.

The size of concrete melons raining down.

Crane knew that he was running out of time. The weapon had obviously started to explode. Or had exploded and the fall-out and EMP was destroying the base.

He knew from his own training that the testing area would have been lead-lined. But the fall out and EMP-tremor would have reverberated right through to the foundations. And would have done serious structural damage. The base was old and not nuclear-proof.

As Crane hooked the Patriot hard left. The tunnel opening to the cavern loomed. And he finally darted through it. He was out and clear. In open sea. But he didn't let go of the throttle. He kept full-bore.

Then finally slumping back into the seat. He pushed the throttle forward and the Patriot slowed and the bow lowered itself back into the surf.

He chest was thumping. And opening his mouth. He could hear his heart-beat. And looking forward he stared at the horizon. The day was starting to dawn and the sun was very slowly starting to rise above the silhouette of the sea.

He gently turned the Patriot and looked back in the direction of the cliff-side and the cavern. It was gone. All that remained of it ever being there was a huge cloud of dust rising from the cliff-face.

But Crane could still see it. Just the rough outline.

Looe harbour was faintly in the distance. He could see the lights of the harbour-markers. He pulled the throttle back slowly and the Patriot started sloshing through the water towards it.

Just as he settled back into the seat there was an almighty bang and Crane snapped his head round over to his left. In the distance a tall thin, green-flamed mushroom rose from the cliff-top. Directly above where the cavern once was.

Crane slowed the Patriot. And watched for a moment. He noticed the base and the aerial tower were now gone.

Then Pam made a sombre murmur. And he knew she'd be awake soon. He gunned the throttle and the Patriot darted towards the harbour.

9

CRANE EASED THE THROTTLE. And the Patriot dipped. And slowly started to glide into the harbour. Looking a-head he could see Davey Parson's little yellow fishing boat. Still moored in its place. The picture of it sitting there haunted Cranes thoughts.

He was gone and so was Sam. And he was made to sit and watch. It was Cranes fault that he and his son had got involved. His fault they were now dead. Used like human guinea-pigs. And then just tossed away like rubbish.

The tide was slowly rising. But it was calm and he gently manoeuvred towards a slip-way that lead from the quayside to the sea. It would take less effort to get up it. Both he and Pam. So Crane punched the throttle and the Patriot sped-up towards it. He guided it in and beached hard. Patriots were designed to still float and manoeuvre in almost six-inches of water. Plus they were mostly made from Kevlar and were basically bomb-proof.

There was a hard shudder. A loud crunch and a sudden abrupt stop. And the engines raced. Crane slumped and switched off the motor. They'd made it. But Crane knew he was now empty. No energy left. His whole body tingled and he started to shake. Like an alcoholic having the DT's

It had been well over twenty four hours since he last had anything to eat or drink and the adrenaline in his body was now spent. He felt all used up and gone.

He literally fell out of the Patriot and onto the wet concrete. He stared back at Pam. She hadn't moved. There was no noise. She was still in a deep sleep.

Crane knew he had to do something to revive himself. And stumbling he was now back on the dock and he looked left and right. For any form of salvation. And then he saw it. The café. The harbour side café. Crane made a stumble pain-racked move towards it. And to his utter relief there was a half-empty milk crate sitting by the front door.

He threw himself down in a crumpled heap and reached out and snatched one up. And placing it to his lips. He managed to stop his teeth chattering and grinding long enough to bite through the silver-top. Then lifted and poured the ice cold milk down his throat.

He gulped and gagged hard but kept on drinking it down. Then he grabbed another and did the same.

Stopping momentarily. He inhaled sharply through gritted teeth. And felt the cold liquid swirling down his throat. And he immediately felt better.

Not 100% but his thirst was gone. And he felt some small pangs of energy return. And the vibrant shaking of his hands and legs slowed.

He glanced out across the harbour and out into the sea. And in the distance. Around the coast. The far cliff-top was still smoking. The plume of lime-green fire and smoke was gone. But the tell-tale sign was still there. With small whiffs still billowing up into the dawn sky. But strangely no sirens.

He snatched another gulp of milk and then examining the bottle. Gulped again and finished it. He placed it down and rubbed his hands on his face. And then down his fatigues.

Getting up seemed easier. And Crane stumbled back to the quayside and looked down at the harbour and the Patriot. There was no change. Pam was still laying there prone and none-the-wiser.

The steep slope of the slipway helped Crane to get to the bottom. And with the aid of almost slipping over on some old seaweed. The sudden shock brought of going 'arse-over-tit' brought Crane back to present life.

He placed his hands on the side of the Patriot. Then he froze. His eyes widened.

He felt the cold muzzle of a pistol jabbing at the base of his neck. Then he caught a whiff of smoke.

Cigar smoke.

He knew the drill. Only too well. And he slowly turned. Raising his hands as he did so.

'YOU..!' – Cranes breath was stolen from him. And he slowly looked the figure up and down – 'HOW THE FUCK.. ? SIMPKINS.. THE REPORT SAID YOU WERE KILLED IN BEIRUT.. ! I READ IT.. !'.

The figured pulled the pistol down to waist height. But still kept Crane covered. Then he slowly and assuredly pulled the small thin cigar from his mouth.

'I was needed elsewhere Crane..!' - he hissed and puffed on his cigar again.

Crane stood still. He stared hard. His muscles once relaxed. Where now tense. And he clenched his fists.

'You always were an evil blood-thirsty bastard Simpkins.. never happy till you got your gun off.. and some poor fucka was laying on the ground.. !'

Then Crane cocked his head to one side and threw Simpkins a sneer – 'So what the fuck have you got to do with shit-show..? Huh ?.. you're the cleaner ?.. aren't you ?.. when it looks like it's all coming on top you get rid of the witnesses.. !'

Crane paused. And nodded to himself – 'Yeah.. that sort of thing would be right up your street..!

Simpkins chuckled quietly. His cigar floating back and forth in his mouth.

'That's right Crane.. and I love it.. I love my work and I'm the care-taker for this op..!'

'Right that's enough of the fucking history lesson.. to the business at hand.. drop that piece into the Patriot and your holstered side-arm.. then grab her and let's get going..!'

Crane pulled the Sig fee of his belt. With two fingers. Knowing Simpkins would be looking for that motion. And threw it into the Patriot. Then made a slow two-finger grab for his Browning.

'So you've still got your Hi-Power eh.. ? your Belfast service weapon.. no serial numbers.. and the one you gave back in was the one you took from that IRA informant.. sneaky Crane.. not strictly 'office' was it.. ! but they let you keep.. didn't they.. keep it all these years.. I wonder why ?'

Crane shot him a side glance – 'Fuck-you Simpkins.. !'

And reluctantly he threw it to the boat. Then he looked at Pam then back at Simpkins – 'She's been drugged.. she can't walk !'

Simpkins just shrugged – 'Well let's hope that milk has revived you.. !' - and he motioned with the pistol for Crane to get on with it.

Crane managed to drag Pam to the side of the Patriot. And got her almost sitting up. She seemed to be stirring. And she murmured and moved her head.

'FUCK-SAKE.. get on with it Crane..!'

Crane glanced at Simpkins again. Then grabbed Pam by her arms and pulled her free and out of the Patriot. She slumped onto the slip-way. A dead-weight.

Bending down he pulled Pam up-right. Placed her arm around his shoulder. His arm around her waist and he started to drag-walk her back up the slip-way.

Simpkins slowly meandered behind. Pistol at the ready.

'Over there.. the black BMW..!' – he barked.

Crane looked behind and Simpkins returned his stare and motioned with his pistol. To once more, get a move-on.

Crane stopped at the BMW and Simpkins opened the back door.

He again motioned with his gun and Crane dragged Pam over and shoved her onto the back seat. And then Simpkins walked around to the other side. Opened the door and cuffed Pam's hands with a snap-tie.

He gave it a last tug and then closed the door.

Then returning to where Crane stood. Crane knew the drill and he lifted Pam's legs into the car and shut the back door.

Simpkins shuffled in his over-coat pocket. Then threw the same cable-tie to Crane. He picked it up off the ground and placed it onto his writs.

Once placed. Crane raised his shackled hands towards Simpkins – 'Use your teeth' – and Crane took the pull-through into his mouth and tugged. They clicked as the cables tightened around his wrists.

Simpkins moved around to the front passenger door. He again motioned with the pistol and Crane pulled at the door-handle and got in.

Driving up the lane out of Looe, Crane upped the ante – 'So where we going Simpkins.. McDonalds drive-through.. coz I'm damn-hungry.. ?'

Simpkins looked at Crane for a second. Then an evil smiled eclipsed the edge of his mouth – 'To see the sun rise.. !'

Crane looked at him and frowned – 'What the fuck you talking about..?'

'Sun Rise !.. the sun rise over Looe is beautiful.. you get a wonderful view from the cliff-tops..!' - blurted Simpkins.

Suddenly the penny-dropped and Crane knew exactly what he meant.

'Yeah well leave her out of this OK.. she hasn't seen your face… she's innocent in all this shit.. OK !'

Simpkins shot Crane a glance. The stone cold look on his face said it all – 'Operational prudence.. remember ?.. she's collateral damage.. nothing more !'

Crane stared at Simpkins then returned his gaze to the passing countryside. Then Crane turned and looked behind him. To the rear seat. Pam was waking up.

'What the fuck.. where am I ?.. what the fucks going on.. ?

And Pam shuffled and pulled her legs down. Suddenly she was trying to sit-up and trying to lean between the seats.

Simpkins raised his pistol at Pam. It brushed her cheek and she winced back.

'We're going for a ride Pam..!' - said Crane. Looking at her and waving his cuffs.

'Last I remember.. was the hospital.. now what the fuck is going on..!'

Crane glanced briefly. His mind flashed and he to play for time. Play for a distraction – 'This man here is going to kill us.. kill us both just like he did to your Nory.. ! and what he tried to do to you Pam.. when the station blew-up'

Pam looked at Crane. Then at Simpkins. She shuffled nearer his seat. She seemed angry and almost fearless – 'So that was you .. ? - pausing, waiting for a reply.

'You killed my Nory.. ? you murdering bastard.. and Pullet.. he was there as well' – Pam glared at Simpkins and then she looked into the rear-view mirror. Glaring at his even more.

Simpkins laughed – 'Oh you mean the fat one.. well he was dead before the place blew.. so was your Nory..! they didn't feel a thing.. I promise you.. not a damn-thing !' - and Simpkins turned and looked at Pam. With a dry smug look.

Suddenly Pam let out a shrill scream and brought her hands up and tried to lash-out at him. Simpkins ducked the blow and the car viscously swerved. And as he fought to regain control. Pam suddenly leap behind his seat and brough her arms over his head. And her cuffed hands came down and landed right across Simpkins's throat. And she pulled.

This caught him by complete surprise. And he tried to make a grab for Pam's arm. Whilst still trying to aim his pistol at Crane.

Crane was dumb-founded. And made a grab for the steering wheel.

The fight raged. And Crane fought for the wheel. As Simpkins tried in vain to release himself from the strangle-hold. Pam's pressure on his neck intensified. She was now a woman possessed.

Simpkins gurgled as he continued to fumble at Pam's death-grip. But she was out for blood.

Crane reacted the only way he could. And heel-palmed Simpkins right across his nose. Just as his gun went off.

There was a blinding flash. And the car suddenly veered to the left and grazed the hedges. Then the windscreen gave a loud crack and the car came to an abrupt stop against a heavy gate-post.

Crane had been thrown forward and had hit his head on the dash. He recoiled and rubbed his eyes and shook his head to clear the fuzz and ringing in his ears. He glanced down. And Simpkin's pistol was now laying in the cars foot-well. Right at his feet. Smoke gently trailing from the barrel. He snapped right and saw that Pam had not relented. Her eyes were closed. And her mouth was open in a silent scream. But her bound hands were still clamped tightly in place.

Simpkins hands slowly dropped. And his eyes were shut.

'PAM.. PAM..' - and Crane now had hold of her hands. Trying to get her to release her grip. But no-one could hear a thing.

Crane fumbled at the car door. It clicked open and Crane pushed with his feet. Then fell on to the grass verge. Balancing on his hands and knees. Crane clicked his jaw several times to dispel the humming. Then he fell back against the car and raised his hands. Then frowned. He pulled at the leather glove and saw he had a large bloody hole in his left palm.

Crane stumbled back to his feet and looked back into the car. Pam had finally relaxed her grip. But her hands and wrists were still firmly around Simpkins's neck. Her head was bowed. In shock at what had just taken place.

Crane slowly walked to the rear door. The handle clanged and the door fell open – 'Pam.. let him go.. he's done.. he's out cold.. !'

Pam didn't raise her head. Just slowly lifted her hands. And uncurled her arms free of her ferocious death-like grip.

She slumped back into the seat and then turned to face Crane. Her mouth fell open and she tried to speak. But all she could was do mouth the words.

Crane nodded - 'It's OK..!' - and he waved his bound hands in a backing-off motion. Then wandering round. He grabbed the driver's door. And It creaked open. Almost pushed. As Simpkins's was now slumped against it. And he spilled out onto the road as it slowly yawned open.

Crane stepped back and glanced down. Simpkins was out for the count all right. Crane had smashed his hands into his face as hard as he could muster. And his top lip was now swelling up. Along with his nose. Plus his face was covered in claret.

Then he realised. That as he struck him. He'd hit him in the face with the muzzle and top-slid of his own gun. That's how it went off. And blew a hole in his left hand. Then he looked at Pam. Her expression hadn't changed. She just stared at Crane. Her eyes were wide in shock and horror at what had unfolded.

He bent down and checked Simpkins's pulse. It was there. Faint but still beating.

Crane walked around to the boot and popped the lock. He made a brief search and grabbed a large leather holdall and placed it onto the ground. He fumbled around inside and then found what he was looking for. A small pair of pliers.

It was tricky but Crane managed to snip the plasti-cuffs off. But his left hand was numb and wouldn't work. And it was still bleeding profusely.

Crane turned his attention back to the boot and searched again. Then lifted the boot cover and found a small first-aid box.

Crane leant exhausted against the car. And pulled off his glove to again inspect the wound. Just as Pam came shuffling towards him. She seemed calmer. And she saw the bullet-hole.

Crane pulled himself back to his feet and reached for her cuffs. And he snipped off the cable tie as gentle and as careful as he could. Pam rubbed her wrists. Then she took his left hand and slowly turned it over. The bullet had gone right through. And luckily Crane was still pumped on adrenaline. So he couldn't feel it. But the wound was cauterized from the muzzle-flash but it was still bleeding.

Crane slumped against the boot again as Pam took the first-aid kit. She pulled out a small squeezy plastic bottle from the kit and tore off the lid. She poured some saline over the wound and through the hole and then placed gauze over it. Poking a little through the hole. In an effort to stem the bleeding. Then with a final knot. The bandage was in place.

As painful as it was. He flexed his hand. Not much. But it was better. And he slid the torn glove back on. 'Now what.. ? what we gonna do.. do with him.. ?' – Pam blurted.

Crane returned her look and then peered round at Simpkins.

'We're gonna end this.. Now.. !' – he replied without looking at her.

Crane reached back down into the leather holdall. And rummaged through it. There was an MP5K machine-pistol. A small lump of C4 plastic explosive. A ring-det. Some spare mags and some red hand-grenades. Indicating to Crane that these were Thermite. And could literally burn through anything. And finally some reels of gaffa-tape and ties. He grabbed-up some plasti-cuffs and looked back at Pam.

'We're going to give that evil bastard a taste of retribution.. it's been long over-due.. !'.

Crane steered the BMW back up the lane. It was limping and making an odd clanking noise. And the windscreen was flapping from the gate impact and bullet-hole.

'Where we going Peter ?' - said Pam. Looking at Crane suspiciously.

'To see the beautiful sun-rise' – he replied. As he shot her a reassuring glance – 'Don't worry Pam.. I'm going to do what should have been.. done twenty years ago.. !'

A sign emblazoned with the words 'Bluff-Point' came into view. And Crane turned left and followed the road. A little tea-hut came into view. And public car-parking but Crane kept going.

He stopped just short of a sign that read 'Beware Cliff Edge'. And put the BMW into park.

Resting his hands on the steering-wheel. Crane breathed hard then shot Pam a relaxed look – 'You OK ?.. you ready for this.. pay-back for your Nory.. ?'

Pam slowly nodded. Her gaze never moved.

Crane popped the boot and looked at Simpkins. He was now awake and his eyes were staring. He still looked arrogant and defiant.

Crane smiled. Then he grabbed Simpkins by his hair and yanked. He gave a muffled squeal through his make-shift sticky gag. The gaffa-tape was tight. But Crane could still hear him protest.

Simpkins hit the grass head first. And he kicked-out with his legs. He was bound. Gagged. And cuffed. But he could walk. And Crane still holding him by the crown of his hair. Pulled him roughly to his feet.

He stared at him hard. Right in his eyes. Simpkins expression had now changed. He now looked broken – 'Quite an experience isn't it .. Fear.. !!'

Then Crane still holding his hair. Pulled him round and shoved him into the driving seat of the battered BMW. He pulled some more cable-ties from his pocket and fastened Simpkins's bound-hands to the steering wheel. And using the gaffa-tape. He pulled his legs back and tied them to the seats bottom adjuster.

Crane pressed a small button on the door panel. And the driver's window hummed as it went down and disappeared into the door. He then slammed it.

Pam walked round and stood beside Crane. she looked at him. No words. Just a solemn look. Then she looked at Simpkins and folded her arms. Cocking her head back. She stood somewhat judgemental. But offered no protest to what was unfolding.

Simpkins snapped his head forward than back at Crane. His eyes where as wide as saucers. His muffled squeals and squawking's got louder. And he started to fight and pull at his bonds.

Crane pulled a Thermite grenade from his belt. Placed it into his left hand and pulled the pin. But kept a firm grip on the spoon-catch.

Crane stepped forward and peered in the car. And looked Simpkins straight in the eye - 'Well it's off to the next life for you.. and I promise.. you won't be lonely..!'

And he reached in further and shoved the BMW into gear. It was an automatic and the tick-over slowly started to draw the car forward.

Then without even looking. Crane eased his grip on the grenade. And the spoon pinged off. And It started to spark and fizz. Then he tossed it. And timed it perfectly. As it sailed through the window and landed squarely in his lap.

Simpkins head shot down and looked at the grenade. Burning away right in front of him. He tried to scream through his gag. He struggled. He fought. But the grenade just sat there fizzing. Then he looked back at Crane and Pam. Tears where welling in his eyes

The car drew past and gathered a little speed. And both he and Pam stood together as it rolled on further. Then it stuttered and slowly sank and disappeared from view.

Straight over the edge of the cliff.

They exchanged no-words. They stood in silence. Just as the Thermite grenade exploded.

The BMW was now just a ball of flame. Tumbling down the cliff face. Then it finally struck the rocks below. And the fuel tank joined in the explosion. The sound boomed. Echoed. And bounced off the cliff.

Both Crane and Pam sauntered forward a little. And they stared at the fire raging below.

'Paid in full and give my regards to Mr Capricorn..!' – mumbled Crane.

'Now what.. and who's Mr Capricorn ?' - said Pam. Turning to look at him.

Crane returned her gaze. His composure now seemed relaxed – 'Where are you staying at the moment ?'

Pam waved her arm down towards Looe – 'At the Rose and Crown.. the Penzance Police have put me there and are paying till the whole thing is sorted out I suppose..!'

Crane nodded – 'Then we'd better get going.. the suns rising fast.. !'

Back in Looe Crane walked up the harbour-side. The patriot was still there bobbing in the surf as the tide was coming in. Crane waded down the slip-way and grabbed the tow-line and fastened it to the quay-side. Then he jumped in and fastened the rear cleat. He placed the leather holdall from Simpkins car on the Patriots pilots seat and grabbed up the Sig and his Browning. And shoved them into the bag.

Along with Simpkins's pistol.

Searching the rear pannier boxes on the Patriot. He found an artic-wrap-around. And sliding this on it almost came down to his knees. But it covered his fatigues. And Crane felt a little more at ease.

Grabbing the holdall. He walked back up the slip-way. And made for the harbourside café. Looking through the window Pam was sitting at a table in the far corner. And he sauntered over and pulled a chair.

A steaming cup of tea sat in front of her. She was staring at it.

Crane breathed hard and ran his good hand through his hair. He felt like shit and knew he looked it too. Pam was no better.

Then Josey came over and placed an old snorkel coat over Pam's shoulders. She looked up and mouthed - 'Thanks'.

'Tea ?' - Crane just looked up at her and gave a slight nod in agreement.

Pam looked at Crane. The horror of what she had been through. What she had witnessed was written all over her face.

'Go home and get yourself cleaned-up.. then wait until you hear from me OK' – Pam just looked at Crane. Then she agreed with a gentle nod.

'But if you go out stay in sight.. in public OK.. your be safer !' - Then Crane got up and made to leave.

'Your tea ..!' - and Josey appeared. Mug-laden.

Crane didn't look back. Then he turned. Grabbed the cup and almost swallowed the hot tea in one gulp.

'Thanks' – and Crane slammed the door and was once more back on the harbour-side.

The bus pulled up over the road. Near the junction. But Crane knew he couldn't take it. He'd have to go across the fields. And come about circular to his cottage.

They could be waiting for him. Ready to ambush him.

Crane threw the holdall up on his shoulder and started walking. And as he neared the outskirts of town. The farmers' fields beckoned. The road was clear. No cars. So he climbed over the gate and kept close to the edge of the field. And the hedges.

He trudged on and glancing at his watch it was a little after 8. The sun was up and it was going to be a warm day. Still wearing the over-coat. He'd draw attention on the main road. So this way was safer in many respects.

And just as he came over the brow of the next hill. His cottage came into view. He could make out the thatched roof and chimney.

Crane ducked into the arms of a low-lying tree. And placed his back against the old boundary brick-wall. He placed the holdall down and rummaged through it again. And pulled a small pair of foldable bino's from the bag.

Through the trees near his cottage he could make out a car. It was black. And someone in a dark rain-mac was standing near the front of it. Almost sentry-like.

Crane threw-off the over-coat. He grabbed up the MP5K from the holdall and performed a brass-check. Then he attached the shoulder sling over and under his right arm. He slid the belt and holster around his waist. Brass-checked his Browning. Re-holstered it. Then checked the Sig.

The Sig was empty and he dropped it in the holdall then he remembered Simpkins's pistol.

He picked it up and looked at it. Then dumped it back into the bag. He didn't want anything to do with that evil Bastard. Let alone use his side-arm.

Crane grabbed the last two grenades and slipped them on to his webbing-belt. Then a final check of his weaponry. He was good to go.

He looked one last time through the bino's then placed them back into the bag. He was at the shorter end of the farmers field. He could cover the ground fast. He grabbed up the holdall and threw the long strap over his left shoulder. Slung it around to the small of his back and was off.

And keeping low and the machine-pistol at the ready. He scampered along the wall and dodged in and out of the culverts.

He stopped short of the final boundary wall near his cottage. Again operation prudence. He clicked and pulled the curved mag from the MP5K. And gave the 9mm rounds a nudge with his thumb.

They moved up and down under the tension of the spring. Then nestled against the feeder-lips. Then he pushed and clicked it home back into the machine-pistol. He curled his fingers around the cocking handle and pulled it down lightly.

A bright shiny 9mm bullet sat in the breech. He took a knee and breathed hard. Then grabbed his Browning from the holster and did the same.

Crane was well-armed. He was ready to go. Then he checked his left hand and the dressing. It was bloody. Still numb. And he bit it hard across the knuckles to wake it up.

Then he ghosted further down the side of the wall. Noting the distance he knew he was almost level with his cottage. He raised himself. Just enough to look over the wall.

The chap standing by the car was looking down the lane. And was standing almost opposite the farmer gates to the field. Crane saw he was wearing a covert head-set. As a thin wire ran from his left ear to his collar. Disappearing the under his shirt.

Crane surveyed the car. And the number plate. This confirmed it. They were from 'The Office'.

His next move had to be quick and quiet. Then Crane had a thought and he fished his Sig from the holdall. It still had the suppressor attached.

Crane took a knee and dropped the mag from the MP5 and thumbed three 9mm rounds from it into his palm. Then quietly pushed the mag back home into the machine-pistol. He release the mag on the Sig and then pushed the three rounds into it.

He raised it slowly and pushed the mag back into it and cycled the action as quiet as he could. Then he wrapped his hand around the suppressor and gave it a final twist. Just to make sure it was tight.

He knew if he had to drop the guy standing watch. It had to be silent.

Crane breathed hard. In through the nose. Out through the mouth. Regulate. Regulate your breathing echoed through his mind. Pace yourself. Be steady and controlled.

He looked up. Then got into a crouch and ghosted further down the wall towards the gate. He stopped just inches from the wooden post.

The adrenaline was powering through him like electricity. Every beat of his heart pounded in his chest. And echoed in his mouth when he breathed out.

Looking down Crane slid the MP5 out of the way. To rest under his right arm. But close enough to grab if he needed it. He flexed his right hand. It felt sweaty in the leather glove. Then tried to do the same with his left.

Then finally reaffirming his grip on the Sig. Cocked the hammer back with a solid double click.

10

THE SOLID DOUBLE CLICK. The weight and feel of the Sig. Crane once more re-affirmed his grip and slowly peered around the gate post. The chap was still there. Still in the same place. Standing guard and none the wiser. No movement. He hadn't heard a thing.

Crane was in a crouch. Balancing on the balls of his feet. Remembering to make himself as small as possible. He looked at the guard. His face. It wasn't familiar. He was young. Very young. Probably part of a yet another new in-take from Oxford.

He had to draw his attention. Get him closer. Then gently peering around again Crane suddenly sprang back. As the guard was now walking towards him. Towards the gate.

Crane back-peddled. Then stood and placed his back square against the wall. And slowly raised the suppressed Sig head-height. In a one-hand salute.

His muscles and senses twitched. His whole body was as tight as guitar-strings. He had the Sig dead-bang for a head-tap. And it fidgeted nervously in his right hand.

Then Crane looked down as a small stream of liquid was now squirting through the gate. With his back still against the wall. He took one side-step and caught the guard completely by surprise.

The pissing stuttered as the cold end of suppressor now rested squarely on his left cheek.

Crane wiggled his thumb on the side hammer-drop. And the guard squinted sideways from the corner of his eyes. They were wide and full of horror and surprise.

Crane tipped his head forward just enough for him to see him. And for them both to lock eyes at each other - 'Make any sudden moves and I'll snatch the life right outta-ya..' – he hissed.

The guard stood with his hands still on his dick. Then he started to tremble – 'Now with your left hand only.. your left hand only.. take the two-way out of your ear..!'

The guard complied. And slowly raised his hand. And the ear-piece now hung limp.

'Who's in there..?' - and Crane nudged the Sig into his cheek.

'J j just the regional commander.. Anderson !' - stuttered the guard.

'You armed.. ?' - the guard shook his head. Crane now shifted position slightly. Knowing he was covered by him.

'Open your coat.. and your jacket..!' – and again he complied. And he clearly wasn't armed. Only a radio 2-way was clipped to his belt.

Crane again shuffled his grip on the Sig - 'What's your name.. ?' - 'P..P..Parkes, he replied.

'OK Parkes.. put your dick away and take two steps back and turn around.. very slowly.. !'

The Guard lowered his arms. And fumbling he put himself away and then stumbled back on the grass verge next to the road. Taking two steps he turned.

Crane sprung like a Gazelle over the gate. And closed in behind him. He gently pushed the Sig into the centre of his back and got even closer.

Crane mouthed to the back of his head - 'Move.. front door now!'

The guard walked forward and Crane ducked in behind him. Keeping concealed. And keeping pace. They went through the front gate to the cottage and slowly sauntered up the path.

Crane nudged with the Sig and Parkes pushed the front door and it squeaked open. Then Crane placed his hand on Parkes's left shoulder and firmly shoved. And raised the suppressed Sig to sit right on the base of his neck. Taking heed Parkes then started down the hallway with Crane very close behind.

As they reached the middle of the hallway. Crane steered Parkes to the left and towards the lounge.

Crane nudged again with his pistol as they neared the door. Parkes pushed. And it slowly swung open.

'Parkes.. what are you doing ?'

Crane slowly pulled the Sig down and waved it just past the guards head. Then he bent slightly and gently peered round him.

'Crane.. ! we're not armed.. ! .. just calm down will you.. ?' – boomed a voice.

Crane shoved Parkes forward and he stumbled towards the sofa. Then he turned. The look of fear still emblazoned across his face. And still in combat-mode Crane crouched into a weaver-stance and waved the Sig back and forth at the two now in his front room.

They both slowly raised their hands in a surrendering motion.

Anderson was sitting on the Chesterfield. He seemed more at ease. Then he started to lower his hands – 'Just take it easy Crane.. will you.. for fuck-sake.. !'

Crane sprang forward – 'Fuck easy.. !.. now you both keep your fucking hands open.. and where I can see them.. !'

Anderson raised them again. With a frustrated look.

Crane looked at Parkes – 'Sit.. !' - and he motioned towards the arm chair with the Sig.

Parkes shuffled to the side. Hands still raised. And dumped himself down. He looked at Crane. His eyes still wide. His face wore a scared and somewhat solemn look.

'We got your signal' – said Anderson, looking Crane straight in the eye – 'We've been looking for that lab for a while.. that German professor and his gang were operating after their op had been shut-down..!

Crane sneered – 'So they were part of the office.. ?'

Anderson lowered his hands – 'Yes.. I'm sorry to say they were.. I was unaware that lab had been recommissioned.. it had been moth-balled back in the sixties.. !'

Crane lowered the Sig slightly - 'So your telling me they were acting under government orders to test that fucking weapon on innocent people..?.

Anderson shook his head – 'No.. that wasn't part of their remit.. as far as I know it was meant to be animals.. you know sheep, pigs and cows even.. there was no official stamp from us.. for human testing.. Von Heben in the end did that on his own.. !'

Anderson leant forward - 'But as I understand it.. in the early days he was given some human test subjects.. BUT NOT BY US CRANE !.. NOT THE OFFICE..! That authorisation came from further up the government food-chain.. career criminals.. multiple-murderers.. child-killers.. but then the orders were to shut him down.. shut it down.. we had the weapon and the plans etc.. it was to be hidden away and Von Heben was to be relocated elsewhere.. Scotland I think.. he was dying from radiation poisoning anyway.. !'

Anderson paused and leant back into the sofa – 'But that was all way before my time.. or yours for that matter Crane'

Andersons blasé attitude infuriated him - 'SO WHO THE FUCK DID SANCTION THAT EVIL BASTARD TO DO HUMAN TESTS ?.. HE MUST HAVE BEEN REPORTING TO SOMEONE ?'

Crane waved the Sig menacingly and took a slight step forward – 'EH.. SOMEONE MUST KNOW ! SOMEONE AT THE OFFICE WAS SUPPORTING HIM !.. and don't give me any of that.. about above my fucking pay-grade bullshit.. he had Black Ops looking after him.. and he was well funded..!'

Anderson raised his eyebrows. And raised his hands again in a backing-off motion and he shook his head.

'I don't know Crane.. I swear it.. why would I lie.. ? he and his operation went rogue'

'But it's over' – Anderson continued.

'We're cleaning-up the mess OK.. a specialist MOD squad have gone in to secure the weapon.. or what's left of it.. clear any bodies and close the whole lab down.. fill it in and back-seal it off forever..!'

Crane lowered the Sig to his side. And looked at the floor – 'Davey Parsons and his son are still in there.. I saw the weapon being used on them.. get them out OK..!'.

Then Crane raised his head and shot Anderson a stern look. Then he dangled the Sig menacingly by his side. And tapped it against his leg.

'Yeah.. don't worry.. we'll do that.. I swear.. !'- nodded Anderson.

Crane gently acknowledged. Then raised the Sig and placed it into both hands. Palming it.

'There's also the case of some reciprocity.. !'

'What you talking about Crane?' Anderson looked at him. Confused by his statement.

The Sig slipped out of Cranes left hand and again he dangled it by his right side. He looked at Anderson and raised his eyebrows very matter-of-factly.

'Well.. first there's Davey Parson's and his son.. if they have family.. they deserve something..?'

'OK.. I'll look into that back at the office. Seems reasonable,' replied Anderson.

'And Pam.. Nory's wife.. Pam North.. she got caught up in this thing.. the C4 blast at the local Police station.. took him out and his colleague Pullet.. but they were already dead.. shot dead.. then the damn place collapsed down on top of her.. she survived and was hospitalized then kidnapped by Simpkins and she was gonna be used next..!

Anderson stood up and let out a short laugh – 'Simpkins !.. he's dead.. Beirut remember.. that's bastards dead and gone… years ago.. I saw that report

229

too remember.. that safe-house came down on top of him.. during that air-strike.. !'

Crane smiled – 'Nope.. he was here.. he was the cleaner.. he grabbed me and Pam in the harbour.. after I got us out of there.. before the damn place blew.. he was gonna toss us both off the cliff at Bluff Point.. probably with a 9milly hollow-point for breakfast.. !'.

Then Crane moved closer and looked Anderson right in the eye - 'But he's fucking dead now !.. I've made damn sure of that.. !

Then he gently passed Anderson the suppressed Sig – 'He's at the bottom of Bluff Point.. with a BMW rammed up his arse and a Thermite grenade chaser.. Mutha-fucka's been paid in full this time.. !'

Anderson sighed and took the Sig. And looking at Crane, he nodded – 'Yeah.. well let's hope he stays dead this time..!

Crane grabbed the MP5K from under his arm and unhooked the sling from his shoulder. He removed the mag and cleared the action. And he offered it to Parkes who was still sitting in the chair.

Anderson looked at Parkes. Then shot him an impatient look. Parkes suddenly jumped to his feet and took it from Crane. Then stood. Waiting for further orders. But still wore the look of sheer bewilderment across his face.

'Easy with that.. !' said Crane. Looking Parkes straight in the eye.

Crane looked sideways at Anderson – 'We done here.. ?'

'Yeah.. we're done.. but I'll need a full report.. there's a new laptop there.. don't use your old one..!' and Anderson pointed to the side of the sofa - 'You can dial-in using your ID.. OK ?'

'You may be retired Crane but you're on a C27 remember.. this situation is hardly a 'recall to duty'.. but it is what it is.. and I'm sure you'll want to tell your side of the story.. ! and I'll check-in on this Pam North in due course' – and Anderson offered a weak smile.

Crane looked at him. He remained ashen-faced.

Anderson tried the smile again. With raised eyebrows – 'So let's get it on paper.. that way there's no grey-area'

'Oh there's one more thing..!' - said Crane.

'Miles !.. he came down here to help me.. but now he's gone too.. he went over the side from the Patriot.. in a pressure-suit.. he said there was more of those packages down there..!

Then Crane looked down at his feet – 'Then we got jumped.. by the professors Black Ops.. he was never reeled in.. so go and get him will you.. get him out of there.. if the tide hasn't washed him away by now.. he was going to be put out to pasture.. so he came down here to prove himself.. !'

He looked at Anderson – 'Don't leave him down there.. we were moored just off the cliff opening.. but there's no vector.. no transponder position.. !'.

Anderson motioned to Parkes. And as ordered he walked forwards. Towards the lounge door. Then he stopped and turned - 'Sir.. what about his sidearm ?'.

And pointed to the holster on Cranes right hip.

Anderson shot him a stern glance – 'What sidearm Parkes ?'

Parkes looked confused. He stared. His eyes darted back and forth at them both.

Anderson was busy unscrewing the suppressor. And he placed it into his left overcoat pocket. Then de-cocked the Sig and shoved it into the other.

With his hands in pockets. Anderson pulled his overcoat around himself and then shot him a hard ordered stare.

'On your way Parkes..!'

Parkes shuffled out of the lounge and trudged back up the hallway.

Anderson took one final look at Crane – 'New Oxford in-take.. so green !.. Oh and the Patriots were retrofitted with auto-transponders.. so we'll have the last longs and lats.. so we'll take a look OK.. can't promise anything.. but I'll do my best to find him.. I can promise you that.. !'.

Crane turned and walked over and dumped himself down on the sofa – 'Are we done now.. Anderson ?'

But Anderson was already through the lounge door and making his way down the hallway. Crane relaxed himself back into the sofa. He ached. His legs felt like lead again. And his wounded hand was throbbing like mad. Crane flexed and shuffled. And he winced as his back clicked.

Then the sound of a car boot being opened echoed through the lounge. Cranes eyes snapped open and he jumped up and spun around. And slowly walked over to the bay window.

He instinctively placed his hand on his Browning.

And through the dusty net-curtains. He could see Parkes placing the MP5 into the boot. And Anderson standing watch.

Parkes slammed the boot and sauntered to the driver's door. And Anderson turned and looked back at the cottage. He looked at Crane through the window. And gave a small agreeing-smile and nodded.

Then offered a small nod again.

Crane returned the same. With a weak smile. Then Anderson gave a short salute and got into the back of the car.

The engine fired into life and they pulled away. Back up the lane.

The steam filled the bathroom. Warm and invigorating and relaxing at the same time. Crane undid his combat trousers and yanked them down.

And smelling himself. He winced at the aroma of stale piss and dried sweaty shit. Then perching on the side of the bath. He aimed them at the corner of the bathroom. And they landed on top of his combat boots.

Standing. Looking in the mirror. He frowned. The face that looked back at him. Looked old. Old and tired. The bruise on the side of his face had remained. It looked deeper. More angry. Or maybe that was just Cranes demeanour.

He looked at his watch. It was almost midday. Then he looked closer. And he sighed heavily. A small crack creased the glass lens.

Staring into the mirror again. He ran his hands through his hair. It was greasy. Matted with sweat and dirt. And blood. And seeing this Crane moved closer towards the mirror. He searched the area on his head. Searched the hair-line. But there was no mark. No injury. No sign of where it had come from.

This must have been someone else's.

Crane moved his head back and forth. Searching for more. Then he realised. The blood was on the left side of his head. It was from his hand. From the bullet wound. And his struggle with Simpkins.

Then Crane un-zipped the combat jacket and allowed it to fall to the floor. It made a slight thud and he looked down and smiled.

Then he stepped into the bath and slowly. Very slowly. Lowered himself into it.

Every movement of his body ached. And stung with pain. But finally in the hot water. He felt soothed. He felt warm. He felt weightless.

He gently swirled the bubbles around him. Gently shuffled his shoulders. Allowing the water to lap around him.

Then Crane leant to one side and looked down at the crumpled black combat jacket. Then he sat back into the bath and raised his hand. And looked at the small computer hard-drive. He smiled and turned it over in his hand.

'Yeah.. you can have your report Anderson.. but I'll be keeping this just in case' – Crane mused to himself.

Then he dumped it back onto his jacket.

He gingerly lowered his left hand into the warm water. And flexed it. The pain shot through his wrist and up towards his elbow. He winced. And grit his teeth till they started to creek. Then after managing to flex it several times. He started to unwrap it.

Finally he waved his hand back and forth. Slowly in the water. The warmth stung but also gently soothed it. But then the dull ache and pain now started to pulse. As the numbness disappeared.

He could see the hole. About the size of a pencil. And it went right though. From his palm to the other side. Like a blood-red porthole. He flexed it again and it started to bleed. And he could now feel the bones grind together as he moved it. The blood mingled with the soapy water and dispersed into the bubbles.

'Well you left me a souvenir Simpkins.. !' – Crane thought to himself.

Wrapped in an old dressing-gown Crane trudged back into the kitchen. And set the old chrome kettle in motion. He gave one last tug on the new bandage around his left hand. And squeezed his hand into a weak fist. It hurt. But felt a little better. The warm bath had done the trick.

Had done the trick all over. Cranes body still ached but he felt warm. And now all he wanted to do was sleep.

He poured himself a large black coffee and shuffled into the lounge. The wrong thing to do when you want to sleep he thought. But he had no tea in the cottage. Matherson was a real tea-gulper. And undoubtedly had drunk one after another. When he was there.

He walked over to the old Chesterfield and stared out of the window. It was a sunny day. The light was starting to eb its way into the front room. It felt warm. The air felt warm. And the overwhelming desire to sleep started to zig-zag its way through him.

He sat at one end and raised his legs. The Chesterfield squeaked and groaned as he shuffled and finally got himself comfortable. He took a sip of his steaming black coffee and then placed it on the floor.

He breathed hard. Flexed his feet. Ankles and legs. The clicks of his joints echoed in the room.

Then reaffirming his head on the arm of the sofa he glanced out of the bay window. And a gull flew past. Squawking as it went. Crane smiled to himself. Then his left arm fell from his side.

He was gone. Sound asleep.

There was a hard piercing scream. The screech of tyres now on the edge. And the acrid smell of burnt rubber. As a hair-pin corner suddenly appeared on the left and Crane fought to get round it. The Fiat was protesting. As Crane had it right on the limit. And he was flying up and down the gearbox like a man possessed.

Round the corner the road stretched out. And in the distance there was a sharp right. Almost another hair-pin. Crane looked and made a judgement call.

On the crest of the corner. The side of the road disappeared. It descended into an almost sheer drop. Just a small feeble barrier to guard the unwary.

He dropped a gear and sped towards it. Driving middle of the road. To make use of the space. He snatched a moments glance in the rear mirror. And weaved back and forth as shots rang out behind him. Spanish Intelligence was hot on his heels and they wanted their tech back.

There was aloud ping of a bullet. A shattering of glass. As the right wing-mirror flew off and tumbled onto the road behind.

Crane glanced again into the rear-view mirror. They were gaining. Their car was faster. An Alfa-Romeo that was probably office and tuned for pursuits.

He had to slow them down. But how ?. These were the Swiss-Alps.

They stretched out before him. Beautiful and stunning. But sight-seeing certainly wasn't the order of the day. It was survival. There was no real cover. It was a case of making a run for it. And staying in front at all costs.

The Fiat he'd stolen in Geneva was old but sturdy. And Crane had it on the max. The engine was screaming with every crunch of the gears. And it felt like it was going to give up the ghost at any minute.

The hard right hander was looming. Then Crane had an idea. The barrier. And looking ahead he could see that part of it was hanging loose. Probably from an old collision.

Crane went wide. Then eclipsed the corner tight and snaked directly towards it. Then jabbed right at the very last minute. He jerked away and clipped it hard with his rear-bumper.

It worked. The barrier broke free and it snaked out across the road behind him. He once more glanced into the rear mirror. Just in time to see the Alfa crash straight into it. They spun and then hit the mountain side. Crane straightened the Fiat and glanced up again.

It looked like one of them had gone through the windscreen. And was now laying spread-eagled on the bonnet

He yelled in triumph!. Then punched the steering wheel. Then punched it again.

There was no movement. Just steam pouring from the front of the shattered Alfa. And as he gunned the

Fiat. The crash disappeared from view as he blazed around the corner. Then another loomed. He was clear.

'You're getting low on petrol' – Crane spun his head round. There was no one there. The back-seat was empty. He was on his own. He was sure of that. But he heard a voice. A soft gentle almost eloquent voice.

Then he looked at the dashboard. *'Shit !'* - the fuel gauge was low. Crane looked at the road ahead and scanned for any road signs. There was none.

He looked again. He had just under a quarter of a tank. And he knew he had at least another two hundred miles to go.

The road was levelling out. Getting flatter. Most of the Alps seemed to be behind him. So Crane sped up and then eased back. Letting the car coast at high speed. Until he needed to jab the throttle again.

'There's a Jerry-Can in the boot' – Crane spun again. Yet still there was no one there. He suddenly started to shake. The voice sounded strange but familiar. He was on a high. Pumped on adrenaline.

He glanced in the rear-view mirror and saw his Grandmother. She smiled. Crane yanked the steering wheel to the left and skidded along a dirt road at the side of the main carriageway. Then slammed both feet on the brake.

He skidded to a halt and looked in the rear-view mirror again. She looked at him and smiled once more and winked. Crane didn't look behind him. With a fumble he opened the car door and almost fell on to the dirt road.

He crawled away and sat on the grass verge. Breathing hard. He looked up at the back of the car. No-one was there. Then scrambling to his feet he opened the rear door. Nothing. Then looking down. There sitting on the rear seat was his Grandmothers floppy summer hat.

He picked it up and examined it. He raised it slightly. And he could smell her perfume.

He placed it back down and closed the door. And stared at it. *'Check the boot'*- his Grandmothers voice. Again echoed through his head again. He frowned. Then walked round and popped the boot lid. And lifted out the stolen tech in its battered black transport case.

Then Crane lifted the boot-floor cover and sure enough. There was a small green jerry-can.

He poured the petrol into the tank and then threw it away into the bushes. He jumped back into the driver seat. Fired the engine and sped off back up the carriageway.

He was on his way. The road to France stretched out before him. His pursuers had been taken out and he was free and clear. Feeling again - *the Victor !*.

He glanced once more in the rear-view mirror. Hoping his she would appear again. He had so much he wanted to say. But there was nothing. No sign of her.

The drive wore on. Crane was getting weary. As the road seemed endless. Straight. And never ending.

Suddenly there was no noise. No sound from the engine. The scenery passing on the road melded into one. The hills started to sink into the ground. Then the road started to rise and go into a deep climb. And Crane let go of the steering wheel.

He looked to the side of him. At the right-hand seat. And sitting there was his Grandmothers floppy summer hat.

Then the window whirred down and the wind started to blow and billow into the car. Her hat started to flap. Then it lifted and started to hit the door. Like a bird caught at a window. Then it rose further and started to bump the roof of the car.

Crane watched it for a moment. Spell-bound. Then as he reached out to grab it. It dodged his hand and flew out of the car window like it had wings.

He turned and looked behind him. And watched as the hat fluttered away behind the car.

Then he returned his gaze forward. The road was now getting even steeper and the car seemed to be slowing down and stuttering.

Then he looked in the rear-view mirror. And his Grandmother was there again. She smiled and gave the same warm wink as she used to. When he was a boy.

Crane smiled back and slowly closed his eyes. Then he opened them.

'Gran.. Gran ?' - he called out . But she was gone. Then Crane turned to look behind once more. And was suddenly shoved backwards.

He sat bolt-up and rubbed his neck. He hurriedly glanced around. He was in the cottage. On the old Chesterfield and his feet were cold and his shins was goose-pimply. He looked down at his coffee. It was long since cold. Crane swung his legs onto the floor. And tapped his feet up and down.

He grabbed the old coffee and ventured back into the kitchen. The kettle came to life and he tipped the cup into the sink.

Then he paused for a moment.

His Grandmother. Crane walked back up the hallway and into the bathroom. He bent and picked up his combat jacket. And placed the small hard-drive on the side. Then searched and fumbled through the pockets. He found what he was looking for. And pulled it free and studied it.

His eyes went wide. And he pulled the photo even closer.

Crane walked back into the lounge and placed the photo on the mantle-piece. It sat landscape. And centre place on the bare mantle. He stepped back and stared at it again.

In the old photo was his Grandmother. A young version of her. And sitting next to her was the Professor.

He grabbed his new coffee from the kitchen side then sat back on the Chesterfield. He reached down and picked up the black leather messenger-bag that Anderson had left. And searched through it.

The laptop was there. And alongside it a mobile. He pulled it out and inspected it. It was new. An apple iPhone. Then he hesitated. If I turn this on. The office will know everything.

He gently placed it back into the bag. And pushed it to one side. Then he ventured back to the kitchen. His mobile was sitting back in its charger near the kettle. It seemed the safer option for the moment. The office would be tracking this new phone. The one that Anderson left him. Not his own.

Squeezing the side button it blinked into life. Then scrolling through he entered 'Rose 'n Crown' and searched for the number.

He dialled and a voice came on – 'Rose and Crown.. can I help you ?'

'Pam North please..!' – 'One moment' - came the reply. And Crane heard the phone stutter through as his call was being transferred.

Suddenly there was a click - 'Hello..!' - came a faint woman's voice.

'Pam.. it's Peter.. you OK ?

'Oh Peter.. yes I'm OK.. just tired.. that's all..!'

Crane eased back in the Chesterfield - 'Good to hear your voice.. we need to talk but not on the phone though OK.. it's nothing to worry about.. and I'll explain all to you later'

'It's easy for you to say don't worry Peter... I just don't understand what the hell's been going on,' replied Pam in a concerned tone.

'Look get a bite to eat and then get your head down.. stay were you are and I'll meet you tomorrow at the café.. OK ?.. say 10 o'clock ?'

'Ok.. see you then..' - Pam replied solemnly. And she hung-up.

Crane looked at his watch. It was a little after 5.

Time for a bite too..! – he thought.

11

CRANE STEPPED OUT OF the little corner shop. And glanced back up the lane that led to his cottage. The tatty thatched roof was clearly visible in the distance. And he stood and pondered for a moment. *So much for retiring !.. I'm on the hardest case of my life..!.*

And he fumbled and folded the local papers for the second time. Placing them under his arm.

A faint distant rumbling showed the bus was coming. And he strolled down the road towards the stop.

Happily it all started to feel familiar once again. He rode these old buses as a boy with his dear Grandmother. Long summer holidays that he treasured. They would ride them into Looe and then spend the day on the beach. She would read or do a crossword. And he would swim or look for crabs among the rocks.

Then the memory faded. Almost as quickly as it came. And it all felt like a life-time away. When the heavy lump and feeling of carrying his Browning in his home country hit him hard. Cranes mood was now dark, cold and purposeful in intent. Almost like flicking-off a light-switch.

He looked at his watch and it was a little after nine. Always be early. Operational prudence.

The bus did a small circuit of the town then stopped just short of the harbour. Crane got off and made for a mini-market.

He strolled up and up down the aisles. Then finally located what he needed. And he paid for the two cheap smartphones and also bought separate sim-cards. They were both PAYG and he topped them up with fifty-pounds credit on each.

He paid cash. So his name wouldn't pop-up on any screen at the office. He knew they would be watching him now. Especially after the last twenty-four-hours activities. And after searching the old MOD base. There's no doubt that they would know that the professors hard drive had been taken.

With the carrier-bag in hand he crossed the road and made his way to the harbourside café.

Glancing at his watch again. He was still early. This would give him time to set them up.

Crane waved at Josey as he took a seat at a far corner table near the windows. He wanted a clear vantage point. And to be ready. Just in case someone appeared that stood-out. And he didn't like the look of.

He snapped the covers back on the smartphones and powered them up. All seemed good. Then he entered his name and number in one. Then Pam's details in the other.

Josey appeared with a large steaming mug of dark Cornish tea and placed it down – 'Anything else ?' – she said with a large beaming smile.

Crane glanced up at her – 'Not just yet thanks.. I'm waiting for someone.. we'll order together'

'No probs' - and Josey turned to walkway away – 'Oh could you dump these for me ?' - and Crane handed her the carrier-bag with the boxes and wrappings from the mobiles.

She smiled warmly and took them. And strolled back to the counter.

Crane placed the local news-papers down on the table. And his eyes scanned the front page. The main title was as suspected. *'Old Derelict MOD Base Explodes'*. Then reading further it stated that some old forgotten war-time ordinance had degraded and gone off. Causing the explosion. Possibly caused by old faulty wiring it added. But no-one was hurt and the MOD have cordoned it off and made it safe. And the base will be dismantled etc.

Crane leant back into the chair and laughed inwardly. A typical office smoke-screen he thought. And it read like a script.

But the less the locals knew the better.

Just then the front door jingled open and Crane looked up. And Pam looked at him and a small weak smile creased the edges of her mouth.

Crane beamed back at her warmly and she walked forward. He stood and ushered her to the chair opposite him.

'You OK..?.. some tea.. ?'

Pam nodded as she took her seat. But she looked very solemn.

'What do you remember ?' – asked Crane. In a low caring subtle tone.

Pam looked down at the table. Keeping her hands in her lap. She grimaced and gently shook her head – 'Nothing at all really.. I can remember when the Police Station blew.. sort-of.. I was coming down the stairs at the time!.. then I blacked out and woke up in the hospital..!'

She looked at Crane – 'Then I kept lapsing in and out.. I remember you.. your visit.. then a different room.. but that was it..'

Crane leant back into his chair and Pam returned her gaze to the table – 'The last thing was coming too in the back of that man's car.. and the fight we had.. letting it go over the cliff.. with him in it..!'

Pam placed her hands on the table and fumbled with her fingers. She seemed nervous. Crane knew the last thing on her mind. The last thing she was thinking of. Was the sight of the car going off the end of the cliff and seeing it explode. With Simpkins shackled to the steering-wheel.

Crane could see she was struggling with this. He took both her hands and gently caressed them. And she looked-up.

'Now what.. ?'

Crane breathed hard and gave her a solemn look. Then Josey placed a steaming cup of tea on the table and Pam suddenly withdraw her hands.

'Thanks Josey.. !' – he said with an upward smile. And he looked at Pam again and motioned – 'Hungry..?'

She just shook her head. And looked again down at the table.

Crane gave a gentle wave and Josey sauntered off.

'Well now.. all you need to do is nothing.. just stay at the Rose and Crown and bide your time OK.. I've spoken with someone from the government and they will be in touch in regard to what's happened and also making sure you get some kind of compensation.. It won't make up for it and all the shit you've been through.. but you need to start somewhere I suppose..!'

Then Pam looked up at Crane. She seemed a little agitated by his comments - 'Who are you Peter.. who are you really.. ? and what the fuck do you mean.. compensation..!'

Crane snatched a massive gulp of his tea – 'I work for the government.. have done since I was in my twenties.. you've probably worked out that something odd.. something bad was going on down here and Nory got caught up in it.. as did Davey Parson's and his son Sam.. and then of course you.. when the Police station blew..!'

Pam looked at Crane. She seemed a little angry. But still interested and concerned all the same.

'The compensation is a side result.. and I'll make sure you get it OK.. nothing else will change what's happened.. nothing !'.

Then Crane leant back – 'I came down here to retire.. and go fishing.. and I got caught up in all this shit too.. but now I want to set it all straight..!

Crane hooked his head to one side – 'But you must stay quiet as to what you've seen and experienced.. you must.. OK.. or we'll both be in danger'

He then placed the smartphone on the table in front of her. She raised her eyebrows and looked at it concerned. Then looked back him – What's that for..?'

'Pam.. from this moment on.. don't use any public telephones or internet OK.. if you have your own mobile.. don't use that either.. switch it off.. just use that one.. it's clean and not registered to you.. my name number has been entered into the contacts..!'

Crane picked it up and handed it to her – 'Call me anytime.. if you feel unsafe or concerned about something.. a man called Anderson will be in touch.. he'll probably call you at the Rose.. main switchboard etc.. OK'

Pam took the phone and palmed it for a moment. Then glanced back at Crane – 'He'll arrange a time to meet with you OK but make sure it's public.. at the hotel bar or here even OK.. and don't get in a car with him either.. or go anywhere with him.. it's important !.. just stay visible.. but I'll be there with you OK.. your be safe with me.. I swear..!'

Pam nodded. For some reason she now seemed a little more relaxed – 'Come-on Pam.. hungry ?.. let's have a bite.. coz I am'

Crane turned and called out – 'Full English please Josey.. !. then he glanced back to Pam and raised his hand in an offering gesture – 'Toast 'n jam please Josey,' called Pam.

Crane smiled and rested his arms on the table – 'Just be cool.. I'll look after you I promise..!.. one step at a time and when all this shit has calmed-down.. I'll tell you all I know.. promise'

Pam nodded. And gave a warmer smile.

'Oh one more thing Pam' - and Crane reached into his inside pocket and pulled out the old photo. He gently placed it on the table.

Pam lent forward frowning and picked it up - 'That's your old Gran.. I know that much Peter.. she's younger but it's definitely her.. but who's the chap sitting next to her in the arm chair..?'

Crane frowned - 'Don't know.. I found that in my Grans bits and pieces at the cottage.. thought it may

ring a bell.. you've lived down here all your life.. I just
visited in the summer holidays from boarding school..
remember'

'Hang on..!' – said Pam. And she studied the
photo even closer. Cranes ears pricked-up.

'I do remember vaguely.. I think.. when I was at
the college in Penzance.. he was a professor there once..
yeah I'm sure of it.. I was only sixteen.. seventeen.. so
we're talking back in the early 80's.. but yes.. I'm sure
of it..!'.

He took the photo back - 'You sure Pam..?' - and
looked at it again. Pam nodded and held her hand out.

Crane passed it back – 'Yeah.. now looking at it
again.. yes he was there.. I'm positive..!'

Pam looked at Crane – 'But I know who would
know..!' - Crane raised his eyebrows in interest - 'My
mum.. she was a teaching assistant there.. for years!'

Pam picked up the smartphone and took a snap-
shot of the photo – 'I'll show this photo to my mum..
she'll know for certain..!'

Crane nodded just as his large English was plonked
down in front of him. And Pam's toast and jam came
next.

They ate in silence. Crane was hungry. And after
continued splashes of brown sauce. He pushed his plate
to one side. And wiped his mouth.

Pam had finished somewhat earlier. And she was
studying the old photo again.

Placing it back down - 'It's him Peter.. yeah.. a professor at the college.. evil piercing eyes.. and a funny accent.. but my mum will know more..!'

Crane nodded – 'Great.. let's hope she can shed some light on who he was.. and hopefully his connection to my Gran..!'

Pam got up and shoved the smartphone in her pocket. Crane got up too and wrapped his arms around her. He pulled her tight. Gave her a warm hug and smiled.

'It's all gonna be OK.. I promise.. just remember what I told you.. stay visible..!'

Pam locked her arms around him. She pulled. Gently at first. Then harder after hearing Cranes words. He looked at her and gently kissed her cheek.

Then smiling she turned and left the café. And Crane watched through the window as she strolled back up the quayside.

Crane wandered over to pay Josey – 'Dunno were Ole Davey Parson's and Sam are ? .. haven't seen them for a few days..' – Crane bit his lip. He didn't know what to say. He just shrugged his shoulders and offered a faint smile.

'Thanks Josey' – and Crane turned. Gathered up his newspapers and gently closed the door behind him.

Strolling back up the quay. He pondered. *What could he say ?* He mused. The official secrets act. Something he always vehemently believed in. Was in some-ways now a curse. He wanted to shout and scream about the injustice of it all. About the innocent people being killed. And used like lab-rats in some horrible game of weapons testing.

They were nothing more than collateral damage. British Intelligence has a way of marking those who fall by the way-side. Who fall in the line of doing their secret duty. As nothing more than that.

But Pam will get some. Gets some compensation. Get some reciprocity. Crane had saved her life and she was owed for having her whole life turned upside-down.

Back at the cottage Crane picked up the professors hard-drive from the bathroom and trudged back to the lounge. He turned it over in his hands. The terminals looked different to normal computers. But then again Crane was no expert.

He wanted to look at this. See what secrets it held. Crane was sure that it held all the information of what that evil man had been doing for the last thirty-odd years or so.

He grabbed up his own bag from the bedroom and returned to the lounge. He pulled his laptop free and placed it on the kitchen-side. He rummaged again and found several leads. One was the mains charger. The other a feed for down-loads.

It had been a while since he'd last used it. In this way. But to his complete surprise the lead fitted perfectly. Fitted the hard-drive like a glove. Then Crane switched on his laptop and it cycled through and blinked into life.

Then Crane attached the small hard-drive and a program popped up. '*Unable to access attached drive*'. Crane knew the professor would have had it security-coded.

'*A 3-bit cypher encryption*' – he mused. Three-codes to access it. You'd get one chance to access the drive. And make one mistake. It would self-delete.

Crane moved the mouse over a program that had been installed on his laptop. He'd used it many times on operations. It was a 'Black-Hat'. A special program for accessing locked data on emails or stolen hard-drives. And even retrieving deleted data.

He clicked on it. And it blinked and stated, '*Waiting to interface – please enter user code*'.

Crane tapped phenetic -'*Mike-Echo-One-One*' - and hit enter. Then the screen suddenly went blank.

'*Oh Shit !*' - Then suddenly a count-down marker appeared centre screen and timer read-out started counting below it.

Crane breathed a sigh of relief. It was working. But the count-down read twenty-four hours.

'*This was gonna take some time!*' – reaching back into his bag Crane attached the laptop to the mains. Then slowly walked back into the lounge. All he could do now, was wait.

Sitting once more he pondered. Then pulled the new smartphone from his jacket pocket and placed it on the arm of the Chesterfield. It was blank. No calls. No text's from Pam. He hoped that all was OK. That she was OK.

Then Crane got up and sauntered back down the hallway. Towards the end bedroom. As far as he could remember. His Gran had always used this as a storage room.

He gave the door-knob a squeeze and pushed it open.

The curtains were still drawn. The room was quite dark and shrouded. Crane went to pull the old moth-eaten curtains but then thought better of it. And flicked the light switch.

A single bulb flickered into life and the room filled with dim light. Low wattage. His Grandmother was never one to waste money.

Apart from some old furniture. A dinner table. And several chairs. There wasn't really anything in there. And obviously when his dear Grandmother had passed. This stuff was of no interest to his family when they cleared the place out.

He sauntered back through the door. And made his way back up the hallway. He stood in the gally between the kitchen and the lounge. And thought – 'Now what..?'. He had quite some time to kill before his laptop cracked through the fire-wall on the Professors hard-drive.

'*Tea.. I suppose.. !*' – mused Crane. And he strode back into the kitchen and set the kettle in motion.

Stirring his tea he glanced at the laptop. There hadn't been any real movement. Time-wise. As sometimes if the 'Black-Hat' makes good progress. Then it will count down quicker. And jump time-spans. But Crane knew he wasn't this lucky.

Aiming his tea-bag at the sink. He snatched-up his tea and made for the lounge. Sitting back on the Chesterfield. Boredom was starting to kick-in. Crane was eager to know what was on that damn hard-drive. But he'd have to play the waiting game.

Placing his tea down. Crane reached over and flicked on the old TV. He was never one for soaps or documentaries. But anything was better than just sitting there waiting.

A picture came into view. And scratchy-sound started to emanate again from the little ancient wooden-clad TV. He flicked through. Hoping for daily news. But there was nothing more than a weather report.

And a soap about doctors and then adverts. He left it on the third channel. West Country ITV. And hopefully there will be something on news-wise. In due course.

He stretched out on the Chesterfield and started to glance through the local papers again. He could have used the laptops. Either his own or the one that Anderson had left him. But that would have been too dangerous. Way too dangerous to use either one for that purpose.

He had to maintain a zero-internet traffic presence. And zero-mobile activity. Or at least a mobile he knew that could be tracked.

Crane read the front page and proceeding. The news flash about the MOD base read like a script from a movie. It wasn't anything that he hadn't seen before. Just normal British Intelligence smoke-screen bullshit. To avert the public from what had really happened.

But the hard reality was. They had to say something. Cornwall was littered with old MOD bases. And when one goes up in green-smoke and flame. The public will want to know why. And of course they will want to know that they are safe.

As long as the government hit that home. With a governmental smiley face. That there was no threat to their society or way of life. It would all eventually go away. And be forgotten. Cornish folk were like that.

Crane finished both papers. And oddly there was nothing about Simpkins. Or even his car. Or indeed any car had gone off Bluff Point.

This concerned him. As this had happened not long after the lab blew.

Even if the local Police had found him. And his car. Thermite grenades literally melt everything to ash. So identifying Simpkins would be nigh-on impossible. Crane had thrown the grenade onto his lap as the car pulled away. When it went off Simpkins would have been vapourised. The only thing left of him would have been his teeth perhaps.

But he knew. Knew it was Simpkins.

Simpkins had gone rogue. Everyone at the office knew that. Just after the Beirut Op. So he was no real loss. Not even collateral damage. And hopefully Anderson would merely enter his name into the report. Then put a line through it.

A simple case of admin. Finished with a full-stop. And paid in full.

Crane pulled the black and white photo from his shirt pocket and looked at it again. Or rather studied it. His Grandmother seemed happy. Sitting there in the sun. Her floppy hat in place. And the professor was looking sideways at the camera. He seemed to be almost trying to avoid it. Avoid being in the picture. He wasn't in a wheel-chair. But a walking stick was evident.

Then something struck Crane. They were sitting on a veranda. The cottages veranda. At the same old garden table and chairs that are still there now.

They hadn't moved in all those years. They still sat in the same place. Just outside the French doors at the side of the cottage.

The professor had been there. Been to the cottage. What was his connection to his Grandmother.

Crane stared hard at the old photo. He stared hard at his Grandmother. He was going to find out. No-matter what. He was going to uncover the truth.

'Stolen car found at the bottom of Bluff Point..!' – came garbling from the old TV and Crane sat bolt up and stared straight at it. With eyes wide. He listened intently.

The TV footage showed a reporter talking from the grassy layby area at Bluff Point. He explained how earlier today a car was found at the bottom. All burnt-out and a body had been recovered.

'It's unclear if this is connected to the old MOD base explosion.. but the local Police are not ruling it out.. however the Army's Military Police have come in and taken over the investigation and once again sealed off this area too..! - the reporter continued

– *'They have yet to make a formal statement to the Police.. but some locals have stated that they have seen the car before.. but it's not local.. so many believe that it is connected to the base.. or at least the explosion.. in some way!'*

Shit ! – Crane knew that if Pam had seen this. It could throw her into a panic. She was there when it happened. And she watched as the car went over the cliff. With Simpkins shackled to the steering wheel. Squawking for his life.

She saw the explosion. She knew everything and also knew that Crane was involved.

'Now what ?' – Mused Crane.

Then he grabbed up the smartphone from the arm of the Chesterfield and feverishly dialled Pam. He had to speak to her. If anything just to make sure she was OK.

The call clicked through. And after three rings she answered – 'Peter ?' – 'Yeah it's me Pam.. you OK.. have you seen the news.. ?'

There was a slight pause – 'Yes.. I've seen it.. but I'm not bothered.. it was him or us right..?'

'Yeah Pam.. yeah it was..!' – Crane could tell by her tone. That she was demure and even - somewhat calm about the whole thing. And he was sure that she could tell in his tone. That he was relieved.

'Well Peter.. that photo of that chap.. the college professor sitting with your Gran.. my mum rang me and yes she does remember him..!'

Crane leant forward and almost dropped the smartphone – 'What.. ? what does she know Pam.. tell me.. !'

'There's too much to say over the phone Peter.. but my Mums coming over from Penzance tomorrow.. she'll be here around 9ish.. I said we'll meet her in Josey's café.. OK?'

Sure.. sure.. I'll meet you there at 9 on the dot OK.. and remember what I've told you.. be careful'

'I will Peter and you too OK.. see you tomorrow' – and the smartphone went dead.

Crane looked at his watch. Time had worn on and it was almost 4. He leant back into the sofa. His mind rambled. The professor had a connection to his

Grandmother. But how far and how deep did it go ? And for how long ?

He grit hit teeth. And breathed in hard. Then it turned to a sigh – *'What went on down here Gran ?'*

The sentiment slowly walked through his mind – *'What was your involvement ?'* – followed suit.

Crane gently shook his head. And glanced down at the floor. He picked up the old photo again from the little side table and looked at it. This itself was telling a short story. But what ? What was it telling him. He just couldn't fathom it out.

Crane popped the cork on the bottle of red wine. It was the most expensive that the little local shop had. It had to be. It had a good old traditional cork. Not a screw-top. So he hoped it would live up to the price tag at least. It certainly had an excellent aroma when he raised it to his nose.

He dumped the dirty dinner plate in to the sink. Along with the fork. Then with a little effort. The tap finally came on and spluttered water into the sink. He swirled it round with a squirt of some washing-up liquid. His mind was still wandering. Everything from the last forty-eight hours came shuffling through his head.

Then finally the photo. The photo he'd found in the professors desk draw at the lab. He knew there was a connection. A strong connection. Possibly a relationship between them.

That evil old bastard wouldn't have kept it otherwise. So that was the key. It had to be.

Crane shuddered at the thought. Then he recalled how the professor had stated that she felt familiar to him.

Crane poured a large glass of the red wine. And lifted it to his mouth. He didn't hesitate. Just took a massive gulp.

Walking back into the lounge. Crane sat once more on the old Chesterfield. He placed the bottle of red on the floor along with the glass. And pulled his Browning from his hip. He looked at it. Ran it over and through his hands. He smiled. As this pistol had saved his life a few times. And never more so than in Belfast.

Crane stared upward. And his mind fluttered. The Belfast operation. It was like outer-space. He was assigned to intercept a new form of tech. Coming from the United States. And into the hands of the IRA. The intel report showed that this new tech. Was a new type of armour-piercing round that could compromise heavy body-armour. Countries all over the world are constantly designing new and improved ammunition. But this was a really bad one.

It had been made from depleted Uranium and in 9mm 7.62 and 5.56 Armalite. Which meant it could be used for both sniper and assault rifles. And also pistols. So if the IRA got their hands on it.

The British squaddies on patrol would be open-season. Because their current issue flak-jackets wouldn't stop these type of ballistics. And the next step would have been .50 cal. Even more lethal and devastating.

It was also a delicate time for the Irish and British people. As the peace talks were supposed to be going a-head in Belfast. But a hard-core splinter faction of the IRA had gone rogue. And it didn't want to quit.

Word of this new tech possibly falling into the hands of this splintered IRA group had ground everything to a halt. Peace would have to wait. And British Intelligence had to act. And act fast.

Crane was under-cover. Acting as a well-funded British sympathiser. Working with a young IRA agent that he'd turned. The negotiations with the American couriers went well. And the plan was firmly based on them being cash-rich and eager to take delivery to continue the righteous cause. And his remit was to meet them just outside Coots Town. Check the goods. Give them the cash. And then take their car. The whole deal had been set-up by a senior high-ranking IRA informant code-named 'Mr Capricorn'.

It all seemed so simple. But in essence these things never work out that way. Too many variables.

Everything was in place. And Crane picked up his agent and drove on to the rendezvous. And as they drove down the dusty track they could see in the distance they were already there. Parked in the shadow of an old barn. This wasn't what was agreed. And Crane was already on the back-foot.

He did a brief circle of the old farm building then parked up. Some hundred meters away. And left the engine running. As soon as the exchange had taken place – he'd be out of there. Along with his contact. The young IRA agent now seemed jittery and nervous. Then with a deep breath he drew his pistol and gently placed it on the floor of the car. Gave a weak smile and got out and approached them. Bag in hand.

The informant had to leave his gun in the car. As they would have found it on him. And the agreement was an 'unarmed' exchange. But just as he got near. Shots rang out. And Cranes contact slumped to the floor. In a withering burst of gun-fire. Then one of them made a dash to grab the money bag. Whilst the other opened fire on Crane.

The whole deal had gone South. And he could have high-tailed it out of there. But Crane knew that if he didn't get his hands on that tech. It would end up with the IRA. And for him that was not an option. He slammed the car into gear. And careered straight towards them. Just as more shots rang-out.

Fortunately it was an 'Office' car and was armoured, plus it had a bullet-proof windscreen. And several clanged-off as he careered and powered towards them. The guy taking pot-shots stood his ground. Thinking Crane would veer-off at the last minute. But he didn't.

Crane purposely hit him smack dead centre. And watched for a second as both his arms went up in the air as he disappeared right under his car. And his hand-gun clattered across the bonnet. The ensuing thump under his feet and strangled scream indicated that Crane had killed him.

Then he aimed for their vehicle. And slammed hard right into it. Hitting it broadside. And almost tipping it over in the collision. Then leaping-out gun in hand he darted around to the passenger side and the bag-man was sitting there. All bloody. Dazed and confused.

Crane tore the door open and without hesitation shoved his Browning straight into his left eye. And with it pushed his head back hard into the seat. Then he drew the hammer.

The bag-man slowly raised his hands.

A loud whirring noise indicated that the cavalry had arrived. And an army Lynx helicopter suddenly appeared and did a low sweep. Then it started to descend into a farmers field some hundred yards away. Then sirens. And the RUC made a magical appearance.

Crane didn't move. Just kept his Browning in place. Securely jammed fast into his prisoners eye socket. But he wanted him to move. To twitch a finger perhaps. And Crane would have taken great-joy in pulling the trigger.

Cranes informant was just a kid. Brainwashed by the RUC and British Intelligence into thinking he was doing good for his people. The Irish people. But he knew this young lad was just like the Dutch boy with his finger in the dyke.

Then suddenly he felt a reaffirming tap on his shoulder. And without turning he slowly pulled his weapon away dropping the hammer. Then stuffed it back into the waist-band on his jeans.

The RUC hurriedly set-up a perimeter. And then the army secured the tech. Later on that day. Back at the army intelligence office in Castlereagh. Crane gave a de-brief. It was short and sweet and then he surrendered his side-arm. But not his. His was still stuffed down the front of his jeans. The one he gave back-in was his informants. The young lads Browning. The one he left in his car.

Luckily the armourer was off-kilter that day. As he didn't check for a serial number. He just dropped the mag and emptied the breech. Then racked it back into stores.

Crane placed it gently down on the sofa beside him and smiled to himself. And gave his service Browning a reassuring tap. Then he gulped at the wine and swirled it around his mouth. It was good. Full-bodied and tangy.

Cranes demeanour relaxed. He gulped again and re-filled his glass. A further gulp and then repeated the same. Then Crane lifted the half-empty glass in a sombre toast - '*To Mr Capricorn*'. He muttered quietly in a respectful hushed tone.

Before long the bottle was empty. And Crane kicked it as he relaxed further into the sofa. He watched as it skittered across the floor. Coming to rest by the old TV.

His head slumped back. His eyes closed. He fought to keep them open. But in the final moments they stayed shut.

Crane looked all around him. There was no-one near. No-one had seen him. As he approached the twin-engine Cessna and peered into the cockpit. They keys were in the ignition. And he ran his hand over the engine cover.

It was warm. This plane had been used a short while ago. So he was in luck. Crane returned to the battered old Fiat and opened the boot. He grabbed the tech and heaved it out on to the floor.

Then looking around he slammed the boot lid shut.

The coast was still clear and it was a warm bright day. And placing the case down at the side of the Cessna he fumbled with the storage pannier. It sprang open and upwards and Crane grabbed the tech and shoved it in.

He closed it. Locked it and checked the catch. Then checked it again.

Suddenly he was he zooming up the runway. The tarmac was endless. And he pulled hard on the controls and the tarmac became green. Lush. Stretching out in front of him.

He was airborne. The clouds were gone. All that he could see was blue sky. He glanced out of the window and below him was the sea.

There was no noise. No sound of the engines. No wind rushing past the plane. Or rattling the windows. Looking ahead he could see the outline of Dover. Crane reached down and pushed the throttle. He wanted to get home. Back to England.

Then a bleeping sound started to echo around the cockpit. A constant annoying pitch. He stared at the dash. At the controls. But nothing seemed out of place.

'You're running low on fuel' - Crane knew that voice. It was his Grandmother. He smiled and glanced over his shoulder and there she was. Sitting in the back. Her floppy hat in place. He looked at her and his smile turned into a wide school-boy grin.

'You should have checked the Jerry-Can.. ! – she said. Returning his smile and raising her hand gently pointing.

'Jerry-Can.. ? – he replied. Looking at her and gently frowning

Then a shooshing sound eclipsed his ears and he turned. And watched as his window was slowly whirring down. And the cockpit suddenly started to fill with a rush of air.

Crane fought with the catch. Then suddenly his Grandmothers floppy hat came flying onto the front seat. It sat there and fluttered for a moment. Then it rose-up and flew past him. Straight out of the window. And Crane watched as it trailed out into the air. It seemed to hover momentarily then it disappeared behind the Cessna.

Cranes eyes snapped open. He breathed hard and filled his lungs. Then glanced down at his watch. It was a little after two. He slowly uncoiled himself from the old sofa. Grabbed up his gun. And picked up the empty wine bottle.

He placed it down on the kitchen side and then gingerly made his way down the hallway.

Jerry-Can..?' - he mused.

'What bloody Jerry-Can..?' – and he stood for a moment and ran these words through his head. Then looked down at his Browning and gently thumbed the hammer as he contemplated. Then looked back into his Grandmothers bedroom.

'What Jerry-Can.. ?'

He then shook his head and wandered into the bedroom.

12

CRANE STEPPED OUT OF the shower. The water was still tepid but at least refreshing. And padding himself dry, he made for the bedroom and pulled some clothes from his case. He didn't have much with him. So opted for an old beige linen suit.

Crane glanced at himself in the mirror. The suit was still a good fit. But crumpled and could do with an iron. But still, with his old raincoat wrapped around him, he was confident that he'd look fine.

Back in the lounge. Crane grabbed up his Browning and did a brass-check. Then slid it into his waist band. Then the photo. He took one last look then slid it into his inside pocket.

Walking back up the cobbled lane. Crane took a side glance at the cottage. It looked peaceful. But who knew what secrets it truly held. It was a sombre thought. Be he'd find out. He was determined too.

Standing at the bus stop he searched his pockets. Hoping for a cigar. But then he realised he'd smoked them all. Suddenly the bus appeared and he got on and wandered to the back. And slumped himself down staring out of the window.

Every time he rode the bus. He reminisced. But this time, when his Grandmother appeared in his thoughts, her words reverberated. *'Jerry-Can !'*. Crane gently shook his head and stared at the swaths of passing countryside. What the hell did she mean ?. He asked himself and shook his head again wonderment. Then glanced down at the floor.

He couldn't make it out. Just couldn't fathom what she meant. But he knew there was a reason.

The bus started it's circuit of Looe and Crane got off early. He wanted to walk and take in the warmness of the day. And ponder on what Pam's mother had to reveal about the professor and his Grandmother.

He ducked into a little paper-shop and picked-up the local news. And at the counter he spied the cigars and saw they had Henry Wintermans. Half Coronas. A good smoke as he could recall. So he took a pack and some matches and made back to the main road.

Looking at his watch. It was just approaching 8.30. So Crane made for a public bench near the front and sat down. He shoved a cigar in his mouth. Lit the end and breathed in hard. And glanced up at the seagulls swooping over-head.

Then flicking the ash, he thumbed through the local rag. The front page said pretty-much the same as the day before. No real updates in any of it. So he leant forward and dumped the paper into the litter bin and sat back, enjoying his cigar.

Then a light sea-breeze breeze blew up and he closed his eyes and allowed it to whirl around him. It was cool and refreshing. And it smelt of salt and old fish. Tinged with a hint of burnt diesel.

Then glancing down. His cigar was almost spent. So he threw it on the floor and stamped on it. And wrapping himself once more in his raincoat he sprang to his feet and started to stroll towards the café on the quayside. The door jingled as he stepped in. But it was empty. He knew he was still quite early.

'Hello Peter..!' – Crane looked round and smiled at Josey – 'Hey Josey.. may I ask.. why is this place always empty when I come in here ?'

'Sailing times.. we open at 5 for the earlies.. it's busy then.. then they come back in when they've finished for the day at around 4.. and during the day a few people pop in maybe.. tourists mostly.. !'

Crane nodded with an understanding smile - 'Tea please.. strong !' - and he strolled over to his normal table. In the far corner and pulling a chair he sat down.

The smell of the hot tea swirled up and mingled into his nose. It felt homely. And reassuring that things today would be fine. He stirred it gently and looked down. And he saw his face. But this time his image didn't really go out-of-shape. It just swirled and gently lapped against the cup.

Sparking back to Miles's office. And his final day. The day he left British Intelligence. And the god-awful putrid coffee. And the haunting look and ghostly apparition as he stirred it. All this once again flashed into his mind. But this time things seemed different.

It seemed softer. Like things were coming to an end. Coffee kept you awake. Tea calmed you. Or so his dear Grandmother had always said.

'Hungry Peter.. ?' – called out Josey – 'Yes' - he replied. 'But I'm waiting for Pam and her mum.. their be here soon so we'll order together'

And no sooner had he spoke, the front door jingled open. And in strode Pam and her mum closely shuffling behind.

She smiled – 'Hi Peter.. this is my mum Anne..!' – and Crane returned the smile and looked at her beaming. She looked old and tired. As if she had a lot to say. But wasn't sure if she should say any of it.

Pam strode to the table and took the far seat and her mum followed suit and sat down next to her. And Crane slipped back into his chair - 'Tea.. ?' - he motioned.

'Yes.. please' – they both acknowledged the same.

Josey strolled over already tea laden. She seemed to know the score – 'Nice to see you Anne.. been a long time..!'. Pam's mum just nodded at her and smiled.

'Bacon sandwich please Josey' – and Crane looked at them both. Initiating the same.

'Yeah why not.. same here.. we'll all have the same' - agreed Pam.

Crane picked up his tea and took a gulp. Then looked up at Pam. Then her mum. He raised his eyebrows and smiled.

'So your Charlottes Grandson.. Peter..!' – she said. Almost expressionless.

'Yeah.. that's me..!' - Crane replied. Smiling warmly.

'So what brought you back here to this little sparrow-fart of a town ..?' – continued Anne.

'My Grandmother passed and she left me her cottage.. Thimble Cottage.. and now I've retired I've moved down here.. hoping for a quiet life..!'

Pam's mum leant back in her chair. She seemed to relax a little. And a weak smile creased the corners of her mouth.

'Your old Nan was quite a character in her day.. or so I heard.. anyway can I see that photo again..'.

And Crane reached into his inside pocket and passed it to her.

'Yeah I thought so.. that's him.. Professor Hebon.. no no.. Heben !.. he had a German accent.. strange man.. he always looked shifty and aloof.. and as far as I can remember he did have a relationship with your Grandmother.. he lived with her for a while in your cottage if I remember rightly.. and he was a bit of a womaniser as I can recall.. but I'm going back to the late fifties.. long time ago.. so it's all a bit fuzzy..!'

Crane frowned at her statement - 'What makes you say that.. a womaniser?'.

'He used to make passes at some of the older students.. he had money.. seemed wealthy and he used to flash it about.. always wore a three-piece suit and cravat.. but he was banned from the college in the end.. as the rumour was that he was doing weird experiments.. !'

Cranes mind flashed – 'What do you mean weird..?'

Both Crane and Pam looked at Anne in curiosity. But Crane was concerned. As this hit a savage and raw nerve. And a small piece of the story fell into place.

Anne threw her head to one side – 'The word was that he paid several of the students to take part in them.. something to do with chemicals.. but it was found out to be radio-waves I think or something like that.. they got sick and their skin turned a funny colour.. and they used to puke up green crap.. it was awful..!'

Pam's mum leant back into her chair - 'I think one of them died.. as memory serves.. but I can't be sure of that.. again it was just a rumour.. I think the authorities stepped in somewhere along the line.. !'

Crane looked in horror at Pam. She returned the look and seemed confused – 'Do you know something about this Peter..?'

He shook his head, back-peddling – 'No Pam.. nothing.. !' – Then Crane looked back at Anne – 'So what was his connection to my Gran.. a relationship yes.. but what else.. ?'

'Not really sure,' replied Anne

'Like I said.. it was a long time ago.. but I did hear that after he was literally run out of Penzance.. he turned up here.. and was with your Gran for a while.. then he disappeared.. never seen again..!'

Suddenly three bacon sandwiches broke the conversation as they hit the table with a clatter. Crane drew his arms back reaction and gently looked down at the table.

Eagerly Pam made a grab for the brown sauce and doused her sandwich. She passed the bottle to her mum and she did the same. They started munching. But Crane left his un-touched.

He glanced out the window and bit his lip. Then he looked back at both Pam and her Mum. Pam's mum shot Crane a concerned look – 'You OK.. you seem a little upset or concerned by all this..?'

Crane managed a weak smile – 'No I'm fine.. I just lost touch with my dear Gran as I got older.. I spent a lot of my time abroad with work.. and I truly wish I'd spent more time with her in the later years that's all..!'

Anne nodded and smiled though brown sauce. Then Crane grabbed up his bacon sandwich and took a bite. Then slammed it down and picked up the brown sauce too.

Crane was busily munching away. Pondering. The bacon sandwich was a little cold but it still tasted good.

'Oh Peter.. I've had a call from that chap Anderson.. he's coming to meet me at the hotel this afternoon..!' – and Pam offered a short brown-sauce-smile with raised eyebrows. Then continued with her sandwich.

Crane nodded – I'll call you about that later.. what time ?.

'4.. 4pm.. or there abouts' – she replied.

Crane nodded again. And finished his last mouthful. Then looking at his watch, it was nearly 10.30.

Then snatching-up his tepid tea, he washed it down and pushing the plate to one side he got up and made for the counter. Josey was leaning on it. Reading the local rag. And she looked up and smiled warmly. Crane pulled out his money-clip and unfolded a twenty pound note. He shoved this into her hand and smiled as he turned and walked away.

Crane put his hand on the café door and glanced back at Pam and her mum – 'I'll call you about midday' – then suddenly Pam called after him – ' Peter.. !' and she picked up the black and white photo and past it towards him. He took it gently and looked at it again. Then nodded a thank you at Pam.

The bus bumped and meandered out of Looe. And Crane sat at the back again. All sombre. And his mind gently went over the facts. And the last few days activities. He pondered on it all. The professor was obviously relocated here to Cornwall after the war. And as far as he could remember his Gran had always lived down here. But he always thought she lived alone.

But the professor stated that he recognised her. And the photo confirmed this. But how far did the connection go. And for how long.

The bus rounded the crest of the hill and Crane jumped up and sauntered down. And it stopped just short of the top. And with a shoosh of the doors he hoped out. The old bus gave a burst of fumes as it pulled away. And through the smoke Crane looked out over the fields and up towards his cottage.

He smiled – *'Oh Gran.. what went on down here..?'* – he asked himself.

He trudged on. And just as he got to the start of the cobbled lane, he stopped and lit another Henry Winterman. Again he breathed in hard and then whirled out the smoke.

The farmers field to the side of the cottage needed mowing. The grass was almost waist high. But it looked calming as he approached. Gently swaying in the breeze. If not a little over-grown.

Cranes shoes rattled and tapped as he made his way down. They cobble were as old as he could remember. Probably as old as the cottage. With some missing here and there.

Nearing the gate Crane stopped and looked at it for a moment. To the left of the cottage, at the end of the driveway, there was an old shed. And the door was slightly open. And gently swinging in the breeze.

Crane frowned. As far as he could remember. He closed it and threw the old rusty latch across.

Again his training and instinct kicked in. He spat out the cigar and pulled his Browning. And performed a brass-check with lightening-speed. He crouched by the brick-gate post at the end of the drive and scanned the area. Nothing seemed out of place.

Then he sprinted down. Straight at the shed. And he stood with his back against it. Then using his Browning, he nosed the door open with the muzzle and peered inside. Remembering to point his sidearm wherever he looked.

Nothing. There was no one there. No indication that anything had been moved or touched.

Just some rags on the floor. Some old rusty broken garden tools. Some string and some scattered pieces of wood. But just as he turned to leave something caught his eye. On a piece of wood appeared to be some kind of writing. Black writing. They seemed painted or printed.

Crane grabbed it up. Yes it was writing of some sort. Then he grabbed another of the piece. And that too had some writing on it.

Crane placed these to one side and checked the rest. And several more were marked. And one had what looked like a symbol of some-sort. He tucked his Browning back in his waist band. And placed his hands on his hips. And looked down studying them.

'A packing crate..?'

Then Crane laid the planks on the floor and started to rearrange them in an almost jigsaw like fashion. Then he stood up and almost stumbled back.

It was a packing crate. A German packing crate. The symbol was a German army eagle with a swastika shrouded in laurel-leaves in its claws. The wording was German. But Crane couldn't make it out. But a Nazi swastika was enough to hit home what it was.

There must be more. And Crane scanned the shed. But nothing. None laying around. Then he glanced up and laying across the support beams were more planks. They looked like a make-shift shelf up in the rafters.

But none had any black print on them.

Crane frowned for a moment then grabbed the old wooden step ladder from the far corner. He opened it and placed it near the leading edge of the shelf.

He climbed and on tip-toe looked over the top. Yes indeed it was a shelf and there sitting in the middle was an old rusty-green jerry-can.

Crane reached out and tried to pull it towards him. But it was insanely heavy and wouldn't budge.

Then he gave a hard tug and it started to inch towards him. Then with a further hard tug it finally teetered on the edge of the planks and they started to bow and creak slightly.

Then there was a crack and the end plank gave-way. Crane stumbled back and almost fell off the stepladder. Then he wobbled and jumped off. Just as the jerry-can came tumbling forward. Crane side stepped as the can hit the floor and it split in two like a broken suit-case.

In one side there was some old paperwork and letters. In the other there was what looked like a block or bar wrapped in old rags. Crane didn't move. He frowned. Then he bent down and gathered up the papers. And he thumbed them for a moment. And saw old italic writing. And something said 'Certificate'. Then he glanced at another. It was a letter in a small plaid envelope. And he turned it over and it had his name on it. Written in his Grandmothers hand-writing.

Crane placed these down for a moment and looked at the other half of the can. And the thing wrapped in rags. He reached over and tried to pick it up. But couldn't. Then he wrapped both hands around it and lifted it. It was heavy. Very heavy. Then he peeled back part of the rags on the end and something glinted in the sunlight.

It was gold.

Gold bullion. And at the top far corner there was a small stamp of a Nazi eagle and Swastika. And trembling, Crane continued to gently unwrap the bar.

This was Nazi gold. From the second world war. And probably part of a stolen consignment.

Cranes mind rambled. How the hell did it get here. And at his Grandmother cottage. She must have had something to do with it. And there must have been more. The remains of the old packing case proved this.

Crane gathered up the papers and the bar of gold Crane made for the cottage. His head was spinning. So many things were racing through his mind.

He placed the gold bar on the kitchen side. And stared at it. Stared at the Nazi insignia. Then he glanced at his watch. It was nearly 12. And then he remembered that he had to call Pam. Anderson was going to make an appearance later that day. At around 4 as Pam had said.

Crane was totally bewildered. This had trumped everything that he'd gone through in the last few days.

Leaving the gold, he strolled into the lounge and slowly lowered himself into the Chesterfield. His eyes were as wide as car head-lights. Then he remembered the papers and he shuffled them into his lap and thumbed through them.

Remembering the letter from his Grandmother. Crane settled on this first and tore it open.

'*My dearest darling Petie.. If you have now found the gold, I truly hope with all my heart that this letter may answer some of your questions, but alas not all. And I truly wish I could be there with you to explain.*

You may recall that I told you once that I was in the army intelligence corps. Well I was stationed in Berlin at the end of the war. My task was the secret evacuations of important people.

Time was of the essence, as the Russians were closing in. One such man, Carl Otto Von Heben, was a man I had personal responsibility for.

A titled man from a powerful Austrian family, who was working for the Nazi's on their secret weapons. And during our mission, we fell in love. But it was only later, once safely back in England, that I discovered the true nature of his work.

But by then in many ways it was far too late. Too late for me.

He truly was a brilliant scientist. And British Intelligence thought his work, could now become our own. But the brain-washing of Hitlers Third Rich was always there just under the surface. And he used me, in many ways to further his own ideals.

The British Government placed him in a local college as cover, so he could continue his work in a small secret but neutral way. But all it did was corrupt him further.

We did marry, but I divorced him when several people died at his hands and the abominable work he was perpetrating. Whitehall didn't care and shortly after he was whisked away to continue.

What truly happened to him, I will never know. And in truth I never wanted to.

We had a son, your father, but as you know he died just after you were born. Damaged by the wealth that we brought back from Germany. I don't know what your mother told you, but your father died of alcohol poisoning. A sad ending to a once brilliant life and career. And she knew nothing of your real Grandfather, I told lies to keep that a secret from her.

Yes I helped smuggle the gold here and in the end, in the later years of my life, I am now truly ashamed for ever having done it. All it did was cause us pain. But what happened to the rest, I don't really know. But I leave this bar to you. To do with what you will, but do some good with it. Don't let it corrupt you like it did your Father.

Your birth name is 'Von Heben' like your Grandfathers, but I changed it to Crane when I finally divorced him. The name Von Heben means 'Lifting' or to 'lift' so to me, the name Crane still has some small connection.

I still loved your Grandfather, but not in the end, the monster he had become.

You were the light of my life Petie, so try to think of me as I was..

Your dear ever loving Grandmother XX

Cranes eyes welled. And he read the last few sentences again and again. And finally he understood them. So there was the connection and the revelation he was seeking. Stolen Nazi gold and a perverted Nazi scientist that was his Grandfather.

He thought he was already dead. Long before he was born. His Grandmother had never mentioned him. Not once. Even when he asked all she would say is that he's dead. Died in the war.

Cranes mother never mentioned him either. And at that moment he pondered. That perhaps was why he was shipped off to boarding school the moment he old enough.

He never had any real connection with her. Only his Grandmother.

Crane folded the letter. His face became tight. Then he burst into tears and held it to his face. And for the first time in years, he felt very close to her. To his dear Grandmother.

Through the tears Crane looked at his watch. It was half twelve. He reached in and grabbed the smartphone and dialled Pam's number.

It clicked through – 'Peter..?' – 'Hi Pam.. all good.. I'll see you at the hotel at 3.30ish.. I'll sit with you and make sure all goes well.. OK'

There was a pause – 'Peter you OK.. you sound upset..?'

'No.. No.. I'm fine' – He replied '.. I've just woke up that's all.. see you at 3.30 OK'.

Crane placed the smartphone down on the arm of the sofa and picked the letter up once again. He kissed it and wiped the tears from his eyes.

Back in the kitchen he looked at his laptop. The Blackhat had finished. The decoding was complete and he could now access the small hard-drive. But he hesitated. For now he knew all he needed to or indeed what he wanted to.

Crane clicked on a file recovery app and copied all the information and files from it. Then detached the hard drive. He now had a copy. This was his bargaining chip.

He shut his laptop and placed it back into his bag then picked up the little hard-drive. He looked at it and ran it through his palms. He'd seen this type before.

Crane glanced at his watch again. It was just after one. Walking back to his bedroom he grabbed up the black leather satchel that he took from Simpkins's car and sauntered back to the kitchen.

He opened it and peered inside. Took out the block of C4. The two remaining Thermite grenades and opened a cupboard and stuffed them inside. Then threw it on the sofa.

Back in the kitchen he grabbed-up the hard-drive and a bottle of wine. And just as he went to walk away, he remembered. A glass. his Grandmother didn't approve of drinking from bottles.

Sitting back on the Chesterfield he gazed at the TV. He wasn't interested. Crane was just biding his time. He refilled his wine glass and took another gulp. And finished it in one go.

His watch said 2pm. Still over an hour.

Before he knew it the bottle was empty and he placed it back on the floor. And drained the remnants from his glass.

Crane picked up the letter and unfolded it once more. His eyes skipped and jumped through the sentences. And a huge lump appeared in his throat again. And he bit his lip to once more to stem the desire to cry. Then he folded it and placed into his inside pocket of his suit.

Sitting here was useless. Operational prudence rang through his mind. So Crane got up and placed the smartphone in his pocket. And grabbed up the satchel and switched off the TV. Then he breezed into the kitchen and placed the hard drive into it and a few other items. He peered into it. Check and double check.

He slid his rain-coat on and then threw the satchel over his shoulder.

He tapped his right hip and made for the front door.

Back on the cobbled lane he walked fast. And he didn't look back this time. Then before he knew it, he was standing at the bus-stop again. And seemed to have timed it perfectly. As glancing up to the top of the lane, the bus came trundling towards him.

With the bumpy winding ride behind him, he was back in Looe. And as before Crane got off at the edge of town and slowly walked towards the harbour. His eyes darted everywhere. He doubted that British Intelligence would stand-out enough for the locals to notice but he would.

Then again they didn't really notice Simpkins thumping around in a big black BMW. To them he was nothing more than a posh tourist.

There was nothing. Nothing seemed out of place. There was no-one walking around. Constantly re-treading their foot-steps. And pacing up and down in the same area. No-one statue-like in a car.

Crane sauntered on and finally stood at the quay-side. He glanced at the little fishing-boats. Then glancing-down further he saw Davey Parsons little yellow trawler. Still in the same place and now forlorn and un-loved. The vision of their horrific deaths shuttered into his mind and he grit his teeth.

Crane decided on a different approach. The time was now 2.30 so he had a while to kill. He walked on and this time went to the other side of the harbour. The far quay. He sat on a public bench and looked back across.

He could see the café and the boats. And Davey Parson's boat. And further up the quay the Patriot was still there. Just where he had left it. Tied to the slip-way.

All seemed quiet.

Crane pulled the last remaining cigar from the pack and unwrapped it. He placed it into his mouth and lit it. And relaxed back on the bench. His eyes continued to scan the far quay-side with radar efficiency but still nothing seemed out of place.

A light breeze got up and swirled past him. And he closed his eyes like before and breathed it in. The familiar odour of salt, fish and boat diesel again tinged his nose. And he smiled. It felt normal now. A homely feeling of the West Country. Of Cornwall. A place he hoped he could now call home.

Crane allowed a himself a moment to reflect - *'I've been on missions all over the world.. car-chases.. the odd fire-fight.. but here at home.. in England.. I'm on the greatest mission of them all.. and in the end.. a revelation as to who I really am and what my Grandparents really were!'*

A squawk over-head pulled Crane back to reality. And he glanced up as a flock of seagulls came racing over-head.

He smiled. Wishing one would crap on him for luck.

His watch said 3. Time to go. Crane gently got to his feet and threw the heavy satchel over his shoulder once more. And shuffled it higher into place.

The Rose n' Crown wasn't far. Just up past the quay and around the corner. Being early was always a good idea. Crane trusted his honed instincts that treating this like any other mission or operation was a normal way to be. *Operation Prudence, step-by-step.*

It had always served him well in the past. And this was no different. Other than the fact that now it was personal. Very personal.

Crane rounded the end of the quay and flicked his cigar over the side. He could see the little hotel. It was painted white. With the odd yellow embellishment. And looked weather-worn. As most of the houses and buildings in Looe did.

He shoved the door. Then had to shove it again as it stuck. This was a good point. A good indicator that you'd hear anyone who comes in. Their entrance would ne noisy and a good trigger-point.

Crane stepped through into a small reception lounge. It was empty. And eerily quiet. Crane froze. His right hand instinctively shuffled inside his rain-coat and jacket and it rested on his Browning.

'Hello..?' – then suddenly a young girl with a huge mop of red-hair, came bustling down a side stair-case. Laden with towels.

'Oh.. Hi.. can I help you ?' – Crane relaxed and pulled his hand away from his side-arm.

'Yeah.. Pam North.. please' – the girl dumped the towels down on the counter and walked around and picked up a phone. 'Hi Pam.. there's a chap down here to see you'.

Then she pulled the phone down and looked at him – 'Oh it's Peter..!' - Crane blurted in reply and she spoke again into the phone.

Crane glanced around then back at the young-girl
- 'I'll meet her in the bar..' - and he followed the little
signs that led down a passageway.

Crane took a seat at a far table. Making sure he
had direct sight to the passageway from the front desk.
He un-slung the satchel and dumped it on the floor
out of sight.

Then the smartphone vibrated and Crane fished
it out – 'Peter..?' – 'Yeah Pam it's me.. I'm down stairs
in the bar.. no worries OK' – and Crane placed it back
into his pocket.

Suddenly Pam appeared. She had a worried and
some-what tired look on her face. Crane got up and
embraced her. And held her tight. She started sobbing –
'It'll be alright Pam.. I'm here OK' – she feebly nodded
and managed a weak smile.

'Come.. sit down' – and Pam slumped herself
down into a chair. She sat opposite. He planned it that
way. Operational prudence. Keep an eye on the main
entrance.

She looked at him. And looked as though she was
going to burst into tears at any second. Crane smiled.
Slowly blinked at her and widened his smile – 'It's
gonna be OK.. I promise..!' and he reached over and
took her hands.

Pam lowered her head and started to sob again
– 'Just stick to what you know.. that's all and keep it
to a simple yes or no to direct questions.. OK!' – she
nodded again.

The red-head appeared – 'Coffee.. Tea..?' – Crane looked up at her – 'I could do with something stronger..! but tea please.. just bring a pot for two.. that would be great..!'

And she turned and sauntered away.

Crane glanced at his watch. Time had worn on and it was almost 4 – 'Anderson will be here shortly.. but I'm with you' – then Pam looked up. And she tried to smile.

Approaching foot-steps and the red-head appeared with a tray. She placed it down – 'Anything else ?'. 'No that's fine.. thank you' – replied Crane and she turned.

Crane looked at Pam again. She seemed calmer now. And a little stronger. She grabbed the teapot and poured them both a cup.

Crane picked his up and took a sip. It was awful. Pale and like gnats-piss as his Gran would say. He grimaced and swallowed hard. Pam had the same look. At least it was the tea this time.

Crane went to speak just as the front door to the hotel shuffled and banged open. In walked Anderson. He was alone and had a brief case in hand.

Crane stared at him. Anderson was looking around. He appeared a little fazed and confused. He instinctively knew this was a very good sign. He hadn't been in here before.

Crane stood up and raised his hand. And gave a short whistle. Anderson spun round and looked down the passageway. He raised his eyebrows and gave a short wave. Then started to make his way towards them.

Pam turned just as he entered the room.

Anderson came bustling over and shot his hand out to Pam. She took it apprehensively and he shook it gently.

'Crane..!' – he acknowledged him with a nod as he pulled a chair and sat down.

'Firstly.. before we begin.. Mrs North.. I need you to sign this' - and Anderson pulled some papers from his brief case. He laid them on the table and aimed them at Pam. She looked at him and then the papers – ' What is it ?'.

'The Official Secrets Act..!' – and Anderson sat back and folded his arms.

Pam looked back at him then at Crane. Crane was expressionless. Then he nodded and gave a grim but resolute smile.

Anderson passed her a pen and she scribbled her name and pushed the papers back towards him.

Anderson bent to pick them up. And just as he reached forward Pam slammed her hand down on them – 'Now what ?'

Anderson cocked his head to one side - 'Now we can discuss things.. your settlement.. your compensation.. so to speak..!'

Pam hesitated for a moment. Then leant back in her chair. She raised her eyebrows and folded her arms. Very matter-of-factly.

Anderson gathered the papers - gave them a brief check and then slipped them back into his case and closed it. Then he leant forward on the table.

'As I'm sure your aware.. Mrs North.. what the Official Secrets Acts means.. so I won't go over that.. but the case as far as your concerned is closed.. your be relocated if you wish and the government will foot the bill for a small house.. and your also receive fifty thousand pounds as a lump sum.. your late husband will be released to you shortly and again we will foot the bill for his interment..!

Anderson paused. He looked at Pam. Her head was bowed.

'So that's it..?' - she said without looking up. Crane placed his hand on hers. But she pulled away and looked up at Anderson.

'My Nory gets killed doing his job.. my home gets blown-up with me in it.. there was a government assassin driving around down here.. he nearly fucking killed me and Peter.. and that's it ?'.

Anderson shuffled back. He nodded – 'Yes.. I'm sorry but that's it..!' – He seemed uncomfortable.

Crane noticed and he relaxed. And he smiled inwardly to himself. Anderson was playing the white-man. The honest man. Even as regional commander there was only so-much he could do. And this was written all over his face. He could see it as clear as day.

Crane leant forward and looked at Pam. But she appeared to ignore him. He took her hand again and this time she clasped her fingers around his. She squeezed tightly and slowly looked at Crane.

Crane offered a small smile and he nodded. Pam looked back at Anderson – 'OK.. where do I sign for that..?'

Anderson reached back into his brief case and then placed a file on the table. He opened it and passed it to Pam – 'Please read it.. carefully.. it states exactly what I've just said.. there's no catches I swear.. just for your complete silence.. you will be properly compensated.. !'.

Pam took the file and sat back. She leafed through the pages then reached forward and picked up Andersons pen. She scribbled then she closed the folder and threw it at him.

It landed in his lap and Anderson fumbled to catch it. Then looking somewhat forlorn he placed it back into his case. He looked at them both then placed a small business card in front of Pam.

'Let me know what you want to do.. in due course.. I'll be your point of contact.. OK'

And he got up to leave.

'Anderson.. we're not finished.. !' - and he turned and looked at Crane.

Crane leant back into his chair and folded his arms. He nodded at the chair and assuredly cocked his head to one side. Very matter-of-factly. Anderson frowned then walked back and re-took his seat.

Crane reached down to the satchel and threw the hard-drive on to the table. Anderson seemed confused. He looked at it then back at Crane – 'That's the professors.. I took it just before the place blew'.

Andersons face went white. He looked surprised and he gingerly picked it and looked at it – 'The clean-up guys said it wasn't there.. said it had been removed.. we assumed hidden in the base somewhere..!'

'Yeah.. it had been removed alright.. I had it.. I needed proof of what was going on.. do you think I would have left there with nothing to back-up my story.. !' – Crane smiled.

Anderson unclipped his brief-case and gingerly slid it inside.

'Oh and you also want this..!' – and Crane threw Simpkins's pistol onto the table. Andersons eyes went wide and his hand shot out and grabbed it. Then worriedly snatched up his case again and hurriedly shuffled it inside.

'That was Simpkins's side-arm.. not his service pistol.. but his own.. and judging by the look on your face Anderson you recognise it.. I don't want it.. too much blood on it..!'.

Anderson sat still. His face ashen. And looked at Crane in sheer wonderment.

'Oh and let's get one thing absolutely crystal here.. I have a copy of that hard-drive.. and if anything happens to Pam.. then I'll make public all I fucking know..!'

Then Crane leant forward and gave a sly-smile – 'Every-Damn-Thing !!'.

Anderson swallowed hard. He knew that Crane meant every word. He just meekly nodded. And went to get up again.

But Crane raised his hand in a slowing motion – 'I haven't finished Anderson.. Davey Parson's family.. what are they going to get..?'

Anderson stuttered slightly – 'Same Crane.. same deal as Mrs North'.

Crane nodded and smiled and he smirked in agreement.

Anderson looked at Crane then at Pam. He seemed resided that it was all over. And he stood up slowly this time. Almost making sure that Crane wanted nothing else. He shuffled his brief case in his hand and straightened his tie.

Then he turned and was gone.

Pam looked at Crane. He smiled and shrugged his shoulders – 'You OK Pam ?'

She looked calm and resolute. She nodded and glanced at the table – 'Teas cold..!'

Crane sniggered – 'I'm fine thank you.. but what about you..? .. you OK with all this Pam.. ?'

She turned fully to look at him – 'What really went on here Peter ?.. what really happened..?'

Crane looked at the table then out of the small window – 'That's a story best saved for another time

Pam.. but I'll tell you one day I promise.. don't worry about me.. I'm a survivor!'

Crane looked round at her – 'But you.. what you gonna do.. what's next for you ?'

'Dunno..' – replied Pam – 'Look at buying a little house somewhere I suppose.. move on.. nothing else I can do.. I suppose..!

'Sorry about the settlement.. it won't make up for what's happened.. no compensation ever will..! – continued Crane.

Then shuffling in his chair he stood-up and pushed it back in. Then he bent down and kissed Pam on her head and ruffled her hair.

Then grabbing up his satchel he made for the passageway. Then he paused and lowered his arm. Letting the satchel slip back down. Then he clasped it in both hands and turned back and faced her.

'Oh Pam.. there's something here that my dear Gran would want you to have.. you'd make better use of it then me.. and she said I should do some good with it.. and you.. deserve it'

And Crane stepped a few paces back and placed the satchel down near her feet. Pam looked down at it puzzled.

'What is it Peter..?'- and she looked up. But Crane was already striding back up the passageway.

He clamped his hand on the door and turned – 'See ya around Pam.. take care OK.. I promised myself

that I would go fishing.. and now it's time to collect..!'
– then with a shuttered clang the door thumped shut behind him.

Pam smiled to herself. Then curiously reached down to the satchel. She tugged at it but could hardly move it. Then she shuffled back in her chair to get a better purchase. And bent down towards it.

She fumbled with the zip clasp. And then with a final hard tug, it opened. Pam gingerly lifted the flap and curiously peered inside.

Her mouth fell open and she blinked hard.

Then jumping to her feet Pam run up the passageway and tore the door open as hard as she could and almost fell out onto the road in the process - 'PETER... PETER..' – she called out. Looking each and every way.

But he was gone.

Pam sauntered back down the passageway and stood once again at the table.

She paused then bent down and looked back into the satchel once more.

And there was the bar of gold bullion.

Crane stood once more on the far side of the quay and looked out over the harbour. The smell. The lovely smell of Cornwall tinged his nose again.

'Fishing Gran.. I think I'll try fishing.. ! – and a wide warm smile started to creep across his face.